Guinevere's Gift

Guinevere's Gift

Nancy McKenzie

ALFRED A. KNOPF

NEW YORK

to
Marian Edelman Borden
whose idea it was

and to
Caroline McKenzie
for all her help

THIS IS A BORZOI BOOK PUBLISHED BY ALFRED A. KNOPF

Copyright © 2008 by Nancy McKenzie

Published in the United States by Alfred A. Knopf, an imprint of Random House Children's Books, a division of Random House, Inc., New York.

KNOPF, BORZOI BOOKS, and the colophon are registered trademarks of Random House, Inc.

www.randomhouse.com/teens

Educators and librarians, for a variety of teaching tools, visit us at
www.randomhouse.com/teachers

Library of Congress Cataloging-in-Publication Data
McKenzie, Nancy.
Guinevere's gift / Nancy McKenzie. — 1st ed.
    p.   cm. — (The Chrysalis Queen quartet)
SUMMARY: When the orphaned Guinevere is twelve years old, living with Queen Alyse and King Pellinore of Gwynedd, she fearlessly helps rescue her cousin from kidnappers who are plotting to seize the palace and overthrow the king, even as the queen despairs of Guinevere's rebellious nature.
ISBN 978-0-375-84345-7 (trade) — ISBN 978-0-375-94345-4 (lib. bdg.)
1. Guenevere, Queen (Legendary character)—Childhood and youth—Fiction.
[1. Guenevere, Queen (Legendary character)—Childhood and youth—Fiction.
2. Orphans—Fiction.   3. Kings, queens, rulers, etc.—Fiction.   4. Cousins—Fiction.
5. Great Britain—History—To 1066—Fiction.]   I. Title.
PZ7.M198632Gu 2008
[Fic]—dc22
2007028782

Printed in the United States of America

February 2008

10 9 8 7 6 5 4 3 2 1

First Edition

Contents

Chapter One	King Pellinore's Daughter	1
Chapter Two	The Fitting	9
Chapter Three	Dreams of the Ignorant	22
Chapter Four	Old Argus's Son	28
Chapter Five	Daughter of Rhiannon	33
Chapter Six	Llyr	39
Chapter Seven	Council of Elders	47
Chapter Eight	The Tracker	57
Chapter Nine	Counting the Days	61
Chapter Ten	The Guest	69
Chapter Eleven	The Banquet	76
Chapter Twelve	The Cairn	84
Chapter Thirteen	Double Trouble	94
Chapter Fourteen	The Headache	105
Chapter Fifteen	Trials of a Scribe	112
Chapter Sixteen	The Warning	122
Chapter Seventeen	The Old Ones	127
Chapter Eighteen	The One Who Hears	136
Chapter Nineteen	Traveling Companions	151
Chapter Twenty	A Dangerous Ride	159
Chapter Twenty-one	By the Garden Door	166
Chapter Twenty-two	Plans for a Princess	175

Chapter Twenty-three   Only an Earl's Son   180

Chapter Twenty-four   Orders from Regis Himself   188

Chapter Twenty-five   A Private Supper   195

Chapter Twenty-six   Discovery   206

Chapter Twenty-seven   In the Lion's Den   212

Chapter Twenty-eight   Escape   221

Chapter Twenty-nine   Rescue   230

Chapter Thirty   The Queen's Choice   239

Chapter Thirty-one   An Arrow in the Dark   249

Chapter Thirty-two   The Cave   256

Chapter Thirty-three   The Guardian   265

Chapter Thirty-four   Queen of Gwynedd   273

Chapter Thirty-five   A Measure of Mercy   284

Chapter Thirty-six   Riding Out   298

Chapter Thirty-seven   King Pellinore's Surprise   308

Chapter Thirty-eight   Promise   318

A Note to Readers   326

Acknowledgments   328

The House of Gwynedd

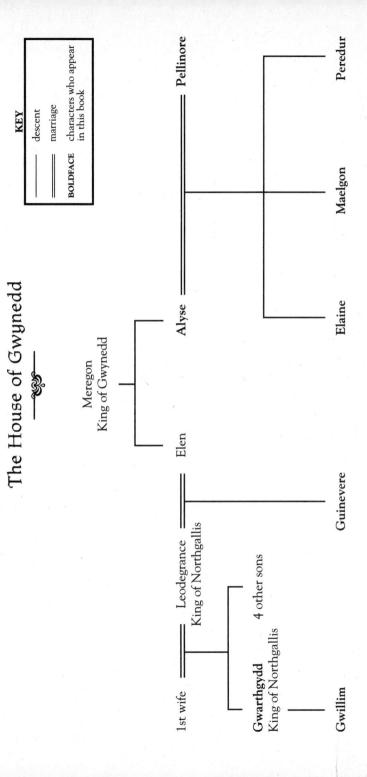

CHAPTER ONE

King Pellinore's Daughter

"Move over, Gwen. It's my turn." Elaine tugged at her cousin's sleeve. The two girls lay flat on their stomachs on the cold stone floor of the parapet. Guinevere had one eye pressed against a break in the mortar low in the castle wall.

"The courier's just coming. He's entered the room. He's making his reverence."

"Move *over*," Elaine demanded. "I let you look first. Now it's my turn. You keep watch."

Guinevere moved aside. "He looks exhausted. I wonder if he's come straight from the battlefield." She wriggled closer. "What's he saying? Can you hear?"

"Shhh! Not if you talk."

They had known that the new arrival was a royal courier by the dragon cipher on his belt, although he had ridden in with a party of merchants and wagons. Everyone had seen him, a young man with a military straightness in his carriage and the dust of travel still clinging to his clothes. He had come while the tables were being laid for dinner, and Queen Alyse had postponed the meal in order to receive him alone. She had been waiting weeks for a message. Elaine and Guinevere had taken advantage of the confusion and excitement at the courier's arrival to sneak up the guardroom stairs and learn firsthand through their peephole whether Elaine's father, King Pellinore, was still alive.

It was six long weeks since Arthur's courier had come at snowmelt to summon Pellinore of Gwynedd and all his men to war. Half of Wales had risen with him. All of them were eager to fight for the young High King who never lost a battle.

Guinevere crossed herself quickly. *Please, God, let nothing happen to King Pellinore.* She missed him dreadfully. He was a rough bear of a man with a jovial nature and a willingness to believe the best of everyone. He *had* to return safely. If he did not, Queen Alyse would rule Gwynedd alone.

"Listen, Gwen!" Elaine cried. "Father is—"

Guinevere clapped a hand over her mouth, but too late. Behind them, the guardroom door squeaked as it opened, and a sentry emerged. The peephole lay near the corner of the western wall, low to the ground and deep in the shadow cast by torches outside the guardroom door. Experience had taught the girls that they could not be seen if they huddled inside their cloaks and kept absolutely still.

The sentry walked along the rampart, sword in hand, and looked warily about him. It had been a cool spring day, and dusk had brought a chill sea breeze ashore. Nothing stirred but the wind.

"Galgan!"

The sentry spun around. "Sir?"

"We've just got word! The High King's done it again! The Saxons are running for their lives, and King Pellinore is on his way home at last. Come, lad, and drink a cup of wine with us."

The sentry's gaze swept the parapet and peered into the shadows. He sheathed his sword. "I'm coming, sir. I thought I heard—but there's no one here."

Guinevere exhaled as the man disappeared back inside the guardroom. Through the open door, she could hear the soldiers' celebration, a chanted victory paean, and the slosh of wine poured from a jug. "That was close."

Elaine sat up and pushed the hood from her face. Bright golden curls danced about her shoulders, and her voice exulted. "Father's alive and coming home victorious! The High King beat the Saxons back—didn't I say he would? He's not lost a battle yet. Admit it, now. He's the best warrior in all the kingdoms. And Father is coming home! Oh, what a feast we shall have when he arrives! I'll wager my last coin I can beg a new gown from Mama." She grinned. "You can have my old blue one if I do."

Guinevere smiled. "Let's hope those wagons that came in tonight carry your mother's order of cloth, for the storerooms are as empty as your purse. Hurry now. We've got to get back before Grannic and Ailsa discover we've gone."

They tiptoed through the flickering torchlight and past the guardroom door. From within, they could hear the guards' joyous cheer: "Long may he live, long may he reign! Praise be to Arthur, King of all the Britons!" The girls just had time to fold their cloaks away before their nurses arrived to usher them downstairs for the evening meal. Elaine's nurse, Grannic, a lanky woman with a sour face and small, calculating eyes, busied herself laying out a new gown for Elaine. She asked no questions about how Elaine had dirtied her present gown; she knew from long experience she would not receive an answer. But Guinevere's nurse, Ailsa, round, plump, and cheerful, pulled Guinevere into the anteroom for private speech.

"What have you been up to, then?" she said half under her breath as she brushed dust from Guinevere's skirts. "You were perfectly clean when I left you. And just look at you, with the roses in your cheeks and your hair pulling loose from its pins. You've worn your hood. You've been outside."

Guinevere bowed her head. She never liked fooling Ailsa, however easy it was to do. But Elaine had sworn her to secrecy long ago on the subject of the peephole and, in exchange for her silence, allowed her to look through it now and again. Having accepted the bargain, she could not go back on her word.

"I'm sorry, Ailsa."

Ailsa's nimble fingers worked swiftly and firmly, replaiting her hair and straightening her gown. There was no question of laying out another; the girl did not have enough to spare. "Now, why, I ask myself, would two young maids want to go outside on a cold spring night? Something to see? Or someone to meet?"

"No, no, nothing like that. Whom would we meet?"

"What, then?"

"We were perfectly safe. Honestly. It was just . . . something to do."

"Are you so idle, then? Perhaps I should speak to the queen. I've no doubt she could find a way to relieve you both of the time on your hands."

Guinevere hid a smile at Ailsa's pretended threat. "Please, Ailsa, I would tell you if I could. But I can't. I've promised. We were perfectly safe."

Ailsa finished her ministrations and lifted the girl's chin so she could look into her face. "I know who it was got the promise out of you, and all I can say is, be as careful as you can. Please, Gwen, for both our sakes."

Guinevere hugged her fiercely. Good, kind, loving Ailsa was more mother to her than nurse. Her actual mother had died at Guinevere's birth, and Ailsa, originally brought in as wet nurse, had stayed on to tend her. She had even left Northgallis with her five years ago, when Guinevere had been sent to her mother's people in Gwynedd for fostering.

Guinevere kissed Ailsa's cheek. "Thank you, Ailsa. Don't worry. I won't get us sent back to Northgallis in disgrace. Although . . . I'm homesick for it sometimes, aren't you?"

Ailsa's brown eyes widened. "Lord love you, child, is that what you think the queen would do? Why, what good would you be to her back in Northgallis? You'd be King Gwarthgydd's half sister, and his to marry off as he pleased. She'd profit nothing. No, Gwen, you'll not be sent back to Northgallis, whatever happens or however much you wish to go. But I might."

It took a moment for Guinevere to comprehend. "You mean . . . she'd send you back *alone*? Without me?"

Ailsa smiled crookedly and patted the girl's shoulder. "There, there, child. It's not likely to come to that any time soon."

"But why should it come to that at all? Why can't you stay with me always?"

This time it was Ailsa who looked away. "You'll be thirteen in two weeks' time and ready for courting. You won't need a nurse much longer. Queen Alyse is beginning to feel that she can manage your future without my help. It's only a matter of finding a suitable husband." She met Guinevere's anguished gaze with consummate gentleness. "This was bound to happen, Gwen. Sooner or later."

Tears welled in Guinevere's dark blue eyes, and she wiped them fiercely away with the backs of her hands. "You're more than my nurse, you're my—my mother, almost."

Ailsa kissed her. "I'm also an extra mouth to feed." She tried for a smile as she patted her ample hips, but Guinevere hugged her tightly.

"I'm going where you're going. I won't stay here without you. If it comes to that, I'll steal a pair of horses, and we'll escape together into the hills. . . ."

Pressed against Ailsa's stout body, Guinevere struggled to force back her tears. When she was calmer, she pulled away. "I ought to be allowed a companion of my choice. All highborn women have companions. I'm her own niece, after all, which I know counts more with her than being Gwarth's half sister. Besides, I'm not ready for courting. Anyone can see that. Let her make a match for Elaine before she starts scouting about for me."

"Oh, she will. No doubt of that."

"Elaine's not yet twelve, so we're safe for a while—if it's age that matters."

But she knew very well that it was not merely age that mattered. Six months ago, at the age of eleven, Elaine had begun her monthlies. This event had made her a woman in the eyes of the world and eligible for marriage. Guinevere, although a year older, was still considered a child. *That* was what mattered.

"What *are* you two talking about?" Elaine parted the curtain and came in from the bedchamber, freshly combed and dressed. "The bell has rung, and I'm half starved, and here you are whispering in secret conference."

Guinevere managed a smile. "Yes, very secret. Ailsa thinks your mother is getting ready to marry us off."

Elaine grinned. "It's about time, don't you think? I was beginning to think she would put it off forever." She linked her arm through Guinevere's and looked at her with dancing eyes. "Guess what Grannic told me? Mama is going to make each of us a new gown to wear to Father's homecoming feast!"

"Good, for I've outgrown mine." Guinevere stretched out her arms to reveal sleeves that fell well short of her wrists.

"*And,*" Elaine continued, unheeding, "there's a rumor going about that the High King has finally been persuaded to start searching for a wife."

Guinevere rolled her eyes at Ailsa. Since well before Arthur's crowning, Elaine had been smitten with an ardent admiration for this warrior son of old Uther Pendragon. Now, after four years as High King himself, and with the kingdoms of Britain beginning to settle into a stable alliance against the invading Saxons, Arthur was ready to marry. How opportune—or was it foresight?—that last autumn Queen Alyse had placed a large order of imported cloth with a merchant in Londinium.

Like a tapestry unrolling, the picture became suddenly clear: King Pellinore, high in King Arthur's graces after his bravery in the field; Pellinore's daughter, pretty, vivacious, almost twelve years old, and already past her menarche; Arthur Pendragon, High King of Britain, just eighteen and still unwed, beyond all doubt the most eligible bachelor in the land. Guinevere's respect for Queen Alyse's foresight deepened considerably.

"So he'll marry at last?" She gave Elaine's arm a squeeze. "It's about time, don't you think? I was beginning to wonder if he'd put it off forever."

CHAPTER TWO

The Fitting

Queen Alyse turned her profile to the window. It was her best feature, and the turn of her head, like the lift of her chin, was not entirely without thought. She held a swatch of sky blue fabric to the light and rubbed it gently between her fingers. "Yes. This will do very well for Elaine."

She glanced at the two girls standing in obedient silence near the door. Predictably, her daughter's face clouded, and her petulant mouth folded in a pout.

"Let Gwen have the blue, Mama. I like the scarlet better. Or the gold."

"Nonsense. You are far too young to wear scarlet. The blue is suitable for a maid your age, and it's a perfect match for your eyes. Guinevere may have the green."

The queen signaled to her women. Cissa and Leonora

lifted two lengths of cloth from a large trunk in the center of the chamber. Leonora carried the green to Guinevere, and Cissa held the blue up to Elaine's chin. Ailsa and Grannic, standing ready with pins of slivered bone, murmured their approval.

Elaine grimaced. "I'm so tired of blue," she muttered under her breath. "She always makes me wear it. Just once, I want to wear something scarlet."

"Hush," Guinevere whispered. "Don't rile her. You will in time."

"I don't want to wait until I'm old and gray. I want to wear it now."

Queen Alyse heard the whispers and ignored them. She did not particularly care whether Elaine liked the cloth. It suited her perfectly, accenting the blue of her eyes, the gold of her hair, and the pink creaminess of her complexion. But she could not help noticing the cloth's effect on the other girl, her ward and niece, Guinevere of Northgallis. Let that child anywhere near something blue—a gown, a tapestry, even a painted cup or the sea in summer—and her dark blue eyes shone like sapphires set in alabaster. Elaine should have the blue so that Guinevere did not.

Queen Alyse looked out at the budding hills and sighed. They were Elen's eyes, of course. Dear, departed sister Elen, the firstborn, the beauty of the family. She had collected admirers the way other girls did trinkets. Even so, she had not married until she was eighteen, when Alyse was already past her fifteenth birthday. Fifteen! The indignity of it still brought a flush to Alyse's cheek. Most girls were married by that age or at least betrothed. She remembered only too well the long parade of suitors who had come and come again, for years on end, to beg for Elen's hand. None of them had spared a glance for little Alyse, eclipsed by Elen's shadow. Hers had been the only dry eyes in all Gwynedd when at last her much-admired elder sister wed King Leodegrance of Northgallis and left home forever.

The queen smiled to herself. Of all the men she could have chosen—young men, handsome men, heirs to kingdoms twice the size of Gwynedd—Elen had chosen a man old enough to be her father, a man with five sons from his first marriage already grown to manhood. Northgallis was a tiny kingdom, ringed by mountains, insular, isolated, and, Alyse was certain, primitive by modern standards. For the sake of love, Elen had made a very foolish match and, as things turned out, a fatal one. She'd been sleeping in her grave these thirteen years while Alyse ruled in Gwynedd in their father's place. So much for Elen's singular beauty. All it had brought her was an early death in childbed, a daughter she never knew, and a sister who never mourned her absence.

Even now, Queen Alyse felt no regret. The threat of Elen's beauty hung over her still, like a lowering cloud, in the presence of Elen's daughter. But without Elen herself, it would not matter. There was only one princess of importance in Gwynedd, and that was Alyse's daughter. History would not repeat itself in this generation. She was not going to allow Elaine to grow up in anyone's shadow.

She turned from the window and gazed thoughtfully at her ward. There was nothing to worry about yet, and she was, after all, in complete charge of the girl's future. She and Pellinore, out of the goodness of their hearts, had taken the child in five years ago when King Leodegrance's health had begun to fail. Even at the time, she had considered it a practical move. If she could decide the fate of Elen's daughter, then she need have no worries for the fate of her own. Elaine had always been a pretty child and was now on the verge of becoming a very lovely young woman. Only a true beauty could out-shine her.

A smile forced its way to the queen's lips. One could hardly call young Guinevere a beauty. Just two weeks shy of her thirteenth birthday and clad in her much-loved leggings and tunic instead of a proper gown, she was still as straight and slim as any boy. Next to Elaine, who was a full year younger, Elen's daughter looked more like a garden scarecrow than a girl on the verge of womanhood. There might be promise in those dark blue eyes, those fine bones, and that rather astonishing white-gold hair, but the child would need a figure to attract a husband. When Guinevere did begin to blossom—a distant event, by the look of things—Alyse would have plenty of warning. There would be time enough to foil the ridiculous prophecy made at Guinevere's birth. Highest lady in the land, indeed!

That's what came of marrying a minor king of an isolated pagan kingdom like Northgallis. People were credulous fools. So many of them still believed in primitive gods, in magic, in witches and enchanters, and in the prophecies they uttered. The queen smiled bitterly. Folk were always claiming pro-phetic insights of one kind or another, and nothing ever came of it. The pagan witch who had descended from the hills and burst in on King Leodegrance on the night of Guinevere's birth had told the old king exactly what he wished to hear. His laboring wife would give birth to a daughter of surpassing beauty who would one day be the highest lady in the land, who would wed a great king and come to glory with him.

Glory! Queen Alyse almost snorted in contempt. How glorious was it for a woman to betray her king and be herself betrayed? For that, too, had been part of the prophecy, the dark part that people never spoke aloud but discussed in whispers behind closed doors. It was a terrible fate, and yet the hill witch had promised King Leodegrance that his daughter would come to glory, that her name would be remembered beyond a thousand years.

Queen Alyse shivered. It was so much stuff and nonsense. It was the result of ignorance, superstition, and a willingness to believe the rankest flattery. In any event, it could be prevented. Once the girl began her monthlies, Alyse would marry her off to the most obscure prince she could find.

"Yes, yes," she said impatiently to Cissa, who still held the blue cloth to Elaine's chin. "That will do. You shall have a gown of that, Elaine, provided you don't pout. And if you behave yourself, you may have your choice of another."

Elaine's face lit. She hurried to the trunk and pawed through the neatly folded cloth, lifting out a pale yellow linen threaded with gold. "Look at this one, Gwen. Isn't it beautiful?"

"Perfect for summer," Queen Alyse agreed. "And there's enough for a shawl to match."

Elaine draped a length of the shimmering cloth over her shoulder and spun around. The fabric floated with her, light and airy, the interlaced golden threads sparkling in the morning light. She would look every inch a princess in a gown made of this. And the other selections inside that trunk—golds, ivories, scarlets, greens, and purples, silks and velvets and linens as soft as down—they were equally fine. Surely her mother had some great project in mind.

"Where are we going, Mama? Tell us what you are planning. Oh, I know what it must be—a journey to Londinium, at long last, to be presented to the High King and his court." Elaine spun on her toes and whirled the linen overhead.

"That will do, Elaine. If you tear the cloth, you shall have nothing from it."

The queen's sharp voice brought her back to earth, and with a sigh, Elaine let the fabric tumble from her arms. Cissa and Leonora hurried to snatch it up and smooth the wrinkles.

"But I've got it right, haven't I, Mama? It's our turn to meet the High King, even if we *are* the last ones in all Britain. We're going to travel across the mountains and out of Wales and meet him and Father at Londinium or Caerleon or Aquae Sulis or somewhere grand and fine where all the court is gathered. Say it's so, Mama. I know it is."

Alyse raised an eyebrow. "Court? King Arthur has no court. He's a war leader. He lives in a tent surrounded by troops and servants. He hardly spends two nights in the same place. Where have you heard this foolish prattle about a court?"

Elaine gulped, trying unsuccessfully to hide her

disappointment. "But he was at Caerleon all winter. I heard the soldiers talking. People flocked to him there, through snow and storm, just to meet him or beg him for favors or offer him service. It was a—a court of sorts."

"He may have been at Caerleon all winter, but he's not there now. He and his men were planning the spring campaign against the Saxons during the cold months, and now they're fighting it. But you know that. You were in the hall six weeks ago when Arthur's summons came."

Elaine's eyes filled with tears. "Aren't we *ever* going to be presented to King Arthur, then? It's been four years since he pulled the Sword from the stone—four solid years—and *still* we haven't been within a hundred leagues of him."

Queen Alyse turned her lovely head to gaze back out the window. A pale shaft of sunlight warmed her cheeks, and she lifted her face to the blessed heat. After a long winter in a dank stone castle, nothing was so welcome as the springtime sun. She basked in it a moment, drowsy with warmth, and let her thoughts drift.

The wheel of time seemed to turn faster every year. Could it really be only four years ago that she had gone to Caerleon with Pellinore to attend the coronation of Uther's astonishing son? It seemed like yesterday. She had not known what to expect of the fourteen-year-old fosterling of Sir Ector of Galava who had turned out to be the High King Uther's only son. A legitimate son, too, born to Ygraine of Cornwall, Uther's queen, but spirited away on the night of his birth by Merlin the Enchanter to be raised in secrecy, away from court, and kept ignorant of his parentage. Indeed, in the way that mattered, Merlin was more his father than Uther. Even when the boy had lived with Sir Ector in Galava, he had been under Merlin's protection. What kind of person could such a heritage produce? She had wondered about it all the way to Caerleon.

The queen smiled to herself as she remembered young Arthur's serious boy's face, the steady calm of his composure, and the burning desire for achievement that shone like a beacon from his eyes. She could still see him standing surrounded by his battle captains, men twice and thrice his age, listening intently, his bright new crown forgotten, with little room in his head for thoughts of anything but Saxons, horses, and fighting tactics. Pellinore thought him a born leader, and he was not alone.

Four years of war had made a man of Arthur, by all accounts. Now, if one could believe the rumors the courier reported, he was on the point of yielding to the advice of his Companions to build himself a fortress and find himself a wife.

Alyse compressed her lips into a firm, straight line. She ought to have foreseen it earlier. She ought to have ordered the cloth last spring and scheduled this fitting months ago. The young King ready to marry, and Elaine with a dowry half complete! There was much to do and perhaps very little time.

She turned from the window and regarded her daughter with speculation. "You are eager to see the High King in person, are you? You'd be disappointed. He is a war leader, not a landed king like your father. He's what my grandfather called a *dux bellorum*, a duke of battles. He lives in a soldiers' camp, full of mud and horses. It's not the sort of place any woman of standing would even wish to visit. If he survives, no doubt in time he'll build a fortress somewhere, if only to have a place to house his horses and his men. But he'll have to do it on some-one else's land. He has none of his own."

"He has all Britain," Elaine returned with a defiant lift of her chin. " 'Arthur of Britain' the soldiers call him. Even Father calls him that."

"It's always politic to flatter leaders. But he's a landless prince. King Arthur has nothing to call his own."

"Then why does everyone serve him? Why does Father answer every summons? Why do men talk of nothing else but Arthur's victories, Arthur's plans, Arthur's Sword, Arthur's horse, Arthur's hound? He's a leader like none we've had before, that's why!"

Queen Alyse allowed herself a smile. "Well, you have caught Pendragon fever, I see. It seems to be sweeping the land. I did not mean to disparage the High King, my dear. He is a surprisingly skillful leader for one so young. Someday, if he ever builds a fortress and establishes a court, I'm sure we'll all go to pay him our respects. You will meet him then. There's plenty of time." She turned to the nurses. "Now, then, Grannic, Ailsa, undress these girls and let's begin the fitting."

"But what are the gowns for if they're not for court?" Elaine cried, unpacified by this vague promise. "You ordered the cloth last autumn, you must have, when that merchant from Londinium passed through Gwynedd. What is it you've been planning? Why won't you tell us?"

Queen Alyse looked at her coolly. "Why do you think I employ Iakos to teach you Greek, Latin, and mathematics?

Why do you study the housekeeping accounts with my steward, Linias? Why do Cissa and Leonora instruct you in spinning, weaving, and stitching and Father Martin in Scripture? We are laboring, all of us, to prepare you for your futures."

"You mean, at last we'll be allowed to receive suitors? That's what the gowns are for?" Elaine clapped her hands for joy. "Oh, Mama, why didn't you tell us so last autumn? Gwen and I could have spent the long winter making plans instead of reading Homer. Does this mean we are done with lessons? Oh, hurrah!" She grabbed Guinevere and swung her around in a circle.

"It means no such thing," Alyse retorted. "Lessons will continue as before. If there are plans to be made, your father and I will make them."

Elaine faced her mother with a mulish gleam in her eye. "Lessons with Iakos are a waste of time. I hate history and mathematics. I can't keep all that information in my head, and writing makes my hand cramp. It's all right for Gwen; she likes it. But I hate it. Besides, we're not going to be scholars or scribes—we'll have servants who can do all that for us—why do we have to know such useless things?"

Queen Alyse drew herself to her full height and scowled down at her daughter. Her women nailed their gazes to the floor.

Guinevere tugged furtively at Elaine's sleeve. "Hush, Elaine. It's an *honor* to take lessons with a scholar like Iakos. It's a great privilege. You know it is."

"Snake in the grass!" Elaine turned on her. "You say that because Iakos likes you best."

"Silence." The word fell, cold and contemptuous, like a stone from a precipice, and stilled Elaine. The queen glared at each girl in turn. "I won't tolerate such impudence. How do you know what it takes to be a queen, either of you? You are ignorant children. You value nothing you don't already know. Your Latin is atrocious. How do you propose to converse with anyone beyond the borders of Gwynedd? Do you think everyone in Britain, or even Wales, can understand your speech? You can read a smattering of Greek and quote a verse from Homer, and you think you're educated. God grant me patience! You know next to nothing about history, government, star-reading, or even housekeeping. You don't know how to keep a castle full of people fed and clothed over a long winter. You don't know how to keep accounts or take an inventory. You can't prepare a feast or preserve food. You can't set out a garden or harvest flax or care for cattle, pigs, sheep, or fowl. If you don't know these things, how will you know whether those you employ to do them for you are doing them well or ill?

"Knowledge is power, Elaine. Never give it willingly into another's hands. If you wish to be a queen, the running of the household will be your responsibility, and if you are a strong queen, the running of the kingdom will be yours, as well, from time to time."

She paused, nostrils flared, her color high and her breathing quick and sharp. "I will not let any daughter—or ward—of mine beyond the borders of Gwynedd until you know enough to keep from being cheated or scorned by everyone you meet. You will be educated whether you like it or not."

The queen approached the girls and stood before them. "One thing more. You are women. You live in a world run almost entirely by men. If you want a modicum of joy in life, you will do well to earn their respect. I called you here to fit you for new gowns, but that is only a small step in the process. I will train you and groom you to attract a prince of standing. I will do everything in my power to see you marry well. But life does not end there. I am trying to fit you for a greater happiness. Beauty is a fleeting weapon. It's the use of your wits that will carve you a place in life and make you the women you will become: powerful or weak, respected or ignored, remembered or forgotten.".

Queen Alyse watched their faces. Elaine pouted visibly and rubbed the toe of her slipper against the cracked mosaics of the floor. It had all gone over her head, the entire torrent of words, because it was not what she wished to hear. But Guinevere's eyes were open wide, and her blue gaze fastened on the queen's face. A rush of appreciation warmed Alyse's heart. Here was fertile ground for the seeds of her wisdom, but she shrank from willing cultivation. She was afraid of the harvest she might reap.

Every time she saw Guinevere, something turned cold inside her and hardened her heart. The child was too much like Elen. Even standing silent, obedient, and blue with cold amid the whirl of women and cloth, she had the power to fill Alyse with dread. Like a vulture, Alyse thought, brooding on a branch, alone and unwelcome, but ready to swoop down and steal the prize when the time was ripe.

She shrugged. Life was full of injustices, great and small. It had been unfair of Elen to delay marriage until she fell in love. It had been unfair of their father to prefer his elder daughter to his younger. Persevering in the face of injustice had made Alyse stronger. She did not pause to consider, as she turned away, that the effect on Guinevere might be the same.

CHAPTER THREE

Dreams of the Ignorant

Guinevere bent over the tablet before her and made deep, careful marks in the pliant wax. Sunlight flooded the school-room. Iakos had unshuttered the windows at long last, and all around her, tiny motes danced and floated in brilliant sun-beams. The day was turning warm and the air soft. She raised her head to gaze out the nearest window, but all she could see was a tumble of outbuildings nestled against the orchard wall. A dull view, no doubt desirable for a schoolroom. But beyond the wall, the slim branches of apple trees warmed to blossom in the welcome heat, and between the outbuildings, a worn path ran down to the stables. The path beckoned to her. It was a perfect day for riding out.

She glanced up to see the tutor Iakos eyeing her down his long nose. With a sigh, she took up her stylus and bent her head obediently over her work. He had set them an easy problem, and she knew she could solve it if only she could muster her attention. But no sooner had she applied herself than her thoughts drifted away again.

The fitting had taken most of the morning, thanks to Elaine's unwillingness to obey her mother without argument. The ordeal had spoiled everyone's temper. In the end, Alyse had marked the cloth herself to put an end to the wrangle over necklines and waistlines. Elaine's new gown would have a low neckline and a high waist to show off her budding figure to best advantage. Guinevere's gown would have a high neckline, all the way to the throat. "No need to accent a bust that isn't there," the queen had said. And so it had gone, hour upon hour, with Guinevere shivering, undressed, while Elaine wheedled and coaxed from her mother the promise of two more gowns, a pair of slippers, an embroidered belt, and uncounted lengths of ribbon for her hair.

"Oh, bother!" Beside her on the bench, Elaine threw down her stylus and yawned. "I don't care what Mother says, I'm *never* going to need to know the Pythagorean theorem and all these rules about ratios and diameters. Old Pythagoras must have been barking mad. Why on earth bother with numbers like pi that aren't really numbers at all? I can think of a thousand better ways to spend the day. Especially after the awful morning we've had. Don't you agree, Gwen?"

Iakos rose from his stool by the window. "Do you find the problem too difficult, Lady Elaine? It's merely a demonstration of the principles we studied all last week." He peered over her shoulder at the scratches on her tablet and sighed a little wearily. "I don't require your calculations to be exact, but I do require that the principle itself be understood." He leaned down and drew another problem for her. "Try that one. You've solved it before."

Elaine scowled. "I'm not in the mood for solving problems."

Iakos glanced over Guinevere's shoulder. "That is correct, my lady. Would you like another, or do you want to get right to the translation?"

"Oh, the translation, please." She smiled up at him. "I'm dying to get out. It's much too nice a day to spend inside."

Iakos retrieved a scroll from the cupboard and laid it on the table between his two students. He smiled a fatherly smile. "I couldn't agree with you more. You may go as soon as you've done the first twenty lines."

"What about me?" Elaine demanded. "May I go when I've solved this problem?"

"A problem you solved two days ago? No, my lady, that would defeat the point of the lesson. You may go when you've solved the original problem or when you've done twenty lines from Homer. You may take your pick."

Elaine fumed at him, but to no avail, and Guinevere bent cheerfully to her task. She liked Iakos for his patience, his evenhandedness, and his innate sense of fairness. He seemed to regard rank as an unimportant accident of birth. To him, it was the mind that mattered, ideas that carried weight. He was the only one she had ever met who looked at the world that way.

Iakos was Greek by birth, a cultured man who had come to

Britain when Uther Pendragon was High King because a priestess in Delphi had read portents of a coming golden age in Britain. Guinevere often stayed to talk to him after lessons were over. She loved learning about life in faraway lands, loved to imagine the sun-drenched shores of Iakos's homeland on the Inland Sea, where rain was a cause for celebration and one could walk outside without a cloak in winter. She liked learning other languages. She loved the mysteries of mathematics, the cerebral magic of symmetries and proportions. And he, like any good teacher, responded with praise and encouragement to her interest.

She hoped his regard for her stemmed only from her willingness to learn. But she knew he had heard about the prophecy made at her birth. His only comment about it had been a subtle one. Once, he had revealed that Delphi was his birthplace, and she had asked him about the old priestess at the shrine of Apollo there. Were the prophecies voiced by the Pythia always true? Did he believe them? Iakos had regarded her for a long moment, replying at last in a gentle voice that prophecies were dreams of the ignorant fostered by the willing.

He had been trying to comfort her. That meant he had heard about her own prophecy. And why not? Everyone in Gwynedd seemed to have known all about it before she even arrived. During her first year here, when she was eight years old, people had avoided her, made the sign against enchantment behind their backs as she passed by, averted their heads when she entered a room, and kept their distance. Now, after five years of acquaintance, they no longer treated her like a strangeling. Only on moments of great occasion would she see that ancient, superstitious fear flicker in their eyes and, reminded of what was expected of her, feel that sickening nausea grip her innards once again.

How many times had she cursed that vile hag, Griselda, for her bold interference? Her dear father, King Leodegrance, bless his proud pagan heart, had believed every word the hill witch said. That was why he had sent his only daughter to Gwynedd when he felt death approaching. Gwynedd was a wide kingdom and King Pellinore a powerful king, although a Christian. She would find her future in Gwynedd, her father had told her at their parting. No one would see her light in small, dark, mountainous Northgallis. She must go to her mother's people in Gwynedd. Her destiny required it.

Guinevere shuddered at the thought of destiny. Curse Griselda for putting such a notion into her dear father's head. She told herself sternly that there was no longer any need to fear the prophecy. It was all nonsense, and even if it wasn't, Queen Alyse was determined to foil it. That had been made perfectly clear. Far from resenting it, Guinevere found the knowledge extraordinarily restful.

Elaine put down her stylus. "I can't write anymore. My hand hurts."

"Rest for a while," Iakos suggested. "It will be better presently."

"Gwen's finished. I want to go. I will go. You can't stop me."

"Nothing is gained without effort, Lady Elaine. Come, we'll work through it together."

"No." Elaine rose. "I don't want to. My head aches. I'm going to see my mother."

Iakos came to the bench and glanced at Guinevere's translation. He nodded, and she rose from her seat. "The queen is beyond your call at the moment," he said. "She is meeting with the captain of her house guard."

Both girls paused, Elaine by the bench and Guinevere almost at the door. "What for?" Elaine asked.

"I understand there was another theft last night. Four head of cattle."

Elaine whistled. "That's enough to ruin her temper for the rest of the week. You'd better not go out, Gwen, if there are thieves in the hills."

But it was too late. Guinevere had gone.

CHAPTER FOUR

Old Argus's Son

Queen Alyse paced back and forth across her workroom. The looms were silent, the women gone. She had dismissed them before she met with her advisors: Linias, her steward; Gelston, the cattlemaster; and Regis, the captain of the house guard. The meeting had been a complete waste of time. Twenty-seven animals stolen since the herds were put out to graze, and not a man among them knew where they had gone. Ten cows, two bulls, eight heifers, three ewes, and four lambs—gone without a trace. The fools would have her believe they had vanished into thin air! In a temper, she had dismissed them from her presence and threatened to dismiss them from their posts if they could not provide her better information.

She whirled and crossed the room again. She had been foolish to rely on such incompetents. She would take charge of the investigation herself. She would begin with Regis's second-in-command.

Marcus, son of Argus, was a young man of twenty, fifteen years younger than his commander, Regis. As a son of one of King Pellinore's chief nobles, Marcus deserved a place in the king's fighting force but had been cheated of this honor by an accident of birth. His right arm was deformed, shriveled, and hung useless from his shoulder. He could not wield both shield and sword; he could not notch an arrow to a bowstring; he could not throw a spear or fight with cudgels as well as other men. But he had trained himself to handle a sword left-handed, and he could throw a knife of any size and any weight with unerring accuracy. He was quick, strong, clever, and soft-tongued. These skills had earned him a place in the house guard. His ability, his obedience, and his even temper had won the king's favor, and over Regis's objections, he had been promoted to second-in-command.

Queen Alyse watched him enter the room and make his reverence. He was a smaller man than his commander, and plain of face, but with a compact, muscular body and an air of quiet self-possession that Alyse found more formidable than Regis's customary displays of bravado. In the short time since his promotion, Marcus had developed a reputation as someone who could be trusted.

As he rose from his knee and raised his head, she met his eyes directly. They were Celtic eyes, gray as the winter seas. She saw intelligence there, and self-command, and no fear at all.

She beckoned him forward. "Sit down, Marcus. There's no

need to stand at attention. This meeting is informal. I want your advice."

He came forward readily enough and took the bench she indicated.

"Let me congratulate you on your promotion. I'm sure it was well deserved. You come from an old and honored family."

The young man bowed his head. "You are very gracious, my lady."

"I've known Argus of Oak Hill all my life. A brave and honorable man, a loyal soldier. And your brothers, all four of them, fight with Pellinore. An extraordinary family. There seem to be fewer and fewer such men born nowadays."

The gray eyes, clear as rain, regarded her with wary amusement. Alyse abandoned the indirect approach. This man was no fool and knew flattery when he heard it. Better to ask him straight out for his help.

She leaned forward in her chair and began to speak. He listened attentively and without interruption as she laid out the problem of the cattle thefts. She told him everything she knew, including the actions she had taken, the reports she had received, the suspicions she had begun to form, and the possibilities that had occurred to her. When she finished, she knew her reading of Marcus had been correct. She had appealed to his intelligence and his loyalty, and both were now fully engaged. More, he had read between the lines and understood what she wanted of him without her having to come right out and commit herself to words. Alyse appreciated subtlety and looked upon him with approval.

"If you are right," he said, "there is more at stake than live-stock."

"Yes."

"You are asking me to risk my post."

"There is no gain without risk."

Marcus flashed her a brief but transforming smile. "I like risk, my lady."

"Good. Then you are the man for it, Marcus."

He rose and stood at the window, looking out. He made a neat figure, with his right sleeve tucked tight in his belt as if his withered arm did not exist. "And if I refuse?"

"I will not hold it against you. King Pellinore will never know. But . . ."

He turned to her, and for an instant, she sensed something fierce in him, something sharp as a dagger point and bright as the flash of a sword. "But I will know, won't I? And that might make me . . . uncomfortable to have about."

Queen Alyse wondered briefly if she had been wise after all. She had counted on loyalty from an offspring of Old Argus, but when it came to wits, the son was twice the man his father had been. An instant later, she realized that Marcus was laughing at her in his polite, reserved way and that his smile was genuine.

"Your suspicions, my lady, run with my own. I would be happy to undertake the task. And whether I succeed or fail, you will never hear any mention of it from my lips."

The queen exhaled. She was too relieved to care if he saw it. "Thank you, Marcus. I will not forget it."

"One thing more." He turned back to the window, where, beyond the castle walls, beyond the thatched roofs of the village, the cold green sea stretched to the horizon. "Your ward, Lady Guinevere, often rides out into the hills unattended. This must cease. Restrict her to the shore paths or provide her with an escort. Better yet, keep her safe indoors."

"Easier said than done," Queen Alyse responded, rising to her feet. "What is it you fear? Abduction? No one would dare."

He shrugged. "Can you afford to take the chance?"

An icicle of fear struck Queen Alyse. The shiver it produced lingered long after Marcus had gone. She sent to the schoolroom for Guinevere and returned to her workroom to oversee the cutting of the fabric for the girls' gowns. She was deep in a discussion with Leonora about sleeve lengths when the page returned with the news that Guinevere had completed her lessons early and had already been dismissed. Alyse glanced out her window at the height of the sun. Again, that needle of ice in her chest caught at her breath.

She left her women, threw on a cloak, and made for the stables. Stannic the stablemaster met her on the cobbled stones of the yard. He ducked his head politely.

"My lady queen, what a surprise—"

"Where is my ward? Where is Guinevere? Is she here? I must see her at once."

Stannic ducked his head again. "I'm sorry, my lady. The young princess is not here. She, er, she rode out more than an hour ago."

CHAPTER FIVE

Daughter of Rhiannon

"Hup!"

Guinevere leaned low over the gelding's withers as the old horse thrust himself into the air, knees bent, and cleared a carefully stacked pile of logs and brush. She murmured to him sweetly as he landed, and one ear flicked back to catch her praise. Calm hands on the reins and firm legs against his sides urged him onward. He complied and opened up his stride.

"One, two, three," she counted under her breath each time his leading foreleg hit the ground. The chicken coop approached, festooned with pine boughs. She knew the coop held a secret terror for him, and she kept her voice and hands steady as she urged him toward it. "Come on, old boy, you can do it, five, six, here we go, and hup!"

He gathered himself for the leap and threw himself over,

hooves recoiling at the tickle of boughs against his fetlocks. She patted his neck for that and called him her darling boy. He bent his head and danced a little, playing with the bit in a burst of exuberance and pride as if he were a youngster and not an aging cavalry mount whose best years were behind him. She laughed and circled him patiently until he settled into his steady canter. At the top of the field, they turned and headed back. He took the last three obstacles in the even, ground-covering stride that had served him so well on the battlefield.

"Well done, Peleth! Good job, old boy. There's nothing like it, is there? Flying through the air, as free as the wind— oh, you are a magnificent old beast!"

His ears flicked back, and he basked in her affection. She dropped the reins so he could stretch his neck out, and when he did, she bent forward and hugged him, pressing her cheek into his mane and sliding her arms around his neck.

The horse dropped his head into a patch of new grass, and Guinevere slid off his back. She led him into the woods toward a nearby stream. Out of the sun, the air was cool, and her eyes, unaccustomed to the dimness, could not see into the shadows. She glanced behind her once, as if she felt eyes on her back, but when she turned to look, there was no one there. Still, the hair rose on the nape of her neck, and she suppressed a shiver. The pagan part of her believed in evil spirits. In Northgallis, they had sown sickness, injury, and madness among the local population and could be driven off only by the most powerful charms and protections. Here in Gwynedd, a Christian kingdom, evil spirits were classed with faeries, elves, and shape-shifters, creatures of myth and fable, not of God's creation. No one paid the slightest attention to them. But *something* was raising the hair on her neck, and she hurried a little faster through the dark parts of the forest.

At the stream's edge, she stopped. While Peleth drank, she hummed a tune to herself and let her eyes stray over the dappled shadows among the trees. She could see much better now, but still she saw nothing that did not belong to the forest of an April morning. Nevertheless, the prickle of fear between her shoulder blades refused to go away.

When Peleth had finished drinking, she led him deeper into the woods to a place she knew, a clearing where grass and wildflowers grew rampant within a rough circle of oak and beech. The sun always seemed to shine inside that clearing. This day was no exception. She hobbled the horse and left him to graze while she took her customary seat on a flat rock to finish her song in a pool of sun.

Looking carefully around one more time to make sure she was alone, Guinevere reached into her tunic and pulled out a little ivory figurine: fair Rhiannon the horse goddess, astride her ivory mare. She held it gently and rubbed a finger over its silken surface. It had been her father's parting gift five years ago on the day she had left Northgallis forever. She turned it toward the sun and watched the tiny sapphires of the divine eyes glimmer deep and blue. Beautiful Rhiannon, protector of horses and of women, so young, so radiantly powerful—this talisman had been her mother's once. And her mother had treasured it, even though she was a Christian, because it had been a gift from Leodegrance on their wedding day.

Guinevere touched the figurine to her lips. It was warm from the sun and radiated warmth into her fingers. But for the sapphires, which her father had added to imitate her mother's eyes, it was very old and roughly carved. The features of the goddess were indistinct, and her white mare might have been any one of the mountain ponies that bred freely in the hills of Wales. Years and years of gentle rubbing by a long line of mothers and daughters had worn all the details away. To Guinevere, the featureless face of the goddess had one outstanding virtue: it could represent any face she wanted. Now, gazing down at the little carving, she gave it the face she imagined her mother might have had—a high-browed, oval face with delicate features and wise, all-knowing eyes.

Again, as she had done a thousand times before, she wondered what her mother had been like. A courageous woman, surely, to grow up a Christian in Gwynedd and marry the much older, pagan Leodegrance. By all accounts, she had loved him. She must have, to leave home for him, to leave behind everyone and everything she knew and start a new life in a tiny mountain kingdom where her husband's was the only familiar face.

Guinevere pulled the stopper from her waterskin and poured a small libation on the ground. Eyes closed, she uttered a silent, heartfelt prayer to Rhiannon to watch over her mother's spirit, wherever it was now, and protect it from harm. She ached to reach out to the woman who had borne her, to touch her spirit, to receive the blessing of her love, as she had already received the blessing of her life.

She kicked at a stone and watched it land near Peleth's

feet. He blew and raised a startled face to hers. She realized she had been thinking a lot about her mother lately. The thirteenth anniversary of her own birth—and of her mother's death—was only eleven days away, on the first of May. She did not look forward to it. Her own birthdays never brought her joy. She could not forget that if she had never been born, her beautiful mother might still be alive.

Even her father, who had loved his daughter dearly, had felt the same. Though he had danced with Guinevere at every Beltane celebration on the first of May and showered her with gifts and kisses, his joy was bittersweet. She knew, as all Northgallis knew, that grief for his young wife still weighed his spirit down. Guinevere was almost glad he could not be here to see her turn thirteen and stand on the verge of womanhood herself. Would he be frightened for her? Would he wake in the night, as she did, filled with doubts about the kind of woman she would make?

Guinevere rose to her feet and went to Peleth's side. She stroked his smooth coat, warm from the sun, and patted his neck, as if he were the one who needed reassurance. For her father's sake, she would do her best to be brave and face the future with confidence, even if it was not the future he had envisioned for her.

All soldiers were superstitious men. Pagan or Christian, they believed whatever came to them from the stars, from the shadows, from the precincts of the Otherworld whose ways could not be understood. Guinevere herself had never believed a single word of the witch's prophecy. The hag had probably been drunk and wandered into the king's house to warm herself at the fire, earning a place at the hearth by telling the old king what he wanted most to hear. Highest lady in the land? The suggestion was ludicrous. Without parents, without land, power, rank, or backing, she would have to be ten times as pretty as Elaine even to attract the notice of a suitor. And she was not pretty. She knew this by Elaine's satisfaction whenever they looked at themselves in the queen's polished bronze. She knew it by Queen Alyse's condescension and by Ailsa's too-frequent reassurances that time would change everything. At least her father had gone to his grave with his dreams intact and would not have to suffer the disappointment of his fondest hopes.

Peleth's head jerked up, ears pricked. Guinevere whirled. Something had moved in the bushes behind her. She tucked Rhiannon carefully back inside her tunic and reached for Peleth's reins. She had wasted enough time sitting and brooding. The sun shone in a sky still free of clouds, and there was time for another gallop through the meadow.

The horse snorted, nostrils sprung wide, his gaze still fastened on the woods behind her. She could hear nothing, but she knew without looking that this time, something was there. Trembling a little, but holding hard to her courage, she turned and followed the horse's gaze into the dappled shadows.

A pair of dark eyes looked back at her.

CHAPTER SIX

Llyr

She blinked once, twice. The eyes were still there, holding hers. They were set into a narrow human face above a lithe body half hidden in the shadows. She bent down to release the horse's hobbles, grabbed a hank of mane with one hand, and prepared to leap onto the gelding's back.

At once, the figure moved. He spread out empty-fingered hands in a conciliatory gesture and took one step forward into the light. He was a young man, lightly built, and no taller than she. His only garment was a wolf skin slung over his left shoulder and hanging halfway to his knees. On his feet, he wore slippers of animal hide and around his neck, his only orna-ment, a double-strung choker of wolf's teeth. His weapons—a small bow, a quiver of arrows, and a long, slender spear with a killing point—lay propped against the trunk of the oak behind him.

Guinevere drew in a deep breath. "Who are you?"

His hair was brown, thick, and badly cut. He had trouble keeping it out of his eyes, and more than once as they stared at each other, he reached up a hand to push it back from his face. Pointing to his own chest, he spoke in a soft, guttural voice. Guinevere shook her head. Hesitantly, the stranger tried again. "Llyr, son of Bran, leader of White Foot hunters of Snow Mountain."

His accent was foreign, but this time, he spoke a dialect of Mountain Welsh, and she could just make out the words. Mountain Welsh was an old language, out of use now except among isolated folk. In Northgallis, people used it to communicate with that ancient race of men who still lived in the hills, men known to modern Britons as the Old Ones. Guinevere's eyes widened as she realized what this meant.

Tentatively, she let go of the horse's mane. "Llyr, son of Bran," she repeated. He had the name of a god, and so had his father. But this was not surprising, for the Old Ones traced their lineage all the way back to the ancient days, when the world was new, pristine, divine. They considered themselves to be descended straight from gods.

"Snow Mountain? Do you mean Y Wyddfa?" This was the tallest peak in Gwynedd, whose upper slopes glittered with snow even in summer and where the gods themselves were still said to walk.

The young man's face lit in a delighted smile. "Y Wyddfa," he agreed. "Home of gods."

Guinevere let go of Peleth's reins and made Llyr a reverence as best she could in her tunic and leggings. "Guinevere, daughter of King Leodegrance of Northgallis."

Llyr lowered his eyes. "Gwenhwyfar," he said shyly. "She With Hair of Light. I am honored." And he made her a deep and solemn bow.

She colored faintly. Strangers always gawked at the pale color of her hair, as if she had chosen it herself just to astonish them. "Never mind that. What do you do here, so far from home?" She glanced at his weapons stacked against the tree. "Not hunting—you're too far from Snow Mountain."

He shook his head. "Not hunting." He searched for the word and found it. "Guarding."

"Guarding what?"

He laughed. "You."

"*Me?* Whatever for?"

He gestured to the woods all around them. "From beasts in the forest. From wild men."

"Wild men?" she breathed.

"You will be safe," he said gravely. "There is no need to be afraid."

She stiffened. "I've been riding out in the woods all my life, and I've never been afraid."

Llyr looked pleased. "Long Eyes guard you well. And Red Ears."

"Red Ears? Long Eyes? Who are they?"

He waved toward the eastern mountains. "The Red Ears live in the land of mountains. In the land of your father-king."

Guinevere gasped. "In Northgallis?"

"Aye. Nort-gal-us."

"Do you mean . . . ," she said, her voice beginning to shake, "that I was guarded in Northgallis? When I was a child?"

Llyr nodded.

Guinevere laughed nervously. "That's enough of your tall tales. You'll have me believing in faeries next."

Llyr pointed up into the heights above them. "I live with the Long Eyes now. In this place, the Long Eyes guard you."

"You mean here in Gwynedd? In King Pellinore's kingdom?"

"Gwynedd," Llyr said, pleased. "In the valley lives the king. In the hills live the Long Eyes."

Guinevere gulped. "You must be jesting. You can't be telling me that the Old Ones have guarded me *my whole life*."

"Old Ones," Llyr repeated happily. "Aye. Old Ones. Earth's Beloved."

She was shaking, and he gripped her arm to steady her. Together they sat down on the warm, flat rock. While Guinevere struggled to come to terms with the enormity of these revelations, Llyr began to talk. As he talked, his command of Mountain Welsh improved, and as she listened, so did hers. After a little while, she found she could follow his speech with ease.

Llyr was no longer with the White Foot, the people of his birth, but with the Long Eyes, who hunted in the high hills above Pellinore's castle. Mapon, the leader of the Long Eyes, had sent his own son to the White Foot in exchange. As far as Guinevere could determine, this was a common practice among the Old Ones, or Earth's Beloved, as they called themselves.

She could see the wisdom of it. In this way, the people in different clans could keep abreast of changing customs, get news from different parts of the country, and intermarry so their lines did not diminish. Llyr had been with the Long Eyes for six months and would not return to his own people until he was twenty. He was now seventeen years old.

Guinevere looked at him in surprise when he told her this. She had thought him younger, perhaps because of his diminutive size, but the longer they sat together and talked, the clearer it became that he was a person to be reckoned with, a prince of standing among his own people. He was not like anyone she had met before. The meanness of his dress, the shaggy hair, the awkward speech, were offset by his natural gifts. His dark eyes were liquid as a deer's and large for his narrow face. His arms and legs, as slim as her own, were tanned and hard with muscle. He moved like a dancer and had a certain air about him, a direct meeting of the eye, that commanded respect.

He seemed very proud at having been selected to guard her today. Apparently, it was considered a great privilege among the Old Ones to be awarded guard duty over She With Hair of Light. According to Llyr, only the bravest men were assigned to the task. He had killed a boar last week to prove himself worthy.

Guinevere stared at him. "You killed a boar? By yourself?" When King Pellinore went boar hunting, he took a troop of well-armed men with him and ropes, too, sometimes. They were often gone for two or three days, returning home exhausted, scratched, and bruised and, when successful, with the carcass of a great beast stuck all over with spears. No one ever went boar hunting alone.

Llyr laughed at her suggestion. All the men in the clan had gone to hunt the boar, a great she-boar who lived in a mountain cave high above their camp. The search had taken one day, the chase another, and the final battle, beast against man, had lasted from noon to sunset on the third. He, Llyr, son of Bran, had thrown the spear that finally dropped her. Thus, he was given credit for the kill. At the celebration— where, he assured her, he had gotten gloriously drunk— Mapon had promised to grant him one request. Naturally, he had asked to be permitted to guard She With Hair of Light.

Guinevere said helplessly, "It is very flattering that your people consider it a privilege to guard me, but I honestly do not understand why you bother. I am not an important person anymore. I have no rank outside Northgallis, no land, no power, no value to anyone. In Gwynedd, I am only the queen's ward. It is a waste of your time to guard me."

Llyr smiled. "You are jesting."

"No, Llyr. I am not jesting."

Llyr drew in his breath sharply as color drained from his face. "You . . . do not know why we guard you?"

"Of course I do not know. How would I?"

Llyr swallowed hard. "Did not your father-king tell you? Did not your people tell you? Everyone knows." He turned to her a face still pale with shock and a gaze focused on something in the distance. "No one ever told me that you did not know."

"Know *what?*" Guinevere narrowed her eyes. "Tell me this is not about old Griselda's prophecy."

Relief flooded Llyr's face. "You *do* know."

Guinevere buried her head in her hands. Even the Old Ones had heard the wretched prophecy! Then a thought struck her that startled her into speechlessness. Of course they had heard of it—it was *their* prophecy in the first place! The hill witch Griselda, who had visited her father on the night of her birth, had been one of the Old Ones herself. It must be so; it explained everything.

Breathing slowly to control the racing of her heart, she looked into Llyr's liquid eyes. "Llyr, listen to me. You must not believe such nonsense. No one can know the future. A prophecy is not necessarily truth."

Llyr smiled forgivingly. "Gods do not lie," he said simply. "Gods speak truth. Always."

Guinevere bowed her head. She could think of nothing to say to change his mind. Divine pronouncements, pagan or Christian, were universally believed. To doubt them was heresy.

"It is written in the stars," Llyr explained. "You will save Earth's Beloved one day, you and the great king who is coming."

Guinevere stared at him. "What king? Your people do not have kings, you told me so yourself."

Llyr stared back at her, enveloped in stillness. His voice, when he spoke, fell so low she had to strain to hear it. "One day, a great king will come. This is a promise to Earth's Beloved from the Goddess Herself. He will save us from oblivion. It is written so in the stars. His name in our tongue means 'the One Unconquered.' "

Llyr paused, searching her face for comprehension. He saw only disbelief. He rose to his feet. "I have said too much, and it is time to be going. Lugh, son of Lugh Long-Arm, will be coming to take my place." Llyr winked. "Although you will not see him."

Bending down and scrabbling in the undergrowth, he collected handfuls of small rocks and pebbles. With deft fingers, he built a little cairn in the middle of the clearing. It was a small construction, deep in the grass and likely to go unnoticed unless looked for.

"If you need me at any time for any trouble, build a cairn, thus. I will come. This is a promise. Between you and me." Llyr pressed his cheek against her own. "Fare well, Gwenhwyfar. Light with thee walk." He stepped back and raised an arm in a formal salute.

The last she saw of him was the flash of his bright smile before he gathered up his weapons and faded into the forest, noiseless as a wraith.

CHAPTER SEVEN

Council of Elders

Deep in a cave high in the hills, a dozen men sat cross-legged around a low peat fire. They were short men, thick-bodied and tough, with shaggy hair and unclipped beards. Their faces bore the marks of the hard life they led, and their sharp black eyes missed nothing. They wore skins, well cured and oiled to a comfortable softness, and most of them wore some kind of ornament as well, of bone, horn, or shell. Each of them had a smudge of ash on his forehead.

The leader, indistinguishable from his fellows but for the carved staff he held and the gray in his hair and beard, led the others in a prayer to the ancestor spirits. Then he struck his staff against the stone floor of the cave and said, "Let them come."

Llyr entered the cave behind Lugh, son of Lugh Long-Arm,

and looked nervously about him. Only once in his life had he been brought before a Council of Elders, and that was during the ceremony that had marked his entrance into manhood. He had been with the White Foot then, and his own father had held the sacred staff. This was very different. He was bound to the leader, but only by a foster-bond, and he knew that he was still regarded as a foreigner by the others. Lugh had been born into this clan, and his father held a high place among the men. Today, Lugh Long-Arm was sitting next to the leader, Mapon.

Both young men stopped opposite Mapon at an open space in the circle and made the sign of submission. Mapon bound them with an oath to answer truthfully all the questions put to them or risk expulsion from the clan. Lugh, the accuser, was the first to speak. He told the gathered men he had seen Llyr in a clearing in the forest, sitting on a stone with She With Hair of Light, sitting right down next to her and actually speaking to her. Lugh had seen him clearly. Llyr had been sitting in the sunlight, closer to the woman than Lugh was to the Elders now. Not only had he sat beside her, he had touched her. He had pressed his cheek to hers.

The sitting men stirred, and their faces hardened. Llyr had broken the prohibition, Lugh continued. Llyr had shown no respect for the rules laid down by the Elders. The gods only knew what secrets he had revealed.

Llyr shot a sharp glance at his accuser. Lugh's color was high, and he spoke with anger. With a sinking heart, Llyr realized Lugh was taking his revenge. Before Llyr had come to live among the Long Eyes, Lugh had been promised to a very pretty girl who, once Llyr arrived, had transferred her affections to him. Llyr had never encouraged her. The girl was coy, flirtatious, and empty-headed, and he did not want her. But this had only infuriated Lugh, who considered Llyr's indifference an insult to his beloved. There seemed no way out of this dilemma except the girl's changing her wayward mind or Llyr's returning to Snow Mountain. This, obviously, Lugh was doing his best to accomplish.

Llyr looked at all the solemn faces around the circle and wondered how many of them knew this, and if those who knew it would take it into consideration. There was no way to tell. Like all of Earth's Beloved, they guarded their expressions. Those lined and weathered faces gave nothing away. Mapon himself might have been made of stone.

The sight of Mapon gave Llyr another sinking feeling. He loved the old man, although he had known him only six months. Mapon had done more than take him into the Long Eyes; he had taken him into his own home, treated him like a son, and dealt with him patiently and fairly. These accusations would pain Mapon every bit as much as Llyr himself. When it came his turn to speak, what could he say? He could not have acted any differently. He had been guided by something far beyond himself. Perhaps if he had turned and run away when he first saw her riding across the meadow on her horse, the rest would not have happened. But how could he leave his post, betray Mapon's trust, on his first day of guard duty? Besides, he was not certain he could have turned away.

The girl was . . . a mystery, a wonder, a revelation. And he, like a summer moth greedy for light, had flown too near the flame.

Lugh had finally stopped speaking. Mapon signaled him to take his place in the circle, and Lugh sat down. Now Llyr was the only person in the cave still standing.

Mapon said, "Llyr, son of Bran, speak. We will hear you."

Llyr took a deep breath. The air was full of peat smoke and shadowy light. He sensed the divine presence all around him. He would obey the god and tell them the truth, but he doubted they would believe him.

As the fire dwindled, Llyr recounted his adventure of that golden day: how the girl had come into the clearing with her gleaming horse, how the light had fallen from the spring sky and lit the air all around her, how his weapons had slid from his hands and stacked themselves against the tree, how his feet had moved forward without his willing it, how still the world had gone in that moment when she turned her bright head and saw him.

He had been powerless to prevent any of it. That was the point he stressed, again and again. Something else had been with them in that clearing, steering his body, commanding his thoughts, guiding him through the difficulties of speech in a seldom-used tongue, opening his eyes to the person behind the dazzle of her presence. She was patient and kind. She had the gift of warmth, of openness, of understanding. Talking to her had been astonishingly easy, like water sliding downhill.

As he spoke, he watched their faces for any sign of com-prehension. He saw none. He glanced anxiously at Mapon but saw no change in that grave and weathered face. Behind Mapon, a curtain of stitched skins hung on the cavern wall. Llyr knew the curtain hid the entrance to a smaller cave where the clan's wise woman lived, the hag they called "the One Who Hears." Llyr had been hoping she would not show herself at this gathering and was glad to find her chamber still in darkness. Only twice had he seen light behind that curtain, and on both occasions it had signaled the appearance of the hideous old woman, half blind, half mad, who could hear the voices of gods. He did not want to see her again.

Llyr came to the end of his tale and stopped. He had told the Elders about everything except the building of the cairn. Lugh had not mentioned that, so perhaps he had not seen.

Mapon nodded to the man on his right. One by one, each man in the circle had the opportunity to question Llyr, to praise or castigate him, and to express his own view of Llyr's behavior. In every council, each man was allowed his say. This time, without exception, they condemned him. He heard anger, horror, and outrage in their voices. They ridiculed his belief in a guiding power. They accused him of falling in love, of desiring her, of lacking the discipline and control required of a hunter, a leader, a man. Only Mapon added nothing to this chorus of disapproval.

When it was the leader's turn to speak, Mapon asked Llyr if he had anything else to say. Mapon's voice sounded sad and weary, and a lump rose in Llyr's throat. He held himself very straight and answered that everything had happened just as he had related. He had not revealed any forbidden secrets. The girl already knew about the prophecy, and she did not believe it. She knew nothing about the great king. She thought he was someone among Earth's Beloved.

The cave grew very still. No one moved; no one breathed. The coming of the great king was never spoken of aloud in any gathering. It was a promise of the gods to Earth's Beloved, a promise of salvation from the violence of the Others, a promise to save them from annihilation. Only seers and wise women spoke openly about events that determined the future of the race.

Mapon rose. His face was no longer unreadable. It was consumed with grief. "We have heard you. Leave us now, and wait for our decision."

Outside, Llyr was surprised to find it was still a beautiful day. He sat down near the mouth of the cave in a pool of sun. He could see no one else about, but he knew they were there: lookouts in the trees, children foraging for wood and edible shoots or tubers, women squatting by the streambed washing wool or gathering reeds, young men checking their snares and following spoor. All of Earth's Beloved knew how to become invisible in the forest. It was their invisibility that kept them alive. It was their invisibility that he had violated.

The heat of the sun on his skin raised gooseflesh on his arms. It was a bad sign. Llyr shivered and tried to look on the bright side. Perhaps Mapon's grief sprang from worry about his wife and not from his foster son's behavior. Sula had given birth to a stillborn son weeks ago and then had fallen into a fever from which she had not yet recovered. Constant tending and the sacrifice of every lamb in the flock had kept her alive, but only just. Any day now, he expected the wailing to begin.

Llyr hugged his knees to his chest. What would the Elders do if—when—they decided against him? They would probably remove him from guard duty, but that was not disaster. He could still keep an eye on the clearing while he was out hunting. Would they bar him from the group hunts because they could not trust him? The thought brought a flush of shame to his cheek. To be excluded from the group in any fashion was the worst punishment a member of Earth's Beloved could suffer. Llyr was certain Mapon would not want to do this. He was not just any youth who had misbehaved; he was the son of Bran, leader of the White Foot, in whose care Mapon had placed his own favored son. Surely Mapon would think twice before bringing public dishonor upon Llyr.

Llyr found that this reasoning did little to console him. All the other members of the council were against him. Would they be powerful enough to sway Mapon's judgment or to overrule him? He went cold at the thought. What would he do—may all the gods preserve him—if they cast him out? He could never return to the White Foot under such disgrace. And he had nowhere else to go. He swallowed in a dry throat. He had heard of such men, cast out from their clans, cast out from the entire fraternity of Earth's Beloved, forced to live in the barren and lonely places of Britain, growing as wild and unkempt as any she-wolf and hunted by every man they met.

They never lived long, these outcasts. No man could survive without his fellows.

A finger tapped him on the shoulder, and he spun around to see Lugh, son of Lugh Long-Arm, standing behind him. The young man looked frightened. "Time to go in," he said.

In silence, Llyr followed him back to the cavern deep in the hill. Mapon stood alone before the fire. Everyone else had gone. Lugh, too, hurried away after a quick salute to the leader. Mapon's face was grave but not unkind.

"Sit," he said. Llyr sat on one of the braided wool mats still in place around the circle. Mapon sat down next to him. The fire had been rebuilt with fresh turf, and both men stared into the flames as Mapon spoke. Like all of Earth's Beloved, when he told a tale, Mapon began at the beginning and worked his way in measured beats to the end. Too numb for thought, and huddling from the shadows all around him, Llyr listened to the story he had himself related a few hours before. Hearing it like this, from other lips, it sounded ridiculous, a boyish prank played by a fool, and he was not surprised the men had not believed him.

Mapon repeated the men's objections, that it was forbidden to show oneself to She With Hair of Light, whatever the circumstances; that it was forbidden to speak to her, to approach her, even to think of her except as someone who must be protected from harm. It was certainly forbidden to touch her, to aspire to any degree of familiarity, to tell her anything at all about Earth's Beloved and their ways. More, it was forbidden to let her know that she was guarded, and it was expressly forbidden to tell her why. Yet Llyr had done all these things, by his own admission. It did not matter what his reasons had been.

Mapon paused and picked up a stick to stir the flames. The Council of Elders had spoken with one voice: Llyr must be cast out from the clan. The final decision, however, was Mapon's. Out of friendship and respect for Llyr's father, Bran, he had decided against the wishes of the Elders, even if it cost him his place as leader of the Long Eyes. He was loath to subject his foster son, for whom he and his family had developed a genuine liking, to a punishment that was sure to end in a wretched and lonely death.

Mapon hesitated, his eyes on Llyr. When he spoke, sadness filled his voice. He wished to give Llyr the chance to realize the gravity of his error and reform. Llyr was to pack his belongings, go out into the hills, and live for one month the life of an outcast. At the next new moon, he could return, and if he could convince the Council of Elders of a change of heart, if he could give proof of his resolution through his actions, Mapon would readmit him to the society of Earth's Beloved.

Llyr heard it all through a steady drumming in his ears. The words made no impression but slid by like dead leaves in a dark current. He was cold, despite the fire, and his head was empty of thoughts. He heard his own voice pierce the silence, as though someone else were moving his lips, forming the words, pushing them out with breath he did not command. He listened, astounded, to what he said.

"Honorable father, I will go."

Mapon's hand came down on his shoulder, heavy and warm. Mapon's rough lips brushed his cheek. "Light with thee walk, my son."

Llyr rose. His chest ached, and he fought to draw a steady breath. "Dark from thee flee, my father." He turned toward the mouth of the cave, blinded by tears, and fled.

CHAPTER EIGHT

The Tracker

Marcus, son of Argus, followed an old goat trail downhill. He paused under the branch of a juniper tree that had rooted in the scant soil between two rocky outcrops well above his head. He squatted and gazed intently at the edges of the trail. He saw, as he expected, that he was not the first to stop here under the shelter of the branch. The mark of a hard heel, a booted heel, stood out clearly in the dirt.

Thunder rumbled in the distance, and he raised his head. In the west, the sea and shore were gray with mist. Overhead the sky sank low with cloud. He could already smell the coming rain, enemy of the tracker. A hard rain would not last long, but it would wash out footprints. A soft rain might last for days and would blur the edges of any mark. It would certainly erase the delicate trail of prints he was trying to follow.

Marcus rose to his feet and continued his slow and careful progress down the rocky mountain pass. Away below him lay the soft green fields of Gwynedd and, to the north, the beginning of the marshes. There was much ground to cover and little time, but he would not rush. Hurry was as much his enemy as rain. He had spent days examining the shore road, the wagon road through the forest, the myriad cattle paths around the grazing pastures, and the animal trails that wound among the hills and snaked through mountain passes. He had picked up traces of horses, cattle, sheep, dogs, mountain cats, deer, boar, rabbits, and all kinds of vermin. He had seen the tracks of men, women, children, and Old Ones. He knew, within rough bounds, the business of the kingdom since the last hard rain. Late yesterday, in the slanting light of the setting sun, he had at last come across the signs he had been looking for. He had spent the night in a cave and now had picked up the trail again.

He smiled to himself. Queen Alyse was right. Where there were tracks, there were the men and beasts who made them. What a woman she was! Old Argus had warned him, when Marcus was offered a post at the castle, to pay attention to the queen. It had proved to be excellent advice. King Pellinore's word might be law, but the king did very little without the queen's assent. Except in matters of war, where she never meddled, Queen Alyse had an opinion on every subject and knew the right way to do anything that needed doing. A powerful woman was an easy target for ridicule and envious remarks, but those with intelligence paid Queen Alyse respect. She tolerated few mistakes and no fools. She ran the daily business of Gwynedd with a deft and efficient hand. In Old Argus's opinion, the kingdom had never been so wealthy, so strong, so powerful, or so respected.

That this was due largely to Queen Alyse, Marcus did not doubt. She was an exceedingly capable administrator. He admired a woman who could be both forthright and subtle, both feminine and cold of purpose. During their entire interview, she had not once stared at his arm. She had met him not as queen to servant, not even as woman to man, but as mind to mind. This was a rare enough experience among his fellow men, and unheard of in a woman. He had found it invigorating.

He stooped to run his fingers over another mark in the dirt, a soft smudge made by a small canvas shoe. It was the tenth such mark he had found that morning, and he regarded it with satisfaction. He had an idea now how the cattle thefts had been accomplished, but he had no proof. No one would admit to having seen the cattle leave. Regis had posted sentries throughout the hills after the thefts had begun, yet no one, young or old, shepherd or sentry, had seen a single sign of anything unusual.

The rain began as he reached the valley floor. He hunched his shoulders against it but kept his gaze on the path ahead. The ground was softer here, but the tracks he sought were fewer. Someone had taken care to wipe them out. If the tracks were not there, the marks of erasure were, and he followed them.

How was it possible for a woman to be as intelligent, as perceptive as Queen Alyse and still have blind spots? He would wager his month's pay she had no idea that Regis of

Wyebridge, the captain of her house guard for more than seven years, despised her. Regis seldom bothered to hide his contempt from his men, and Marcus had always assumed the queen must be aware of it. He knew now that she was not. Regis might not be her favorite, but he was King Pellinore's choice for the post, and she found him acceptable. Marcus wondered what she would say if she knew the truth. He wondered if he would have to be the means of enlightening her. He hoped not. He could not cast stones at Regis when the man was his commander.

He peered into the thickening mist. A hundred paces ahead, the path forked. One trail headed north into the marshes, the other west to the meadows and the shore. Soon now he would know where the cattle had gone. But he could not return to Queen Alyse until he also knew why.

CHAPTER NINE

Counting the Days

Guinevere lifted her head from her needlework and listened to the rain clattering against shuttered windows. It had been raining for three days now, penning everyone but the shepherds within doors. It felt almost like winter again, for the stone walls of the castle still held their winter chill, and braziers blazed in every room. This imprisonment, after days of sun and warmth, had not improved anyone's temper.

Queen Alyse's ill humor, like the rising storm outside, seemed to grow in power with every passing day. She had been furious with Guinevere for riding out alone and returning late to her lessons with Father Martin. She had scolded Elaine for greediness at supper, Leonora for a misplaced stitch, and Grannic for a mistake in the pattern on the loom. Ailsa she berated for negligence, laziness, general incompetence, and anything else that occurred to her. No one was spared the queen's attentions. Folk either rolled their eyes behind her back or hid from her altogether. Everyone in Gwynedd seemed to be counting the days until King Pellinore's return.

Guinevere certainly was. Queen Alyse had not done the very worst thing imaginable, threatening to send Ailsa back to Northgallis, but she had done the next worst. She had banned both girls from the stables. Permanently. If they wanted to travel about, she had told them in icy tones, they would go like ladies, in a litter. If they wished to ride, they would have to wait until there were armed men enough to escort them. That would not be possible before King Pellinore's return and, depending upon the state of things in this impoverished, wartorn land, perhaps not even then.

Guinevere and Elaine were to spend their days in work, study, and prayer for the improvement of their souls. Lessons with Iakos were to begin midmorning, when they would share the schoolroom with Elaine's younger brothers. Since Guinevere was so facile at her studies—racing through her work in order to sneak out early—she could spare the time to help eight-year-old Prince Maelgon with his figuring and five-year-old Prince Peredur with his letters.

There would be no more early dismissals. The girls would spend a part of every day learning household management from Queen Alyse, her steward, and her women. Lessons with Father Martin would increase to four times a week, and Guinevere should prepare herself for baptism. It was high time she became a Christian. Queen Alyse had no intention of harboring a grown pagan in the family.

The girls were assigned the additional responsibility of constructing their own gowns. They must stitch every stitch themselves. It was time, the queen declared, that they learned the art of dressmaking, learned how to put together and take apart a garment, to refit it for another use or a changing fashion. It was high time they learned to do something useful.

The queen's workroom had become a place of refuge over the past three days, for Queen Alyse was too busy about the castle to spend much time there. Now, three of the queen's women huddled together near the brazier, spinning basketfuls of washed wool into thick, yellow-gray thread. Side by side on the long bench against the wall, Ailsa and Grannic worked the looms. Normally, the chamber would have hummed with the women's gossip, but today the only sound was the muted clacking of wooden shuttles as Ailsa and Grannic tried without success to weave in silence, attempting even in her absence to avoid the queen's notice.

Guinevere focused her attention on the fabric in her lap. For the hundredth time, she paused in her stitching to marvel at the feel of it against her skin. The thick silk was the color of oak buds, a spring green that made her think of the wooded hills above the castle warming to life in the April sun. Queen Alyse might have a famous temper and a tongue that could slay a man at sixty paces—or so the soldiers claimed—yet she was capable of a gift like this. Guinevere slid her hands under the heavy silk to feel its weight again. The quality of the cloth amazed her. It was superior in strength and texture to Elaine's blue, and the color was unusual, being both rich and delicate, with a sheen like a polished apple's. A gown of this fabric would flatter any shade of skin or hair. She thought she might actually look well in it. Not for the first time, she wondered what had moved Queen Alyse to give it to her.

"Pay attention, Gwen." Elaine poked her in the ribs. "You're three seams behind me. Pity you can't stitch as fast as you can ride."

Guinevere stifled a protest. Elaine's bone needle raced across the sky blue fabric, as quick and erratic as a darting bird. As usual, her seams were crooked and her hasty stitches far too large to withstand the stresses to which she would inevitably subject them.

"A great pity, for I'd be done by now."

"Jest if you like, but there will be trouble if you don't finish your gown on time."

"Your mother is overreacting. I didn't ride far, I wasn't very late, Father Martin didn't mind at all. I am not responsible for her rampage."

"Well, you began it."

Guinevere colored. "She has no right to ban me from the stables. My father taught me to ride when I was three years old. He was proud of my skill. And King Pellinore is the one who gave me Peleth. She has no right to forbid me to ride him."

"Shhhhh." Grannic shushed her from across the room, scowling. "Have some sense, girl. Keep quiet."

"She's right," Elaine said firmly. "Whatever you do, don't start that again. She'll put us all on bread and water."

Once before, Queen Alyse had banned the girls from the stables, saying they had outgrown their ponies and were getting old enough to put away childish things. Elaine had objected on principle, but Guinevere had been devastated. King Pellinore had intervened and stemmed her grief by giving her Peleth, a retired cavalry mount he was about to put out to grass. Queen Alyse had not spoken to the king for an entire month afterward, but she had been unable to alter his decision.

Unfortunately, King Pellinore was still a week from home, and in his absence, Queen Alyse ruled the kingdom. Her word was law. Guinevere knew very well there was nothing she could do or say to change the queen's mind. Yet riding had become a necessary part of her life. It was the only time she could be alone. It gave her a sense of freedom and independence in a world growing every year more circumscribed as she neared marriageable age. Riding restored her sense of self. To wait an entire week for another chance of a gallop through the woods was more than she thought she could bear, yet somehow she would have to bear it. And she would have to hope that King Pellinore would, for his ward's sake, once again be willing to cross the queen.

She would ask the king as soon as he got home. He was due on Beltane Eve, but she would not ask him then.

The mischievous spirits of spring were abroad on Beltane Eve, even in a Christian kingdom like Gwynedd. The castle inhabitants might not celebrate the ancient rites but the villagers, like most common folk across the land, believed in the old ways and worshiped the old gods. The springtime festival of Beltane was one they looked forward to all winter and would celebrate with or without the king's approval.

Up at the castle, however, the first of May was a day like any other. And if she missed the dancing, the ribbons, the flowers braided in her hair, and the footraces, which she always won, Guinevere was glad, on the whole, not to be in Northgallis now. Her half brother Gwarthgydd, King Leodegrance's eldest son from his first marriage, was king there now and would sit at the head of the feasting board in their father's place. Gwarth's only son, Gwillim, her best friend and companion for the first seven years of her life, would be fourteen now and training for a warrior. He would sit at the king's right hand on Beltane Eve, while she, if she were there, would be packed off to bed with the rest of the children, to watch from the window as the celebrations moved from the king's hall into the woods and bushes. This would be the year of Gwillim's initiation into the orgies of Beltane. For this birthday, Guinevere preferred to be in Gwynedd, where religious festivals, however joyful and exuberant, never spilled over into worship of the oldest arts.

The looms stopped, startling Guinevere from her thoughts. In the sudden silence, the girls could hear what the women had already heard: the horn at the gate followed by the clatter of hooves on stone. Elaine ran to the window, un-latched the shutters, and threw them open. She craned her neck to see around the corner of the castle wall and into the courtyard below.

"Horses!" she cried. "And a troop of men. I can't see a banner. It can't be Father, can it?"

"Not likely," said Grannic, coming up behind her. "Close that window, my lady, before your mother catches you staring out like a common bawd."

"But there must be thirty horses," Elaine protested. "Whose can they be? What could they want?" She turned, her face alight with excitement. "Whoever they are, they're stay-ing. I saw bedrolls behind their saddles."

Grannic pulled the shutters closed. "At least we've room for them, with all the men away."

"Go find out who they are, Grannic. I've got to know."

"Not on your life, my lady. Your mother told me to stay here, and here I stay. We'll find out soon enough."

Elaine reddened at this challenge to her authority. "These visitors could be important. For all you know, they could be suitors. If you won't go find Mother, I'll go myself. I'm tired of stitching."

Grannic scowled and beat Elaine to the door. "You'll do no such thing, my lady. Not without permission."

"Are we prisoners, then? Oh, I'm so tired of all my mother's rules!"

"Nevertheless—" Grannic stumbled as the door she

leaned against opened and pushed her forward. Cissa and Leonora swept into the room, eyes shining.

"You'll never guess what's happened—" Leonora began, but Cissa could not contain her excitement.

"A lord has come to visit, and we're to have a banquet tonight!"

CHAPTER TEN

The Guest

Cissa and Leonora took seats before the brazier, with the girls at their feet and the rest of the women clustered around. All thoughts of weaving and stitching were forgotten in a wholly feminine impatience to hear the news.

"He rode in the gates with an escort and a gift of twenty fleeces," Leonora began. "He asked the queen's pardon for coming unannounced. She had little warning, and she was furious at the presumption until she saw his face."

"He wore two gold wristbands and a jeweled torque around his neck," put in Cissa. "And he's as handsome as the day is long."

"Who is he?" Elaine cried.

"We weren't close enough to catch his name," said Leonora. "There was such a clamor and a bustle, with all the house guard on display, and Regis snapping orders left and right, and the horses stamping and blowing—"

"The queen dismissed us," Cissa said, "to come prepare you."

"Hurrah!" Elaine jumped up and twirled about in a celebratory dance. "I know why he's come. He's here to look me over—he's a suitor. He's the first of them!"

Guinevere saw Cissa and Leonora exchange glances.

"I don't think—" Leonora began, and stopped. Footsteps were coming down the corridor, sharp, brisk footsteps that everyone recognized.

Ailsa, who was nearest the door, opened it as Queen Alyse swept into the room.

Guinevere noticed at once a difference in the queen. Her gray-blue eyes were shining, and to judge by the curve of her lips, she had recently been amused. Gone was the sour temper of the past three days, of the past month, of the long winter. Queen Alyse looked lovely, vivacious, and young, even though she was nearly thirty.

"Elaine, Guinevere, attend me. I am arranging a banquet tonight for Sir Darric of Longmeadow. He has come to visit for a few days. I want you both to be there. You are old enough to be included in formal company, and it will be good practice for you."

Elaine's eyes danced. "But we have nothing to wear, Mama. Our gowns are not ready yet."

"You have others. Add a new ribbon or belt to the best of them, and it will be good enough. Your gray gown, Guinevere, has just come from the fuller's. You will concentrate on your table manners and on learning to make polite conversation when you are addressed." She turned to Grannic and Ailsa. "Bathe them, dress them, and have them in the hall of meeting at lamplighting."

"Yes, my lady," they replied together.

The queen swept out with Cissa and Leonora in attendance.

"Hurrah!" Elaine threw her arms into the air. "A banquet! And I've got a new ribbon and a new belt out of her, too. What shall I wear, Gwen? My yellow, do you think, or my russet and blue?"

"The blue is warmer," Guinevere said. "But don't get your hopes up, Laine. I don't think Sir Darric is a suitor."

Elaine gave a toss to her bountiful golden curls. "What do you know about it? Of course he is. Why else would he come?"

"Your mother hasn't had much time to get the word out."

"She's had time to get it as far as the Longmeadow Marshes," Elaine said defiantly. "They're only half a day's ride away."

"Now, now, lass," Grannic clucked. "There's been no talk of any suitor. Whatever gave you such a notion? Put it out of your head this moment and don't let your mother hear you."

"Why not?" Elaine turned on Grannic. "What's the matter with him?"

Ailsa said evenly, "He's the second son of Sir Gavin, Earl of the Longmeadow Marshes, who serves your father."

"So he's young, then," Elaine rejoiced. "And good-looking, too."

"He's eighteen and a troublemaker," Grannic said bluntly. "Stay away from him."

Elaine's gaze was coy. "How can I, when Mother's just invited us to dine with him?"

Grannic shook a finger at her. "Now don't you go getting silly ideas. Your mother will skin me alive if he looks at you twice, she will, indeed."

"But why?" Elaine pouted. "Why should his admiring me upset her? Is he someone important?"

"Yes and no," Grannic said, a frown of disapproval darkening her narrow face. "He serves a purpose, you might say. If you want to keep your mother sweet, you'll not get in her way."

An hour before lamplighting, Guinevere sat on her stool in the anteroom of Elaine's bedchamber, bathed, gowned, and scented, while Ailsa stood behind her, braiding and arranging her hair. The gray gown, an old one, was very plain and unadorned except for a band of dark blue that had been added to the hem during her last growth spurt. Now it needed lengthening again. So did the sleeves.

"Ailsa, don't I have anything better than this old gown? I've outgrown it again."

"Never you mind," Ailsa said. "This is the one the queen chose for you, and this is the one you'll wear."

"But it doesn't fit. I look ridiculous."

"Nonsense." Ailsa patted the last strand in place and turned Guinevere around to look at her. "Listen to me, Gwen," she said quickly, under her breath. "Stay as far away from Sir Darric as you can. I've heard tales I dare not repeat. He's no end of trouble to his family. I don't know what Queen Alyse thinks she's doing, allowing him to stay here with King Pellinore away. I hope and pray she won't regret it."

Guinevere looked up at her. "Why do *you* think he's here?"

Ailsa avoided her eyes. "I'm sure I don't know."

The evasion confirmed a suspicion Guinevere had formed that afternoon in the workroom, when the queen's women had given her the impression that they knew quite well why Sir Darric had come, or at least why the queen had received him.

"He's come for Queen Alyse, hasn't he? Not Elaine."

"Hush, child! I've no idea why the man is here." But Ailsa's worried eyes belied her words.

Guinevere frowned. "But why would she want to see him if he's no one of importance? Why would she throw a banquet for him? It can't be just because he's handsome. Can it?"

Ailsa began to look alarmed. "Put all thought of him out of your head, Gwen. Until we know what his game is, pray you can stay in the shadows and go unnoticed."

"I don't know why you're worried. No one will ever notice the ward in this old gown."

Ailsa sighed. "You have much to learn about men, my little chicken, and it's my duty to keep you safe until the right one comes along." The word *right* was accompanied by a grave wink, and Guinevere scowled.

"Don't start that again, I pray you. You know what Iakos thinks of prophecies? 'Dreams of the ignorant fostered by the willing.' And I agree with him."

Ailsa paled. "You haven't been telling that foreigner about the prophecy? Oh, Guinevere, he's only a tutor—"

"He didn't hear it from me. I've told no one, *ever*. I don't even know all of it, anyway. I've only heard the first part. No one will tell me the rest. But Iakos knows it already, I can tell he does. He probably heard it gossiped about, like everyone else's secrets. There's probably no one in all Gwynedd except me who hasn't heard the whole of it."

"You know all you need to know," Ailsa said darkly. "If your father had wanted you to know the rest, he'd have told you."

"He didn't have time," Guinevere countered. "He died too soon. If he were still alive now, he'd tell me. I know he would."

"He might. He could never deny you anything for very long."

"Then why won't you tell me, Ailsa? Please? What harm could knowing do?"

Ailsa half smiled. "So you can foster the dreams of the ignorant? No, Gwen. Knowing will only cause you worry. If it is to be, it will come in its own time. Meanwhile, mind you keep clear of Sir Darric. He's dangerous. Let Queen Alyse handle him, if she can."

Guinevere sighed unhappily. What an evening lay ahead! She must go downstairs in her plain gray, ill-fitting gown to dine with a dangerously handsome scoundrel without attracting his notice. She wished she could be sure that in the adjoining chamber, Grannic was giving Elaine the same advice.

CHAPTER ELEVEN

The Banquet

As dusk fell, Elaine and Guinevere sat patiently on a cushioned bench in the hall of meeting, waiting for the queen. At last, the rain had stopped, and a soft spring breeze crept through the unshuttered windows, bringing with it the light perfume of blooming flowers and the gentle, earthy scent of hardwoods bursting into leaf. But the thick stone walls of the castle still trapped the winter cold, and the log fire in the grate was very welcome.

Guinevere pulled at the sleeves of her gray gown, but still they did not reach her wrists. She glanced at Elaine, sitting motionless and expectant, eyes on the doorway. Her yellow gown had been recently refitted, lowered at the neck to show off the gentle rounding of her shoulders and belted high to accent the definite curves of her breasts. Grannic had dressed her hair with yellow ribbons and borrowed a blue and yellow embroidered belt from Queen Alyse to wrap tight about her midriff. She looked older than her years, pretty, confident, and ready for anything.

A servant opened the door, and Queen Alyse entered with her women. The girls rose and made their reverences. Guinevere tried not to stare. Queen Alyse looked even lovelier and younger than she had that afternoon. Her pale cream gown, banded in rose and gold, flowed in a graceful line from shoulder to heel. A net of tiny river pearls embraced the careful coils of her wheat gold hair, and earrings of mother-of-pearl glimmered like moonbeams on her ears.

Three men followed her into the chamber, all of them laughing at some recent jest. The leader was the youngest, richly dressed, with the kind of features no woman could forget. Tawny and lithe from his doeskin boots to his rich, blond-streaked brown hair, he reminded Guinevere of a hunting cat. He was dressed entirely in leather so soft and pliant that his clothing clung to his supple body and sighed as he moved. Gold flashed from rings, wristbands, and belt. The jeweled torque around his neck was a half a handspan deep and etched with flying birds. Hot hazel green eyes flicked from face to face as he entered the room, then found Queen Alyse's smiling gaze and returned it.

The queen performed the introductions. White teeth gleamed in a charming smile as Sir Darric of Longmeadow bowed and pressed his lips to the women's fingers, one by one. Guinevere shivered. She could not escape the impression that however witty his banter, however smooth and pleasing his social graces, something sinister lurked within. He watched them all with the sulky gaze of the predator.

Wishing that King Pellinore had never left home to follow the High King Arthur, Guinevere trailed along behind Elaine as Queen Alyse led them into dinner. The high table in King Pellinore's great hall was unique in Britain: it was round. With so many men away at the wars, the hall was nearly empty, and Queen Alyse allowed her women and Sir Darric's men to sit at the round table, normally reserved for the king's family and his guests. The advantage to the round table was that everyone sitting at it could see and speak to everyone else. The disadvantage, Guinevere decided, was that no one could escape anyone else's notice. Whenever she raised her eyes from her plate, she found either Jordan or Drako, Sir Darric's companions, watching her and Elaine with knowing smiles.

Sir Darric sat beside Queen Alyse and gave her most of his attention, leaning closer as time passed and the wine went continually around. He drank wine as if it were water, but instead of getting drunk, he grew silkier in his speech and more audacious in his flattery. He knew a thousand amusing anecdotes and kept Alyse in buoyant humor throughout the meal.

Guinevere tried to listen to Sir Darric's conversation. She could catch only snatches, because Cissa and Leonora were doing their best to flirt with Jordan and Drako, who were doing their best to flirt with Elaine and her.

Sir Darric, she gathered, had been left in charge of his father's lands in the earl's absence and had been having a rather dissolute time of it. Left to his own devices, he had held feast after feast and, to clear his head, had rampaged through woods, fields, and water meadows in pursuit of any animal he could chase, although it was planting season. Guinevere wondered why he had come to King Pellinore's castle. Had all his own wine casks run dry?

Sir Darric signaled the winebearer to refill his cup and the queen's. He drank thirstily, then lifted his long-lashed eyes to hers. "Tell me, Alyse, when may we expect the return of your honored husband?"

Guinevere stifled a gasp. *Alyse?* No one but King Pellinore dared address the queen so informally. She waited with held breath for the stinging rebuke that was sure to follow.

"About the same time we may expect your honored father," Queen Alyse replied with a lift of her lips. "Why do you ask, my lord? Are you so eager to see your dear brother again?"

Sir Darric laughed shortly and leaned toward her. "Exactly as eager as you are to see your dear husband," he said into her ear. Her smile warmed all her features, and his lips slid along the delicate scroll of her ear to plant two lingering kisses at the edge of her jaw.

Eyes bulging, Guinevere looked down at her plate and exhaled carefully. She knew very little about the relations between King Pellinore and Queen Alyse, but she had always sensed liking, if not harmony, between them. Her parents had married for love, Elaine had often told her, and she knew from her own observation that King Pellinore admired his wife. She could not therefore imagine what drove her aunt, who was always careful to mark the distinctions of rank, to allow such intimate attentions from a man so far beneath her.

When she looked up, she found Jordan grinning at her.

"Pretty as a bud in springtime," he said, with a glint in his eye, "but no more sense than a day-old chick. He don't mean nothing by it, m'lady. Beltane's coming. The fever's in the air."

He pursed his lips in an imaginary kiss, and Guinevere, coloring fiercely, bowed her head to escape his insolent eyes. She knew exactly what he meant by a fever in the air. At Beltane, everyone suffered from the same disease. She had not known that Christians, too, could fall under the Goddess's spell, but it was clearly so. That languid, laughing look in Queen Alyse's eyes was a sign even she could not fail to recognize.

She ignored Jordan and Drako, who could not hold their wine as well as their master and, as the evening progressed, grew bleary-eyed and sloppy in their speech. She concentrated on listening to what Sir Darric and Queen Alyse were saying. They were talking, of all things, about sheep.

"Three newborn lambs, my steward tells me, and nine cattle. Just in the last three weeks. They disappeared into thin air, apparently. No one saw them go. There were no signs of violence or predators." The queen's voice carried, and heads turned as others fell silent to listen. "I've had men out searching, and they found a few cattle tracks which led into the hills and disappeared. But no human tracks. I've half a mind to set fire to the forest and burn them out, whoever they are."

Sir Darric drained his winecup. "Hillmen. They're the culprits. I've suffered from them, too. Lost about ten animals, in all. Lambs, ewes, heifers, cows. Thieving savages." He raised his cup, and a servant hurried to refill it.

"Hillmen?" Queen Alyse frowned. "Pellinore had trouble

from them once before, but years ago. He met with their leader, and we've had no difficulty since."

Sir Darric snorted. "They're an uncouth race. Live like animals. Can't trust a hillman's promise." He looked to his companions for confirmation. Jordan and Drako vigorously agreed. "They're always after sheep and cattle at the end of a hard winter. Their own herds are tiny. By now, they're probably down to a few goats. And they don't wear boots like normal folk. Whatever it is they wear on their feet leaves no mark."

Guinevere remembered the soft leather slippers on Llyr's feet. She looked anxiously at Queen Alyse, who was still frowning.

"They had an agreement with Pellinore. What would make them break it after so many years?"

Sir Darric laughed. His teeth were very white. The jeweled torque gleamed at the open throat of his tunic. "Who knows? Hard times. Probably ate their last ewe before the thaw and had no lambs for their crazy magic."

"Lambs for magic? What nonsense is this?"

"You didn't know? You surprise me, royal lady." Sir Darric downed a liberal swallow of wine and relaxed in his chair, his tawny hair loose about his shoulders and his hazel eyes alive with interest. "They need the skin and the blood of a newborn lamb to perform some kind of ritual healing. Sometimes they need two or three. They like cattle for the marrow in their bones. They think it gives the elderly new life."

Queen Alyse looked skeptical. "Everyone knows the value of marrow. The rest sounds like witchery to me."

Sir Darric gazed at her with sultry eyes. "They're a primitive people. But I have it on the best authority." He leaned closer, and his voice dropped to a soft, seductive drawl. "I caught one when I was fifteen. Bit and clawed like a wildcat, the little savage. But I made him talk."

The queen's eyebrows rose. To Guinevere's astonishment, she seemed attracted, not repelled, by this admission and the violence it implied. "I'm sure you did. But I cannot go into the forest after them; I have not enough men for more than a patrol, and thus far, patrolling has not stopped them."

Sir Darric bowed his head politely, but his eyes never left her. "Never you worry, my lady queen. I'll hunt them down for you, if you give me leave. My men are itching for some action. Say the word, and we'll clean these hills of those thieving vermin for you."

"Thank you, Sir Darric. I'd be most grateful." The queen's smile was almost coy. "You must let me know if there is anything I can do for you in return."

"I'm certain I'll be able to think of something. My lady."

Jordan and Drako chuckled and nudged each other. Elaine blushed prettily and set her ringlets bouncing with an arrogant toss of her head. Guinevere glanced swiftly at Ailsa, who kept her eyes on her plate and concentrated on picking the bones from her fish. There was more going on here, she sensed, than she could understand, but one thing was clear: the Old Ones were in danger. Sir Darric meant to drive them from the hills. Whether or not they were the thieves Queen Alyse was seeking, she owed them at least a warning.

She had been forbidden to ride out, but someone had to

rebuild that cairn. Someone had to meet Llyr in the clearing and pass on the message. Whom could she send? To send anyone at all would mean revealing that she had been in contact with the Old Ones. The gods—God—only knew what Queen Alyse would do if she should learn that. Guinevere's hand shook as she reached for her watered wine. She could think of no alternative. She would have to go herself.

CHAPTER TWELVE

The Cairn

Elaine dashed into the bedchamber and flopped on the bed, arms outspread. "Did you see the way he looked at me?"

"Who? Drako?" Guinevere followed her in.

"Drako!" Elaine's voice was full of contempt. "That fat oaf? No, I mean Sir Darric, of course. He was staring at me all night; you *must* have seen him. Isn't he beautiful? Have you ever seen such gorgeous eyes?"

"But . . . Sir Darric had eyes only for . . . your mother."

"What would he want with my *mother*? Don't be ridiculous, Gwen. Oh, he flirted with her, of course, but couldn't you see through that ruse? He *had* to make her think she was the object of his attentions, else she might throw him out on his ear. He came uninvited, after all. He had to make himself welcome."

Guinevere nodded warily. That might be one interpretation of what they both had seen, but it wasn't hers.

"You *must* have seen him glancing over at me every time he paused to drink. Oh, Gwen, I blushed until I thought I'd burn. Have you ever seen such a handsome man? Half the time, I could not lift my eyes from my plate. He winked at me twice. Oh, I can't wait to see him alone."

"Alone!"

"Shhh." Footsteps sounded in the corridor. Elaine jumped up to pull closed the curtain between her bedchamber and the antechamber and leaned close to her cousin's ear. "Say nothing of this to Grannic or Ailsa or it will get right back to Mother, and she'll send him home. I know he'll try to contact me secretly; I know he wants a chance for private speech. You'll be the go-between. Come, Gwen, you're the only one who can. You've got to promise me that you'll carry messages between us, that you won't run away if he approaches. Quick, Gwen, promise."

Guinevere's breath came short and fast. "You *can't* be alone with that man. Your mother will—"

"*All right.*" The footsteps came through the door and into the antechamber. Elaine grabbed Guinevere's wrist and held it hard. "Then you'll have to come with me. Promise me. Swear it. Or I'll tell Mother where you *really* go when you're out riding." Her eyes glittered hard and blue. "When she hears about all those silly obstacles you built and how you never use a saddle, even when you're jumping, she'll throw a monstrous fit. She'll never let you near a horse again."

Guinevere paled. How on God's sweet earth had Elaine

learned about the jumping field? "All right—I promise," she gasped, pulling out of Elaine's grip as the curtain behind them parted and Grannic and Ailsa entered the room.

"Come, come, my lady," Grannic grumbled, still puffing from the stairs. "It's time for rest after all that drinking and feasting. Why your mother didn't water the wine better, I hate to think. Come, Elaine, and let me unlace that gown."

Elaine rolled her eyes with exaggerated weariness. "I can't *wait* until I'm a woman grown and can stay up as late as I choose. You may be tired, Grannic, but I'm not. Not at all."

Ailsa led Guinevere back into the antechamber, which served as a sleeping place for both nurses and as a dressing room for Guinevere. She drew the curtain closed behind them and pointed to the stool. Obediently, Guinevere sat. "Now," said Ailsa, as she plucked the pins from the girl's hair and began to comb it out, "what was all that about?"

Guinevere kept her eyes in her lap. "What was what about?"

"You know perfectly well what I mean. All that whispering just before we came in. What's Elaine up to now, eh? Something to land you in the soup and leave her looking innocent as daisies, I'll be bound."

When Guinevere did not reply, Ailsa knelt down before the girl and looked up into her eyes. "I'm not your mother, may the Good Goddess bless her always, but I love you, Gwennie, as if you were my own. You don't have to tell me, of course. You're a king's daughter, and I'm naught but a laborer's widow. But your dear father charged me with your care, and I can't look out for you if I don't know what's going on."

A hot flush of color rose to Guinevere's face, and her eyes

brightened with tears. She slid her arms around her nurse's neck and rested her cheek on Ailsa's plump, comfortable shoulder. "Oh, Ailsa, I do want to tell you everything, but you can get in trouble, too, just for knowing."

"There, there," Ailsa crooned, patting the white-gold head. "If there's trouble afoot, you'd best share it with me. You may swear me to silence, if you like."

Guinevere dried her eyes. Ailsa had a heart as big and as deep as the open sea, but keeping secrets was beyond her. Still, it was comforting to have such a loyal and willing confederate. She swore Ailsa to secrecy for form's sake and told her about Elaine's designs upon Sir Darric and her own promise to act as chaperone. Before Ailsa could open her mouth to protest, Guinevere told her of the threat Elaine had made to ensure her compliance.

Ailsa frowned. Horses had been part of the girl's life since King Leodegrance first put her on a pony at the age of three. In Northgallis, with no mother to keep her close and teach her feminine skills, Guinevere had spent her childhood on horseback, racing across the countryside with young Gwillim and his hawk. Here in Gwynedd, where her life was more circumscribed, riding gave the child a little freedom and the only privacy she had.

"I knew about the riding bareback," Ailsa said. "You've done that all your life. But what is this about leaping over obstacles? How long has that been going on?"

"Not very long. I only built them last autumn, and then winter set in." She looked away. "I needed something vigorous to do when . . . when Elaine got her monthlies."

Ailsa hugged Guinevere to her breast and kissed the girl's damp cheeks. "I've told you over and over, Gwen, you will be beautiful someday. I can see it in you already, and I think your aunt Alyse is beginning to see it, too. Each person, each animal, each tree and flower, has a beat of life inside it that marks its own time, proceeds at its own pace. Your mother was late to blossom, by all accounts, but what an exquisite bloom she was! It's beneath you to be jealous of Elaine. This is her time in the sun. Yours will come soon enough. Mark my words, in three years you'll be looking back on your days in Gwynedd and thinking how carefree and easy life was when you were an innocent girl."

Guinevere pulled away, blinking hard. "In heaven's name, why? Is adulthood so horrible?"

Ailsa chuckled. "Men, my dear. Men disrupt everything. They may be our fate, and even our blessing, but they do change everything they touch." She nodded toward the curtain. They could both hear Elaine's voice from the bedchamber, imperious, arrogant, and excited. "Young Sir Darric's not been in this house an entire day, and look at everything he's changed."

Guinevere bit her lip. "I don't like him. I have to keep my promise to Elaine, but I don't want to go anywhere near him."

"Nor will you, if I have anything to say about it. Elaine is playing with a fire she doesn't yet understand, and you were foolish to promise to help. But since you promised, I will go with you."

"That might work for taking messages back and forth, but she wants to see him in private. What if he agrees?"

Ailsa shook her head and smiled. "He won't. Even a half-wit would think twice before wooing the queen's daughter behind her back. I'm certain he's got at least that much sense of self-preservation."

But Guinevere did not smile back. "I don't think he has any sense at all. Did you hear what he told Aunt Alyse about the hillmen?"

Ailsa blinked. "What hillmen?"

"The ones Queen Alyse thinks are stealing her livestock. Or rather, the ones Sir Darric convinced her are stealing her livestock."

"That's nonsense," Ailsa said firmly. "The Old Ones don't steal. And what they borrow they always repay."

As Ailsa unlaced her gown and helped her out of it, Guinevere reflected on the stories she had heard in Northgallis about the Old Ones and their interactions with the valley folk. They were a shy people who honored the old ways and kept to themselves, but occasionally, the villagers, who lived close to the land, had traded with them. Someone would leave a newborn lamb, trussed for slaughter, at a wayside shrine in the forest. Within a fortnight, the gift would be repaid. On a dark night with little moon, a slab of venison, a sack of newly sheared fleece, or a stack of cut timber would mysteriously appear in the giver's yard. Few words were ever exchanged, but gestures were always understood.

Guinevere looked at Ailsa anxiously. "But Sir Darric doesn't like them. Do you think he means to kill them or just chase them from the hills?"

"I couldn't say, I'm sure. It does sound as if he means them harm. But King Pellinore is due back by Beltane. He'll settle everything."

"But that's a week away. Anything might happen in that time. Sir Darric will kill them if he finds them, Ailsa. I could see it in his eyes. And he has plenty of time to do it."

Ailsa nodded thoughtfully as she folded the gown and put it away in the carved clothes chest at the foot of her pallet. "Aye, he can be a cruel man, Sir Darric. I've been hearing tales about him. Wild as the day is long, for all his courtier's manners, and jealous of his elder brother, Mathowen, the earl's heir. He's got a reputation for devilry, for all he's just eighteen."

"I can't let him do it!" Guinevere cried. "I have to warn them. I owe it to them."

Ailsa looked up sharply from the chest. "Owe it to whom? The Old Ones? Guinevere, what have you been doing up there in the hills?" She glanced nervously toward the curtain. "Out with it. Quickly."

Hesitantly, her face flaming, Guinevere confessed her meeting with Llyr in the forest. Ailsa grew thoughtful. Silently, she pulled Guinevere's shift off over her head, rubbed her body with an herbal balm she had prepared to protect against agues and blemishes, and wrapped the girl's nightdress around her. Finally, she spoke.

"So they've been looking after you all these years? It does make sense. That's why the journey to Gwynedd went so smoothly, in spite of all the tales we heard about thieves and bandits along the road. That's why you've never come to harm riding about the forest as you do. That explains who returned your cloak after you lost it in the high meadow in that storm." Unthinkingly, she clutched the amulet at her throat. "Oh yes, that explains so many things. Even in Northgallis."

Guinevere shivered. She hadn't wanted to tell Ailsa about her adventure in the forest, because Ailsa, with all her superstitions about magic and unseen powers, was sure to believe Llyr's tale, just as she steadfastly believed every word of old Griselda's prophecy. To Ailsa, the world teemed with a thousand invisible deities who scrutinized her every movement. The Christian God, whom she had accepted with alacrity, was merely one among the many.

"Maybe there were no thieves and bandits," Guinevere suggested. "Maybe I've come to no harm because I'm a better rider than you think. And I always thought it was Stannic who retrieved my cloak. He was willing to take credit for it, as I remember."

Ailsa hesitated, and Guinevere hid a smile. Her nurse was always taking baskets of kitchen tidbits to the stables or apples from the storerooms or loaves of new-baked bread filched from the bakehouse. Her gifts did not go unnoticed. Ailsa's liking for the stablemaster was returned. Now, watching the struggle on Ailsa's face, she waited to see who would win the credit for finding and returning the lost cloak.

Ailsa shook her head. "The cloak is a small matter. But it's true you've been under a powerful protection, that I've always known. I just didn't know whose it was."

"Then you agree I should warn the Old Ones about Sir Darric?"

Ailsa swallowed hard, then nodded.

"Then I've got to ride out to the clearing tomorrow, early, before dawn, and build a cairn to signal Llyr. I'll be back before the queen can miss me."

"Who will miss you?" Elaine said, pulling open the curtain. "What are you up to now, Gwen? What's all this whispering about?"

"Just gossip. That's all."

Elaine looked at her sharply. "You're up to something. I can always tell. And you don't want me to know. Well, I suppose I could keep my eyes shut." She smiled. "You know those three whole columns of Herodotus that Iakos gave us?"

Guinevere sighed. "I've done the translation already."

Elaine grinned. "Excellent. Then you can do mine in half the time."

At dawn, Guinevere led Peleth silently from the stable into the shelter of the nearby wood, mounted, and headed uphill. The pale sky, watery blue, was clean of clouds. Dew clung to the meadow grasses, and a rich, fragrant earth scent rose from the forest floor. She felt no eyes on her back as she cantered quietly along a trail soft with damp earth and pine needles. Overhead, birds awakening in the treetops trilled at her approach, singing a sweet descant to the steady thud of the horse's hooves.

There was no one else about when she dismounted in the clearing. She and the horse and the warbling birds were the only living creatures to disturb the peaceful silence of the morning. A hundred wildflowers grew helter-skelter in the young green grass. Gathering the scattered rocks and pebbles, she carefully rebuilt the cairn. Then she reached for her waterskin and poured a small libation on the ground.

"Llyr, son of Bran, leader of the White Foot hunters of Snow Mountain, guest-son of the Long Eyes in these hills." She paused. She felt a little silly speaking aloud to someone who was not there, but perhaps someone *was* there, listening. "Gwenhwyfar, daughter of Rhiannon, calls you forth. There is trouble, urgent trouble. The Long Eyes are in danger." She glanced around at the empty woods, willing someone to be there. "Come forth, Llyr, if you can hear me." But the woods were still. Nothing moved, nothing breathed but the horse among the grasses. "I will come back as soon as I can."

She reached for Peleth and leaped upon his back. "Don't fail me, Earth's Beloved," she whispered, and gave the horse his head for home.

CHAPTER THIRTEEN

Double Trouble

Marcus pressed himself against the rough wall of the cowshed and paused to catch his breath. No one had seen him cross the meadow from the woods; there was no one near to raise an alarm. He had dirtied his face, his hand, and his clothes with dust. If anyone should see him, he would look more like a peasant, a peat gatherer, a woodsman, or a cowman than a spy in the queen's service. For once, his withered arm served him well. No one ever paid much attention to cripples.

He inched his way around the corner of the shed. He saw no guard, no shepherd, no dog, only ten beasts with soft brown eyes who lifted their heads from their grazing to stare at him. He waited until the animals lost interest and began to graze again. One quick glance into the darkness of the shed confirmed that it was empty. Only ten cows, then, in this meadow, unless there were more over the rise. Moving slowly to keep from frightening the cattle, Marcus approached each one with a fistful of green grass and examined the animal's ears while it chewed. Nine pairs of ears were bare of markings. But the tenth revealed the scars of an old knife cut, two short lines meeting at the top and angling out below. Marcus recognized the mark. It represented the mountains of Gwynedd, and it belonged, like the mountains, to King Pellinore.

Marcus gazed thoughtfully at the cattle. It was only the third time that day he had seen the mark, and he had examined over one hundred seventy beasts. He had expected more. Out of the stolen twenty head of cattle, why had he found only three?

His gaze slid across the fertile valley to the fortress. This was not a castle built of stone but a rambling wood and wattle villa with a tiled roof. It was well placed on a low rise and looked well defended. Great earthworks rose around it, topped by a wooden palisade. The entrance seemed to be a tunnel dug into the earthworks. It would not be an easy place to enter uninvited.

Marcus thought of Queen Alyse's firm blue gaze and smiled. He would think of a way to get in. He would cross that valley and find a place to snug down, invisible and unnoticed, until dark. He would observe the sentries, the changing of the guard, the traffic in and out. By dawn, he would be inside. But what he wanted most to know before he walked under those earthworks was whether the lord of the place had stolen the cattle himself or merely bought them from the thieves.

His careful planning proved unnecessary. By nightfall, the

guards at the gatehouse were so drunk that those still standing were incapable of speech. He joined a group of laborers coming in late with a wagonload of timber. No one looked at him twice. The wagon rumbled through a tunnel arched in stone and emerged in a courtyard still bustling with the business of the day. He turned and made his purposeful way to the nearest door, pulled it open, and walked through.

He found himself in a square room littered with scraps of parchment and lined with shelves of scrolls. At first, he thought it was a library, and his mind reeled at the wealth of a man who could afford so many books. Then he realized that the scrolls were thin and tied with twine, not ribbon. They were not books at all but lists of things, perhaps accounts. This was the steward's counting room, and the thin, anxious man behind the desk must be the steward.

"So you are here at last, are you?"

Marcus looked at the man blankly.

The steward rose, uncertain. "Brynn the scribe from Glaston? That's you, isn't it?"

Marcus bowed and ducked his head again and again to make clear his submission. "Yes, my lord. Brynn of Glaston. At your service."

The steward came out from behind his desk. He was frowning now. "It took you long enough. I expected you at midday. You've had a dirty trip, I see. They never told me you—I didn't know the school took cripples."

Marcus shrugged. "I'm not typical, my lord. The school owed my father a favor. As my arm barred me from warrior training, I chose a more settled life."

The steward still looked doubtful. "How do you write, then?"

Marcus took a deep breath to still his panic. He *could* write, thanks to Queen Alyse, who had taught Old Argus, but he certainly could not write with a scribal hand. If it came to that test, he would fail it.

He pointed to the scroll on the steward's desk, held open by two heavy, polished stones. "Just as you do, my lord."

The man accepted it. "I'm not the lord. I'm Jacobus the steward." He pointed to another desk, littered with pieces of parchment. "That's yours. Sit down. There's more to do than I can keep up with, as you can see."

He lifted a large basket stuffed with scraps and scrolls of parchment and set it down in the midst of the litter on Brynn's desk. "This lot's got to be sorted tonight. After that, I'll show you to your quarters. You'll be treated fairly as long as you do your work. You can file, can't you?"

"Yes, sir. But where?"

Jacobus waved a distracted hand at the crowded shelves. "There. And when that's done, God help us, we've got to get them into jars, corked and sealed, and into the storerooms underground. Six months' worth of records. And no assistant worth his salt."

The door opened and a burly, bearded man looked in. "Timber's here, Jacobus."

The steward grabbed his stylus and wax tablet and hurried outside, leaving Marcus alone in the candlelit room. Quickly, he scanned through the scrolls on the shelves behind him. His excitement grew as he progressed. Here were the records of everything that came into or went out of the fortress: meat, drink, cloth, oil, grain, weapons, salt, skins, inks and parchments, tools, building supplies, charcoal, wool, dyes, spices, furnishings—every single thing necessary to the running of a household. He could hardly believe his good fortune. He couldn't have stumbled onto a better source of information.

He grabbed a couple of thin scrolls from the basket. They were lists of wine casks imported, used up, and sent back to the coopers during the past six weeks. Marcus put them with the other wine import records on the shelves. It was a lot of wine, he thought, for a place half the size of King Pellinore's. And liberally dispensed, to judge by the guards at the gate.

Jacobus returned while he was still sorting the records in the basket. The steward copied his record of incoming timber from his wax tablet to a fresh scrap of parchment and tossed it on Brynn's desk.

"I'm off to the kitchens," he said. "I've a constant pain in my stomach unless I'm eating. It's my curse. Did you get any dinner on the road?"

"No, sir."

"I'll have something sent up to you, then."

"Thank you, sir. That's very kind."

Jacobus sighed as he gazed anxiously around the littered room. "My last assistant died a month ago, hunting with my young lord. What possessed the fool to ride with that wild lot I'll never know, but he's paid well for his mistake. I don't seem to be able to keep assistants. I hope you'll stay."

Marcus feigned disinterest, shuffling through the lists. "The lord is young? They told me otherwise at Glaston."

Jacobus groaned, a hand pressed against his stomach. "They'll be referring to the father. He's away at the wars." He lowered his voice. "He can't get home too soon for me." And with that odd admission, he left and shut the door behind him.

Marcus worked for almost an hour before a servant arrived with his dinner: hot soup with chunks of beef, thick-sliced brown bread, boiled eggs, sausages hot from the frying pan, and to top it all off, an entire flagon of warm, spiced wine. Marcus stared at it in wonder. If the steward's assistants ate this well, what must it be like in the feasting hall?

Marcus ate half the food and got back to work. A meticulous man, Jacobus kept records of nearly everything, including the number of animals brought from each meadow into the butcher's shed, their gender, age, and day of slaughter, but, alas, not their markings. The number of cattle slaughtered and eaten in the last six weeks staggered Marcus. It was enough to keep King Pellinore's household for half a year. Perhaps the place was bigger than it looked; perhaps there were more mouths to feed than he had estimated. He would have to ask Jacobus. If they kept consuming beef at this rate, those cattle in the meadows would not last long.

Jacobus was a long time returning, and when at last he came, he was running. He darted across the room and threw open the door to the courtyard. "Hurry! The master's coming!"

Startled, Marcus followed him outside. The master coming now? It must be the middle of the night, yet there in the courtyard stood the entire household staff, lined up in order of rank. As assistant steward, he stood at attention beside Jacobus near the center of the greeting party. The signal horn blared from beyond the earthworks, and a moment later, hooves thundered through the tunnel.

Three horses galloped into the cobbled, torch-lit yard and came to a sliding stop. The first was a flashy chestnut, and the young man who slipped so gracefully from the saddle had flash to match. He glittered with gold and jewels in the torchlight and wore an expression arrogant enough for a king. Predatory hazel eyes slid over the waiting company. Marcus held his breath. He had never seen this man before, but every instinct he possessed warned him of danger. The lord's gaze slid over him, passed on, and then returned.

"Who's this, Jacobus?" he said, coming toward them with a deceptively casual step. "Another new assistant?"

Jacobus straightened defensively. "Yes, my lord. Brynn of Glaston, from the scribal school. He just arrived today."

The hazel eyes regarded Marcus lazily. "Think he'll stay?"

"I hope so, my lord. He's done more work in half a day than Evart did in the two months he was here."

"An accomplishment, indeed, with half as many hands." There was a light in the eyes, now, a devouring intensity. The hair rose on the back of Marcus's neck.

"So you're a scribe, are you?"

"My lord." He bowed low.

"From Glaston?"

"Yes, my lord."

"You speak with the accent of Gwynedd."

"I was raised in Gwynedd, my lord."

"So you're not from Glaston, after all?"

"I beg your pardon, my lord. I meant I was from the scribal school at Glaston. I grew up in Gwynedd."

Something flickered in the lord's eyes, and Marcus knew the man did not believe him.

"Who's your father? Perhaps I know him."

"Argus of Oak Hill, my lord."

"Argus. I've heard that name before. Have you finished your day's duties with Jacobus?"

"Not yet, my lord."

"Not yet? It's past midnight."

Jacobus cleared his throat nervously but did not speak. Marcus met the young lord's eyes. "There's a lot to do."

A hint of a smile crossed the arrogant lips. "Jacobus, when you release him for the night, bring this 'scribe' to me before you show him to his quarters. I think he can be of use to me." He smiled, showing teeth. "Welcome to the Longmeadow Marshes," he said, and laughed as he turned away. His two henchmen followed at his heels.

Jacobus was white as a sheet. "Why did you make him angry? Why did you answer back? Every fool in the land knows better than to antagonize Sir Darric. He has a temper, he does, when he's roused."

Marcus watched the retreating figure with open curiosity. "So that's Sir Darric of Longmeadow, is it? I've heard of him." He smiled, in spite of himself. "He's the kind of man who likes to pull the wings off flies."

Jacobus scowled and urged him back to the counting room with flapping hands. "He did when he was six. He's moved on to larger beasts since then."

Llyr sat at the edge of a precipice in the early light and watched the night recede from the western sea. His mind was numb from so much thinking, and he ached with hunger. But he could not eat. Each day for five days he had snared a rabbit and cooked it, and once he had brought down a plump dove with his arrow, but he could not bring himself to eat much. Food could not fill the emptiness inside him.

The first thing he had done when he left the Long Eyes' cave was to climb to the top of the mountain ridge. He had always felt at home in the heights. This was a barren place of rock, sky, thin soil, and stunted trees, but it was not so barren or so high as Snow Mountain. Like Snow Mountain, it was an open place, open to the ends of the world—a strange kind of place for a boy raised in caves to love.

It was also a dangerous place, for it was full of predators. Wolves, hawks, eagles, mountain cats, and vultures hunted here, feeding on vermin and nimble mountain goats who capered among the rocks as if they were meadow grasses. He had already come face to face with a hunting cat. He had not reached for his weapons but stood before the crouched animal gravely, with understanding and a sense of brotherhood, and stared it down. The cat had switched its tail in heartfelt annoyance and vanished. It was a sign to Llyr that life was losing its importance.

He would survive the time of exile because he knew it had an end. But what would happen when the Long Eyes took him back? Would they let him guard her? Would they let him into their fellowship again? Would they let him hunt and feast with them? Or would he be an outcast forever even if he lived among them?

He knew there was no alternative but death. He could not go home without Mapon's blessing, although the memory of his family—of his mother; his father; his little sister, Leatha; and his brother, Lydd—brought tears to his eyes. His longing for them was so intolerably painful he shut his mind against the hope of ever seeing them again. To go home in disgrace was the last thing he could do. Better to die an outcast in a strange land than bring dishonor upon his family.

He gazed out over the cold, gray sea and watched another set of storm clouds blot out the horizon. It was a terrible punishment, this casting out from the only society he had known. It was death to the spirit. Those who had survived it lived in the hills like animals, like the predators they were, but not like men. They had lost all human feeling.

His own feelings, like his interest in living, had already dimmed a little. He could still feel resentment at the way he had been treated, but it was no longer the hot spurt of anger it had been. He could still summon a sense of peace when he sat like this, alone in the heights with the sky far-flung above him and the sea spread out below. It was a melancholy peace, however, and tinged with regret. He was not afraid of leaving life, but he did not want to be alone.

He wiped a hand across his eyes. How well he could

remember the soft shine of his mother's hair in the summer sun, the sound of Lydd's laughter and of Leatha's songs, and his father's dark eyes filled with pride. Even dearer was the memory of a sunlit forest glade and the haunting voice of a girl like no one he had ever known. Llyr pressed his fists to his eyes and tried to squeeze out the memory of that morning. But it was only five days ago and as clear in his mind as the memory of his mother's smile.

He got to his feet. It was a long walk down the mountain to that clearing in the forest, and he was weak with hunger. It would take him half the day. But now that she had entered his mind again and plucked out a song on the last strings of his human feeling, he had to revisit the place. She would not be there, but it did not matter. For a little while, he would be in a place where she had been, and he might feel near to her again. It would be enough.

Llyr turned his face to the west and started downhill.

CHAPTER FOURTEEN

The Headache

The day dawned cool and cloudy with a fitful wind blowing in off the sea. Elaine and Guinevere spent the morning with Father Martin in a tedious reexamination of the Commandments, followed by an explication of Scripture that nearly put them both to sleep.

Elaine grew petulant as the morning dragged on. Guinevere knew she had not had an easy day. Before breakfast, Maelgon had stolen a fistful of her hair ribbons from her chamber. He had used them to fashion a leash and, with the leash, had stolen a puppy from the kennels, right under the kennelmaster's nose. Maelgon had been punished for his willfullness, but Elaine had received a tongue-lashing, too. The theft was half her fault, Queen Alyse told her, for leaving her ribbons scattered about her chamber and not packed carefully away.

The level of tension in the household was giving Guinevere a headache. She gazed out the open window with apprehension. The sky was dark and oppressive with the threat of more rain. She had been unable to return to the clearing yesterday, and today looked to be just as busy. Sir Darric had left for home the previous afternoon to raise the men he would need for his campaign against the hillmen. He was due back today. Somehow, she would have to sneak away to the forest, even if it meant risking discovery.

By the time she and Elaine met for lessons with Iakos, the throbbing in her temples had blossomed into a beating ache. For Iakos's sake, she tried hard to concentrate on the tasks he set them. But whenever she looked down, she saw Llyr's narrow face in the wax of her tablet, and whenever she looked up, she saw how dark the sky was and how fast the day was passing. It was impossible to think of anything else.

Someone coughed gently. "I see that something is amiss."

Iakos stood at her side, his dark gaze sharp with concern. She saw she had made three mistakes in five lines of translation and wearily rubbed the waxen letters out. "I have a headache."

But when she reached for her stylus to begin anew, Iakos took it from her. "You have done enough, Lady Guinevere. I'm dismissing you for the rest of the afternoon. If you take my advice, you'll get some rest."

"But the queen—"

"I will answer to the queen," he said. "Now go."

"What about me?" Elaine demanded. "I have a headache, too. *And* a sore throat."

Iakos gazed at her wearily. "Do you, my lady? You don't look it."

Elaine gave her curls an arrogant little shake. "It's this awful weather. That brazier is useless. I'm numb to the bone. It'll be your fault if you keep me here and I get sick."

Iakos's long mouth twitched. He knew when deference was required. "Very well, my lady. You may go."

Back in their chamber, Guinevere shrugged off her gown and reached for her tunic.

"Where are you going?" Elaine cried. "Not out riding, for heaven's sake. Not in this weather. It's forbidden."

"I have to."

A sly look crossed Elaine's face. "You're going up into the forest, aren't you?" Guinevere froze, boot in hand. Elaine's smile widened. "I knew it. You're going to meet him. I know you are."

Guinevere pulled on her boots and reached for her good wool mantle. If Elaine knew her errand, there was no hope of keeping it from Queen Alyse. But it didn't matter, as long as she made it to the clearing in time to warn Llyr. They could do what they wished to her afterward. But how on earth had Elaine found out?

"How did he make contact?" Elaine asked, following her to the door.

Guinevere blinked. "We have a sign."

Elaine giggled and clapped her hands together. She fairly danced across the antechamber and sank down on Ailsa's stool. "I'll cover for you, Gwen. You can count on me. Does Ailsa know?"

"Well . . . ," said Guinevere, puzzled. "She knows I've seen him. But she doesn't know I'm going out today. She's been at the looms all morning."

"Then I won't say a word. Not a single word. I'll tell her you're in the chapel with Father Martin. She won't dare to interrupt."

"Well . . . thank you, Elaine. But it's not Ailsa I'm worried about. It's your mother. I don't like to disobey her. I wouldn't do it if it weren't so important."

Elaine jumped up from the stool and flung her arms around Guinevere. "You're an angel, Gwen! I won't forget this. Not everyone would brave Mother's wrath for me. Find out when he wants to see me and where. Suggest he make it after dark. I can sneak anywhere at night."

Guinevere stared at her as if she spoke in a foreign tongue. Elaine pushed her toward the door. "No cold feet," she said. "Tell him to meet me somewhere about the castle after dark. Go on. Go."

Guinevere was out in the corridor and running for the stairs before the sense of Elaine's words came home to her. She almost laughed. Her headache must have slowed her wits, or she would have caught Elaine's mistake, but the mix-up suited her perfectly. What she would say to Elaine when she returned empty-handed, with no message from Sir Darric, she had no idea. She would just have to cross that ford when she came to it and hope that her head was clearer then.

Slipping unseen out the garden door, she dodged between

the outbuildings and headed for the stables. Elaine would cover for her, that was the important thing. She wouldn't learn of Guinevere's real mission until later, and by that time, it would not matter. Llyr would have taken the warning to his people.

She pushed open a heavy oak door and slipped silently into the fragrant warmth of the stable. She loved the smell of horses, leather, and hay and did not much mind the heady stink of manure. Peleth stood where he always did, tied to a ring in the wall halfway down the aisle, his nose buried in hay. She slid in beside him and patted his neck, whispering words of comfort as she loosed his rope and began to nudge him away from his hay.

She had known from the beginning that the chances were slim she could get past Stannic unseen, so she was not surprised when she heard footsteps approaching and a large hand came down on Peleth's rump.

"And just where do you think you're going, Lady Guinevere?"

"Good afternoon, Stannic. I've got to go out. It's important."

"In this weather? It'll storm soon."

"I've got my mantle."

He shook his head slowly from side to side. Guinevere's heart sank.

"It's more than my life is worth," he said. "You'd get soaked to the skin and die of a coughing fit before the month is out. And where would I be then?" His dark gaze never left her face, and she bowed her head to escape it. "If the queen didn't have my hide, the king would, in no uncertain terms."

Stannic guided the horse out into the aisle. "I've been in Pellinore's service since I was twelve years old. Don't you think I owe him all the loyalty that's in me?"

Miserably, Guinevere nodded. The pain in her head was becoming unbearable. "Yes. Of course."

He handed her the halter rope. "Then stand there like a good girl. I'll be right back."

He retreated quickly into the shadows at the rear of the stable. Guinevere could hear him moving about among the trunks and saddles. She pressed her fingers against her temples. It would take her a long time to get to the clearing on foot, even if she ran. She touched the carving of Rhiannon tucked inside her tunic and whispered a quick prayer for help. Then she touched the cross at her throat, as well. She could not believe in every god, as Ailsa did, but neither could she yet choose between them.

Her eyes opened wide when she saw Stannic returning. His right hand held Peleth's bridle, and over his left arm he carried a thick, gray cloak.

"It's a soldier's cloak," he said gruffly, dropping it into her arms. "It's the smallest I've got, but it's plenty warm, and it'll keep the water out. Try it on."

She obeyed while he bridled Peleth. The hem of the cloak dragged on the dirt floor. It was long enough to keep even her leggings dry. It was thick, heavy, and gloriously warm.

"Stannic," she said, following him and Peleth to the stable door, "are you letting me go? You know about the queen's orders, don't you?"

"I do." He gave her a leg up onto the horse's back. "There

isn't anyone in Gwynedd who doesn't know. But King Pellinore is my master, not Queen Alyse." He glanced quickly over his shoulder as he spoke, which made Guinevere smile.

"Ailsa came to see me yesterday," he said, holding the gelding's rein. "Just you remember my neck is on the line as well as yours. Don't take chances. Do what you have to do and get back here fast."

He slapped the horse hard on the rump and watched Guinevere and Peleth fly past the paddocks and into the safety of the woods beyond.

CHAPTER FIFTEEN

Trials of a Scribe

Marcus ducked behind a tree at the sound of hoofbeats and lowered the sack he carried to the ground. He did not want to be caught in the hills of Gwynedd weaponless and dressed in a peasant's tunic. He had no way to explain himself. He was supposed to be at home on his sickbed, and if he was found out of it, he would be instantly dismissed from the king's service. Regis would see to that. Queen Alyse would not be able to save him. She had already warned him he was on his own.

He peered out from behind the tree as the hoofbeats retreated. A bay rump, a black tail, and a gray cloak disappeared at a quick canter into the forest greenery. A young soldier on his way—where? No one lived in the direction the horse was headed. It could not be a messenger. Who else would be riding out with a storm coming on but the newest recruit on some whim of his commander? Yet, something familiar about that slender back produced a qualm of doubt.

He turned away and slung the heavy canvas sack over his shoulder. Queen Alyse was waiting for him. So might Regis be. After the long night's walk from the Longmeadow Marshes, he had neither the time nor the energy to follow the lad. With an effort, he pushed the young soldier from his mind and concentrated on the task before him.

It would not be easy to sneak into the castle, meet with Queen Alyse, get out again, and return to his home unseen. There, he could at last change his clothes and collect his weapons. With luck, he'd be reporting to Regis for duty before the midnight change of watch.

As he made his way downhill, he considered again last night's encounter with Sir Darric of Longmeadow. Jacobus had insisted on making an occasion of it. He had not permitted Marcus to return to work when they were dismissed from the courtyard but had devoted himself to making Brynn the scribe presentable. He had borrowed a clean tunic, combed Brynn's hair, and even loaned him his own pair of polished boots. He had worked with speed but with an air of melancholy, as if he knew that a visit to Sir Darric spelled the end for his new apprentice. Marcus had begun to wonder if he was heading for his doom. But doom or no doom, there was no way out of that fortress without Sir Darric's permission, at least not until the gates opened in the morning.

He had followed Jacobus meekly through the villa. Each room he entered looked larger and finer than the one before, and there seemed an endless sequence of them. Finally, Jacobus stopped at a carved door and spoke nervously to the guard outside it.

"My lord has asked to see Brynn the scribe. Announce him, please."

When the guard stepped inside, Jacobus whispered hurriedly to Marcus, "I will pray for you, Brynn. Do whatever he asks. Don't argue; don't refuse him; don't speak unless you are told to. Remember the boy who pulled the wings off flies."

The steward was gone before the guard returned to usher Marcus inside the grandest chamber he had ever seen. No expense had been spared in its furnishings. Three Roman couches draped in silks and velvets and plump with cushions circled a low central table piled with bowls of fruit and a basket of fresh-baked bread. Even after the dinner Jacobus had provided, Marcus's mouth watered at the scent of new bread. Tapestries hung on the plastered walls to cover the cracks and keep out drafts. Two shining copper cauldrons filled with logs stood between the couches, but only one was lit. Gentle flames warmed the wine jar in its tripod stand. A double-flamed lamp stood in each corner of the room. By their light, Marcus could see into the bedchamber beyond, where skins and cushions in colorful profusion decked a huge carved bed.

Sir Darric rose from the central couch and smiled his dazzling smile. "How good of you to come—Brynn, is it? Please, have a seat."

He gestured to one of the couches, and after a moment's hesitation, Marcus sat stiffly on its edge. Sir Darric, too, had changed his clothes. He wore a long, flowing robe of dark green velvet trimmed with fur. He had removed the heavy torque from about his neck, but gold still gleamed from wrists and fingers. He poured wine from the clay jar into a glazed ceramic bowl and handed it to Marcus. "Relax. Drink up. The night lies before us."

Marcus sipped carefully. The wine was unwatered, warm, and sweetly spiced. He watched Sir Darric fill his own bowl and drink it down. He knew by the unconscious fluidity of the gesture that this was a habit of long standing.

Sir Darric draped himself on his couch with catlike grace. "You interest me, Brynn. I'm willing to wager you're the only one-armed scribe in all of Britain." He smiled invitingly. "In truth, I'm willing to wager you're not a scribe at all, are you?"

It was a rhetorical question. Marcus quelled his impulse to answer attack with attack and tried to look cowed. "Yes and no, my lord. I was not born to it, if that is what you mean."

The smile faded. "I mean that the scribal school at Glaston is select. They don't take cripples." He filled his bowl again with a steady hand. "I think you're a fraud, Brynn, and unless you can convince me otherwise, you'll be dead before dawn." He looked up to see how Brynn was taking this and smiled charmingly. "That gives you time to think up a tale I might believe."

Marcus couldn't help himself. He rose and squared his shoulders. "I beg your pardon, my lord. I don't mean to give offense, but I was raised in a noble household and am not used to being called a scoundrel to my face."

Sir Darric looked pleased. "Noblemen's sons do not become scribes," he said smoothly. "Even ones with two hands. You're an escaped slave, most likely."

"I am a scribe by choice, my lord. My father considered me unfit for warrior training because I could not wield both shield and sword. He wanted me to join the priesthood, but I chose the scribal school instead. My uncle Sir Lucius of Glaston made a large donation to the school, and the master took me on." While these bold words left his lips, Marcus prayed inwardly that Sir Darric knew little of Glaston society and the school only by its reputation, for every word he spoke was fabrication.

Sir Darric took another long swallow of wine. "What about your father, then? Why couldn't he pay the entrance price himself?"

Marcus almost swayed with relief. The man believed him. "My father had five sons, my lord, and four to equip for warrior training. My uncle Lucius, my mother's brother, was unwed. He was able to pay, and my father was not." He lifted his shoulders and let them fall. "I worked on my uncle's estate when I left the school. When he died at midwinter, I had to look for another place. The school sent me here."

Sir Darric watched the wine swirl around the bottom of his bowl. "And your father's name? . . . You knew it earlier."

"Argus of Oak Hill," Marcus said promptly. "He's an old man now, and ill. You'll not have heard of him, my lord."

The savage eyes held his. "On the contrary. The name's familiar. He's one of Pellinore's men, isn't he?"

Marcus bowed politely even as his heart raced. This was a

dangerous game when Sir Darric knew the ground. "He was, my lord."

Sir Darric emptied his bowl, placed it on the table, and clapped his hands for a servant. "Well, well. As a story, it isn't bad. Let's put it to the test."

A boy appeared at the door. Sir Darric sent him off to fetch pen, ink, parchment, and another wine jar. He gestured to Marcus's bowl, still full. "Drink up, my noble friend. If your story is true, you've nothing to fear."

That was an old and hallowed lie, but Marcus could not say so. He sat down and took a decent swallow of the wine. His only hope lay in Sir Darric's education. If it had been a good one, Marcus was lost.

While they waited, Sir Darric regaled him with a tale of his recent visit to Pellinore's castle and his meetings with the lovely Queen Alyse. Marcus hid his surprise. The visit must have been a short one. To have returned already, Sir Darric must have arrived at the castle soon after he himself had left. The idea that the queen had befriended this man repulsed him. It couldn't be true.

"I've been getting the queen's advice," Sir Darric said. "I've met with the captain of her house guard. What's his name? . . . Regis?" He waited for confirmation, but Marcus gave no indication that the name was familiar to him. "I'm grateful for all the help he's given me. We need a complete reorganization here. It's my father's job, but he's past it, frankly. Been getting old in the head, if you know what I mean."

Marcus took another sip of wine. It gave him a chance,

however brief, to hide behind the bowl and avoid the direct, assessing stare of those feral eyes.

"My aim is to get this place into proper order before the earl gets back from the wars. But I have so little time. I can't spend all my days in conference with Alyse and her house guard when I'm needed here."

Marcus flushed. *Alyse.* By God, the arrogant rake bandied her name about as if she were a common wench. If the queen knew, she would cut his tongue out.

A scratch came at the door. Marcus almost jumped. The servant placed parchment, ink, and quill on the table; replaced the empty wine jar with a full one; and retired.

"Now," said Sir Darric, pouring himself another bowl. "Your life is in your own hands, Brynn. Or should I say, hand?" Sir Darric grinned. "You're going to write a letter for me. To Regis, captain of the royal house guard. If you do well, you may have the honor of taking it to him yourself. If you fail, I shall have the pleasure of taking your life with my own hands. Very, very slowly." Again, that terrifying smile. "Much more entertaining than a sword thrust to the heart. I've known men who could scream from daybreak to sunset without pausing for breath."

The memory of those words still made Marcus queasy. He knew a bit about blades himself and, for an awful moment, had thought Sir Darric was onto him, was tailoring the torture to suit him. He remembered all too vividly the eager light in those unforgettable eyes. But his suspicion had been unfounded. Sir Darric knew nothing of his own skill with knives; he had simply enjoyed threatening a man completely in his power.

Now, safely back on King Pellinore's lands, Marcus found he resented this manipulation very deeply. Yet he was not in a position to take revenge. He was on a delicate mission whose outcome was still uncertain. The contempt he had felt for Sir Darric when the man accepted his careful scribbles as a good scribal hand had dissolved when he realized the nature of the trap the man had devised. "To Regis, son of Gaius Paulus," said the letter he carried in his tunic, "I send you greetings by the single hand of Brynn, my scribe." Those were the only words in the message. What followed were merely numbers: "III, V, VII."

"Don't worry," Sir Darric had assured him with one of his awful smiles. "He'll know what the numbers mean. And who they come from. Just take it to him."

Therein lay the problem, for Marcus could not take the message to Regis himself. If Regis and Sir Darric were really in communication, Marcus and his secret mission would be discovered, with only one result for Marcus. If they were not in communication, he still could not take Regis the message without revealing his presence in the Longmeadow Marshes while he was supposed to be sick in bed at home. If he did not take Regis the message, Sir Darric would surely discover it, for if he had visited Queen Alyse once he was very likely to do so again, if only to check up on Brynn, the suspect scribe. A one-armed man was easy to find when actually sought.

What interested Marcus most was the idea that Sir Darric

was clever enough to communicate by code, for what else could the numbers be? If the code was really intended for Regis, it was something Queen Alyse should know. On the other hand, Sir Darric's evident familiarity with the queen suggested another possibility. Perhaps the coded part of the message was meant for her. If Regis received the letter and was confused by the code, his first step would be to show it to the queen. Marcus appreciated the subtlety of this indirect approach, and so, he was certain, would the queen. But coded communications between the queen of Gwynedd and Sir Darric of Longmeadow suggested only one thing to Marcus, and that was treason.

He slung down his sack and seated himself at the foot of a giant oak tree, head in hand. Any way he looked at it, he came to the same conclusion: he was being used as a tool by someone powerful for an evil purpose, and he was doing it willingly. Before he could go any farther, he must weigh his options and make a decision about whom to trust. He must prepare himself for the consequences of his choice if he was wrong. He did not want to believe Queen Alyse capable of treachery, but she was a mother, and mothers would do absolutely anything to protect their young. Could someone have threatened her sons? Or either of those girls? Was that why she wanted Sir Darric? For protection? Or was it merely for her own amusement?

Marcus started. Thinking about the girls had awakened a memory. That had been no soldier in the gray cloak—that was young Guinevere on Pellinore's old cavalry mount, riding into the woods without a saddle. He remembered now that he had seen the bay rump and the lithe, gray back, but no cantle. No saddle. And after his express warning to the queen to keep her safe within the castle grounds . . .

He rose to his feet and took up his burden. His decision was made.

CHAPTER SIXTEEN

The Warning

The sky was growing darker and the wind beginning to gust when Guinevere arrived at the clearing. She rode forward among wildflowers dancing madly in the wind and halted. The cairn she had built the day before was gone. No, not gone, but leveled neatly and precisely. She scanned the woods around her but saw no one. Peleth had already dropped his head to graze when a soft voice spoke behind her.

"Daughter of Rhiannon."

Peleth's head jerked up. Llyr stood at the edge of the clearing, his dark eyes immense in a face grown taut and thin.

"Llyr!" Guinevere slid off the horse. "Whatever has happened to you?" He looked gaunt and uncared for, with circles under his eyes and hollows beneath his cheekbones. "Are you sick? Has there been trouble?"

He came forward and gestured to the place where the cairn had stood. "You called me. Here I am."

Guinevere hesitated. His eyes had a glazed look. Something terrible had happened to him, but whatever it was, it must not interfere with the crisis at hand.

"I have grave news, Llyr. A man came to the castle, a visiting lord. He told Queen Alyse that it is the hillmen—the Old Ones—who are stealing her cattle and her sheep. He has gone home to get troops, and when he comes back, he is going to track down the Long Eyes and . . . and destroy you all."

He stared at her unblinking.

"Llyr, do you understand? He will be back *tonight*. He wants to kill your people. *He is coming to hunt you down*."

Still, Llyr did not respond.

Guinevere came closer. "Llyr, you must take this message to the leader of the Long Eyes. *Now*. There is no time to waste. I must get back at once—I am here without permission, and if the queen catches me, she will never let me ride out again."

Llyr seemed to sway in the rising breeze. Guinevere ran to him and took his hands as he sank to the forest floor. They were cold.

"Llyr!" She reached inside the heavy cloak, drew out her waterskin, and pressed it to his lips. As he drank, she pulled the cloak off and wrapped it around him. Gradually, his color improved.

"Pellinore's men—come to kill us?"

"Of course not. King Pellinore's men are patrolling the hills as they did before. These new troops belong to the lord of the Longmeadow Marshes. But the lord himself is away with King Pellinore, fighting Saxons. His son leads them now."

"We do not steal."

"I know. I know that. But he has convinced Queen Alyse that you do. He does not care whether or not it is true. He likes to kill, and there is no one to stop him."

Llyr rose. His lips twisted with some strong emotion. "Earth's Beloved will not listen to any warning I bring."

"Why not?"

"They have cast me out until the next new moon."

Now it was Guinevere's turn to stare. "*You?* But why? You are a prince among them! Your father is leader of the White Foot."

He turned away from her, and in the slump of his shoulders she read his shame. She took him by the arm and turned him back until she could see his face.

"Llyr," she whispered, "how long have you been . . . outcast? How many days?"

He shrugged and avoided her eyes.

"Tell me," she pressed. "Two days? Three? Four? Five?"

His eyes met hers briefly and dropped again. "Five."

"Five days ago, I met you here. Is that the reason?" Her voice began to shake. "Llyr, tell me the truth. Did they cast you out because of me?"

He shook his head. "I broke an oath."

"How?"

His hands lifted and cupped her shoulders. They were warm hands now, and welcome. Her body had grown cold without the cloak.

"Good guards stay hidden."

She stifled a gasp. "Because you showed yourself to me? Is that why? . . . Oh, that is unfair! It is not the secrecy of the guard that matters, but his presence, his loyalty, his courage." She smiled at him. "I know you are loyal, and you must be courageous, or you would not have come back here."

At last, the glazed look left his eyes, and he attempted a smile. "Thank you, Gwenhwyfar." He did not tell her that his own need, not her call, had driven him to the clearing. He lifted the cloak from his shoulders and replaced it gently on hers.

"You must take my warning to your leader," she insisted, teeth chattering. "Only you can save the Long Eyes from an-nihilation."

Llyr's smile faded. "They cannot hear me or see me. That is what it means to be outcast. To them, I do not exist."

Guinevere stared at him, and pity nearly overwhelmed her. But knowing Llyr did not want pity, she said firmly, "Then we will go together. They will have to believe *me*. If they are my guards, they cannot harm me. And they cannot prevent you from coming if I am the one who brings you."

Llyr hesitated. "It is forbidden."

"There is no time to worry about that. We have to hurry. Peleth can take us both if you will show me the way. All right?"

Llyr did not move. "There is only one way I can return to the Long Eyes," he said, searching for the words that would explain it. "I must go as supplicant. I must ask for a meeting with the One Who Hears."

"Who is that?"

He shied from the question. "An old woman. Once I do that, my life is hers."

Guinevere frowned. "What does that mean?"

Llyr's hands twisted together, and he looked away. "For an outcast to approach her—a terrible act, almost a heresy—means I put my life in her power. Forever. To disobey the One Who Hears is death."

Guinevere paled. "I would not have you risk your life, Llyr. Is the One Who Hears such a harsh judge?"

"She speaks with the voice of the god," he whispered. "Her judgments are absolute."

"I cannot let you risk it. Never mind. I will take the warning to the Long Eyes myself. Tell me how to find them."

Llyr gripped her arm. "No. Do not go alone. It will make great trouble. As long as you live in Gwynedd, you bring them honor and status, but no one is allowed to approach you. They will not know what to do."

"But, Llyr," Guinevere pleaded, "I cannot leave them to be killed and persecuted by the Marsh Lord's son. I *must* warn them."

"We will warn them together," Llyr said at last, after a long study of the forest floor. He did not look happy about it.

"But I don't want you to submit yourself to the One Who Hears if it could mean death for you."

"It is the only way."

He spoke with finality, and Guinevere saw that Llyr had made up his mind. She made him a reverence to honor his courage and reached for Peleth's reins. "Then let's go."

CHAPTER SEVENTEEN

The Old Ones

It was one thing to set off on a mission that honor demanded and quite another to enter a world one knew nothing about, meet strangers whose customs one did not understand and whose language one could not speak. Anything might happen. Guinevere steeled herself against second thoughts as they trotted into a clearing high in the hills where a spring and a small stream flanked a low-mouthed cave.

Rising wind whipped the trees and bushes around them. The gray sky had a greenish hue. Any moment Guinevere expected the lowering clouds to release their burden of rain and drench them both. Already thunder rumbled in the distance.

They slid off the horse together. Guinevere tied Peleth under a tree and took Llyr's hand. It was trembling.

"How do we announce ourselves?" she asked. "Or do we want to take them by surprise?"

Llyr almost smiled. "It is difficult to take Earth's Beloved by surprise. There are lookouts everywhere. They know we are here."

Inside the cave, the floor tilted down at a gentle angle. As they descended into the heart of the hill, the air grew warm and thick with the scents of burning peat and human habitation. Squat oil lamps every thirty paces gave them just enough light to see.

Llyr stopped at the threshold of a wide, torch-lit cavern and released Guinevere's hand. She blinked at the scene before her. The cavern was full of people. Every man, woman, and child in the entire Long Eyes clan must have come to meet them. They stood clustered around a central fire, staring at her openmouthed and making the ancient sign against enchantment.

Guinevere scanned them with frank curiosity. They were a small people, most of them shorter and stockier than Llyr, with weathered faces and thick, dark hair. It was easy to tell which of the men was the leader. He was the only one who did not have black tufts of hair sprouting from his chest, arms, and chin. His hair, as bountiful and unkempt as his fellows', was uniformly gray. He wore a copper armband around the hard swell of muscle on his upper arm. It was his only ornament. A thick bearskin cloak, hanging from shoulder to heel, lent him an air of primitive majesty. In his right hand, he held a staff made of ash wood, one end curled like a shepherd's crook and carved with runes.

Llyr slid to his knees and spoke quickly in the guttural tongue of the Old Ones. When he had finished, he translated quietly for Guinevere. "I have told them who you are and why we have come. The leader's name is Mapon. He speaks your language."

Guinevere waited for him to rise. But Llyr remained kneeling, forehead to the floor, in an attitude of abject submission. A low mutter of voices ran like wildfire around the walls of the cave. The leader, Mapon, glared at Llyr and struck his staff against the floor. The voices died away to utter silence.

Guinevere took a deep breath and made the leader a graceful reverence. "Mapon, leader of the Long Eyes, greetings. I beg your pardon for coming uninvited into your—your abode, but I bring a warning of dire importance to your people."

At the sound of her voice, another murmur swept through the crowd. Mapon raised his staff in the air for silence and took one step forward from the men gathered behind him. All of them, Guinevere noticed, had daggers stuck in their belts.

"We are honored by your presence, princess," Mapon said gravely in excellent Welsh. "But it is forbidden."

Guinevere flushed. "I will leave at once if you'll allow Llyr to speak for me," she said quickly. "Otherwise, I must stay."

Mapon's face darkened. "The one you refer to is outcast. He may not speak."

"Then I must stay. I am very sorry if it is forbidden."

After a short, stiff silence, Mapon nodded in Llyr's direction. "The outcast asks for a hearing with our wise woman. It is his right, but as an outcast, the cost will be high. Does She With Hair of Light wish this cost to be paid?"

Guinevere shivered. "It is not my wish," she said evenly. "But it is Llyr's wish." She spoke his name deliberately, even though it shocked them. But she refused to call him "outcast." He was not outcast to her. "He would not let me come here alone. He said it would make trouble. But the warning must be delivered. He came the only way he could. As a supplicant."

The stiff lines in Mapon's face relaxed. "Very well."

Mapon turned to his people and spoke quickly in his own tongue. Quietly, they dispersed into branching passageways and interior caves, leaving Mapon, twelve men, and twelve women behind in the cavern. The women began to distribute mats in a circle around the hearth, while the men fetched wineskins, horn cups, and an offering of mealcakes on a bone platter. These were arranged near Mapon's place toward the back of the cave.

At Mapon's signal, everyone took a seat around the low peat fire. The women sat cross-legged on the mats, knee to knee with the men. Guinevere was given the place of honor at Mapon's right hand. Llyr was not offered a seat around the fire but remained kneeling, forehead to the floor, a little outside the circle.

Mapon began the meeting by introducing each of the Old Ones in the circle. This took a long time, for each name contained an ancestry. He ended by introducing himself as Mapon the Long-Sighted, son of Lugh Strongheart, son of Bran the Wise, son of Mapon the Mighty. He was the fourth generation of his family to be chosen leader of the Long Eyes.

Guinevere inclined her head politely. "I am honored to make your acquaintance."

Each of them gave her a shy nod in return. Their faces were uniformly grave and disapproving but at the same time alight with curiosity. Mapon began speaking to his people in their own tongue, and Guinevere took time to look around.

The Old Ones were not the primitive people she had imagined. Their clothes of animal hides stitched with sinew were not as fine as her own, but their weapons, from what she could see of them, were beautifully crafted and honed to a bright edge. They looked to be a strong people, strong of build and strong of feature, but they were not the savages some folk thought them. They lived by rules and customs, paid obedience to their leader and their gods. The women wore amulets around their necks, and most of the men had drawings of animal heads etched into the flesh of their upper arms. Their society was different from her own, but it was not uncivilized.

She knew from Llyr that they raised sheep, yet none of them wore anything made of wool. The mats they sat on were made of thick, coiled ropes of braided and twisted wool stitched together in tight, concentric circles. The wool was unwashed, unbleached, and undyed. Smelly and oily as it was, it made a mat that would stay dry on any ground.

Perhaps the Old Ones did not know how to weave. Perhaps they had no spindles to spin fine thread, no looms to weave the threads into a fabric. They were, after all, a season-ally nomadic people who followed the game over the hills and through the forests, and sometimes even down into the settled valleys of their ancestral territories. They had no use for looms or anything too heavy to carry on their backs.

The Old Ones spent their days close to the land, in tune with its rhythms and under the protection of its gods. They put up no fences and owned no property but lived on the earth's gifts, unfettered as the birds of the air, as free and as wild as Father Martin's lilies of the field. Clothes of skins and oily wool mats seemed a small price to pay for such a privilege.

She wondered what it would be like to be on the move so often, to own not a single clothes chest, to sleep in a cave instead of a castle, or better, out under the stars, free of the constant encasing of cold stone walls. A yearning for it gripped her forcibly. No more worries about combs or gowns or the latest fashion in dress, no more feeling pampered and useless until a forced marriage to some stranger tore her away from home. No more wrenching away from the old gods and trying to form allegiance to a deity who had never lived in Wales.

On the other hand, the Old Ones were not sleeping out under the stars; they were living deep within the cave. To the Welshmen she knew, this was sacred terrain. Caves and tun-nels dug into the mountains, the "hollow hills," were consid-ered to be gates to the Otherworld, and to pass into them meant passing into an unknown territory from which travelers did not always return. Great warriors were sometimes buried in the hollow hills. It was considered a high honor to lie at the threshold of gods. Did Welshmen fear the Old Ones because they dared to live at the gates of the Otherworld? Because they claimed to be the mortal descendants of the gods themselves? Or was it just the distrust that always arose between cultures with different practices and beliefs?

Guinevere gazed up at the vaulting roof of stone above her head and shivered. She recognized the feeling that had gripped her on the threshold of the cavern, the feeling that had forced Llyr to his knees. It was awe. Here, in this hallowed hall, she sensed an unseen presence. Someone else was with them, watching, listening. The hair rose on the back of her neck, and in response, she pulled the borrowed cloak tighter around her.

Mapon's voice, speaking in Welsh, jerked her from her thoughts. "I have explained why you are here, princess. The Great Council has agreed to hear your warning. Please, tell us what danger threatens."

Guinevere quickly explained how Queen Alyse had been made to think the Old Ones were stealing her livestock and that she had permitted a young nobleman to organize a force of men to chase them from the hills. Guinevere did not name Sir Darric. It was important that Mapon's people know what the soldiers intended, but she did not want to begin a war between the Old Ones and Sir Darric. This was just the sort of trouble King Pellinore had worked so hard to avoid.

The Old Ones listened carefully as Mapon translated her report into their language. Muttering broke out around the circle, and sharp glances were exchanged. Guinevere did not blame them for their anger. Would they view Queen Alyse's actions as betrayal of the promises King Pellinore had made? If they did, she could not blame them for that, either. The queen's actions were inexplicable to her. Mapon did not translate the discussion that now ensued, even as it boiled into argument. Guinevere hoped the dissension was about strategies for escape or about fighting tactics, but she had no way of knowing. More than once she glanced at Llyr, but he remained in the posture of abasement, kneeling with his forehead to the floor.

Guinevere waited impatiently for some resolution, for a decision to be made or action taken. Time oppressed her. It must be growing dangerously late. If she did not leave soon, she would never get home before dark. She would certainly be missed if she did not appear at dinner, and she did not have much faith in Elaine's ability—or Stannic's—to weave a tale Queen Alyse would long believe.

The forgotten pain began to throb again between her temples. Smoke from the peat fire stung her eyes. She reached into her pouch and clutched the little carving of Rhiannon, uttering a silent prayer for strength and help. Just when she thought she could stand no more—when another moment of it would drive her outside into the clean, smokeless air and blessed silence—the voices stopped.

All eyes turned to the back of the cave. There, half a dozen paces behind her, a light appeared. The wall at her back had been all the time in deep shadow, and she had assumed it to be made of solid rock. It was not. Light seeped around the edges of a curtain of stitched skins covering the entrance to another cave. No one spoke. She glanced hastily around the circle and saw every face alert, intent, waiting with bated breath for whatever was behind the curtain to come forth.

CHAPTER EIGHTEEN

The One Who Hears

The curtain parted and a girl appeared, little more than a child, with a stone oil lamp between her hands. An older girl followed, carrying a pallet stuffed with straw. They placed the pallet and the light before the only empty space in the circle, on Mapon's left hand, and retreated into the background. Two young women came forward, supporting between them a bent figure wrapped in a black cloak. The women deposited their burden carefully on the pallet, then withdrew into the shadows.

Guinevere stared at the cloaked figure, her heart hammering in her ears. Her head felt as if it were about to split apart. Like the others in the circle, she bent forward until her forehead touched the floor, and because the cool stone felt so wonderful against her throbbing head, she lingered in this posture a moment longer than everyone else. When she straightened, the hood of the cloak had turned her way. Guinevere looked up into a pair of black eyes set deep in a tiny, hideously wrinkled yellow face.

"Mother," she whispered in Mountain Welsh, "a thousand pardons. I came to warn you, not to disturb your peace."

The people in the circle inhaled sharply. Llyr raised his face from the floor, his eyes stretched in horror. Guinevere saw she had made a terrible mistake. Perhaps it was forbidden to address the old woman, but she hadn't intended to speak. The words had just spilled out, propelled by a power she could not resist. She pulled the folds of her cloak tighter around her and resolved not to say anything more. She had delivered her warning. The rest was in Mapon's hands.

Mapon spoke softly and quickly, addressing himself to the Crone. For that's who this must be, Guinevere realized, once her mind had begun to work again. This was their wise woman, their sage, their seer, a woman who had grown up in the Mother's service from a child and who represented to the Long Eyes the divine Three-in-One: Maiden, Mother, and Crone. Some part of herself—the unthinking part—had known this instinctively the moment the bent figure had come through the curtain. She knew she ought to be afraid of this old woman, so frail and bent and surrounded by an aura of power, but she was not. The black eyes that regarded her so directly held no malice. Exactly what they did hold, however, she could not say.

Mapon finished speaking. The Crone regarded the circle of people and fixed her dark gaze on Llyr. At once, he bent forward and again pressed his forehead to the ground. The

Crone's lips parted, and Guinevere heard a dry crackling sound emerge. It drifted over the silent throng like wind through a field of grass. Guinevere noticed that no one in the circle looked directly at the Crone, as she had, and that Mapon did not face her when he spoke to her. This in itself did not disturb Guinevere—the indirect approach was a common practice when addressing gods. Even the Christian God required a bent head for direct communication. But the Crone was one of the Old Ones themselves, a mortal being, like the hill witch Griselda who had made such a nuisance of herself in Northgallis. To accord her this degree of respect, the Long Eyes must think her a very powerful old woman, indeed.

A dry chuckle sounded from the dark shroud of the cloak. The ancient eyes were watching her, the seamed face crinkled in amusement. Guinevere pulled her hood forward to blot out the sight. The Crone laughed.

Daughter of Rhiannon, freedom is not thy destiny. Do not yearn for it. Guinevere heard the words perfectly clearly. They came out of the air, borne on a strong, young voice. At the same time, she was aware of total silence in the cave. It was so still that she could hear the faint drip of moisture sliding off a rock face deep inside the hill. No one had spoken aloud.

She knew then that it was the Crone's true voice she had heard, her inner, ageless voice, which bypassed the failing body and spoke directly to the mind. More astonishing, this old woman had the power to read one's innermost thoughts. There in the back of the cave, she had felt Guinevere's yearning for a life free of strictures, for a bed out under the stars.

Guinevere shivered at the thought. How did one keep anything secret from the One Who Hears?

Mapon turned to Guinevere. "The One Who Hears wishes me to translate for you. She wants you to understand and participate in everything that passes here."

Guinevere could hear his disapproval in his voice, but no one could deny the Crone's request. She nodded weakly.

"The One Who Hears knows of the warning you bring." Mapon cleared his throat. "But the Council is divided. Some do not believe that King Pellinore's queen would betray us. Some think we will be safe enough, this high in the hills, without taking further action. Some—a few—think that the outcast has persuaded you to tell us a story that will serve to soften his punishment and get him readmitted to the clan." Mapon averted his eyes as he spoke. "The Council must decide with one voice. We cannot take action until the people all agree. If we split apart, we die."

Guinevere thought she understood. Among the Old Ones, it was said, the leader was not a ruler. He led, but he did not lay down the law. He was not king. It took a consensus of the clan to come to a decision. She had always thought this a very fair way to govern, especially if women were allowed a voice in the discussion, but now she saw a difficulty. If they could not take urgent action until they all agreed, they could be destroyed by a swift attack.

She looked across the circle at Llyr, who had raised his head and whose dark eyes burned with fury. She realized, with a glimmer of delight, that Llyr's anger was all on her behalf.

Some among the Long Eyes did not believe her. Mapon had not said so directly, but that was what his words had meant. Llyr's enemies did not believe she was the one called She With Hair of Light. They did not believe her message; therefore, they could not believe in the messenger. The realization lightened her heart in one respect. If there were doubters among the Long Eyes, there must be doubters in other clans, as well. The hag Griselda had been a local woman and her prophecy a local event, not a universal truth to be accepted everywhere beyond the borders of Northgallis. She almost smiled in her relief.

Her pleasure vanished when she saw Mapon's drawn face. He had been ashamed to tell her of the doubters, and he would not have done it if the One Who Hears had not commanded that Guinevere be told everything. Mapon would have to change some minds before he could unite the Old Ones.

Wasn't this why they called upon the One Who Hears, to guide them through their deliberations, to show them truth? Guinevere glanced toward the Crone, but the old woman's face was hidden by the hood of her cloak. She sat slumped and motionless, supported by the acolyte beside her. She made no movement, gave no indication that she held the power even to discern truth, never mind make it manifest to her followers.

Guinevere looked away. A great grief rose within her. If the Long Eyes were to withstand Sir Darric, they must be united. Uniting them meant convincing them that Llyr had not deceived them, that he had not forced her to come here on his own behalf but on theirs. They must be made to believe that the threat was real, that the warning came from a reliable source, from an outsider they could trust and believe. A sob caught in her throat. The only way to do that was to convince the doubters that she was indeed the child of the prophecy, the one person in the whole world she did not want to be.

The black hood turned toward her again, but this time the eyes that looked into hers were not smiling. There was a question in them, and a stillness that seemed to strike at her very soul. *Daughter, what is thy choice?*

Angry tears rose to Guinevere's eyes. Why should this burden be hers? Why was she the one who must decide? Her choice might mean the death of many . . . or the sacrifice of one. She was only a girl, an orphan and a ward, without the power or standing to command belief. She stared back into the Crone's eyes and read in them only a reflection of her own defiance. She looked away, head held high, too furious for speech. Gathered around the smoking fire, the silent congregation of the Old Ones watched her fearfully, as if waiting for a storm to break.

She looked again at the faces around the fire, and gradually her anger drained away. They were a superstitious folk, after all, to believe such tales as Griselda's. A prophecy wasn't a prophecy unless one believed in it. Hadn't she made that argument to Gwillim over a hundred times? Her childhood playmate returned to her mind as vividly as if he were sitting with her in the circle. Over and over, they had discussed the truth of unseen gods, of magical powers and foretelling, of charms and spells and the crazy incantations of charlatans who practiced on the faith of the credulous. If she didn't believe a prophecy, Gwillim had agreed, it could have no meaning for her, it could not control her life. It could only affect her future if she allowed it to. A great weight seemed to lift from her heart as she looked around at all the waiting faces. She was safe, perfectly safe, from all their superstitions. For it did not matter what they believed, so long as she did not believe it herself.

Guinevere squared her shoulders and turned back to the Crone in time to see her toothless smile. *Daughter, thy courage is a gift from the Goddess. It shall serve thee well.* Guinevere rose and made her a proper reverence, not the self-abasement reserved for deities but a deep curtsy of obedience and respect to a very clever old woman.

With lightning speed, the Crone pulled something from her robe and flung it on the fire. Black smoke billowed from the flames, rising to the rock roof and hanging above them all in a menacing cloud. Huddled deep inside her cloak, the Crone began to rock gently back and forth, mumbling a low chant. One by one, the others around the circle joined her. Their music snaked around the walls until the open space vibrated with a low thrum of excitement. Quick as a flash, a clawlike hand whipped out from the black cloak a second time. The fire leaped and spat as a shadow lighter than peat smoke took shape above the flames, a brilliant shadow rising against the dark ceiling smoke, a soaring shadow that gave the impression of wings outspread.

Guinevere swayed on her feet, dizzy with headache,

chanting, and firesmoke. Out of the darkness came a shrill, in-human voice:

> He comes, he comes,
> The Unconquered One,
> With crowns and swords and rings.
> She waits, she waits,
> The white hart's child,
> For him to bring her wings.

"The white shadow!" Mapon croaked, pointing with one hand and with the other making the sign against enchant-ment behind his back. "It comes!"

Guinevere shrank back as the shadow drifted toward her. The chanting had stopped. No one in the circle breathed, but their eyes, all turned upon her, shone like shield bosses. The wings of the shadow descended and embraced her, cold against her cheek. She sank to the floor, shivering. The white hart was the emblem of Northgallis. And the word Mapon had used for the winged apparition was the one the witch had spoken the night her mother died. *White shadow. Gwenhwyfar.* It was her name.

A cup of hot liquid was pushed into her hands and guided to her lips. Guinevere swallowed, sputtered, and swallowed again. Warmth flooded her limbs, and her throat burned. Llyr knelt at her side, his face aglow. Behind him, the entire com-pany sat around the fire, eating mealcakes and sipping from horn cups. She glanced quickly at the Crone, but the old woman had retreated back into her dark cocoon, and all Guinevere could see of her was a wisp of white hair beneath her hood.

Llyr's face, bent close to hers, was filled with awe. "Drink," he whispered, urging the cup against her lips. "A potion for reawakening."

"Have I been asleep?"

Mapon appeared beside Llyr and smiled down at her. "Don't worry," he said in Welsh. "It's a sleep of blessing. It often happens when the One Who Hears speaks with the god's voice. Even secondhand, the divine voice exhausts mortal ears."

Guinevere sat up and took a sip of the hot liquid. It tasted bitter and sweet at the same time. Ailsa sometimes gave her something like it when she was sick, a mixture of herbs, bark, and honey, and it never failed to make her feel better. She took a long swallow and looked up at Mapon.

"Father Martin said the same thing once. He said God's voice was too much for us sometimes." She glanced quickly at the dark huddle on the pallet. "What a burden it must be for *her*."

Mapon agreed. "It is the burden of power. The One Who Hears carries no other burdens. But even so, it is a heavy weight to bear. As you can see."

Guinevere wondered if this explained the extreme age of the old woman. Or perhaps it was her extreme age that enabled her to hear the god's voice. Either way, she did not envy this divine gift, as some people did. Life was proving hazardous enough without seeking for hidden haunts of power.

"And the warning?" she asked Mapon. "Does everyone understand the danger now?"

"Yes," Mapon said. "The truth has been made plain."

"And Llyr? Has he been restored to his place among you?"

Mapon chuckled. It was the first sign of cheerfulness she had seen in him. "Not quite. Llyr has been honored with a different fate. He is to be your guardian. No longer will the Long Eyes share that duty. It is Llyr's duty now. Wherever you go, Llyr will watch over you. He will have no other life. If he summons us, we will come to your defense. You, and those who love you, will always have friends among Earth's Beloved."

Guinevere turned to Llyr with a worried face. "That is her judgment? But what about your father? What about your place among the White Foot?"

She had spoken in Welsh, and Llyr looked blank. It was Mapon who answered. "He lost that place when he was cast out. Now the god has given him another. It is a place of honor, with a status higher than the leader of any clan. His father and his family will be proud."

Guinevere was still not certain she understood. Llyr was not a member of any clan, but neither was he an outcast. What had the Crone done to him? Where was his place?

"I stood at the brink of death," Llyr said gently, seeing her confusion. "On the edge of a cliff. And the god sent me away from that place and into the clearing. To meet you." He nodded toward the Crone's bent back. "She knew this."

Guinevere looked at the Crone. She must have seen at once the necessity of uniting the Old Ones in the face of Guinevere's warning. She had given Llyr a status that did not require accepting him back into the clan, which might have divided the Long Eyes at a time when they needed to be united. It was a clever strategy, but Guinevere was not at all sure it was in Llyr's best interest. There were sure to be some among the Long Eyes who resented Llyr's elevation, even if he was still outside the clan. Although that resentment had not prevented a coming together for defense, it might still simmer, unexpressed, and endanger Llyr at some future time.

"And now," Mapon said carefully, "we have something to tell you, if you are well enough to hear it."

"I'm perfectly well," Guinevere replied, straightening her cloak, which had fallen from her shoulders when she fainted. "Go ahead."

"We have taken council, and the One Who Hears has advised us to tell you who the thief is."

Guinevere stared at him breathlessly. "You mean, you *know*?"

"Three times in the past month, we have seen a group of men on horseback, eight of them, steal cattle and sheep from King Pellinore's herds in the upper meadows. Always in the darkest hour of the night. Always on horseback. Always eight men."

Guinevere cleared her throat nervously. "But how did they do it? The herds are guarded, night and day, by men and dogs."

Mapon nodded. "The dogs obey the men. The men look

the other way. They receive a copper coin for this. Afterward, they may feel shame—who knows?—but they say nothing. By the time morning comes and the commander makes his count and discovers animals are missing, the tracks are old and impossible to follow. They wrap the horses' feet in cloth, and the cattle's, too. They make no sound and leave a trail almost impossible to follow."

Guinevere swallowed hard. "Who is it who pays them to look the other way?"

Mapon paused. He looked uneasy, and Guinevere saw that this tale-telling was difficult for him. "King Pellinore has a friend. He is lord of a wide valley in the north, where the river comes down from the hills and floods the marshes. It is a rich land, with fish and marsh birds plentiful all summer and deer moving through each autumn and spring."

"The Longmeadow Marshes?" Guinevere whispered. "Belonging to Sir Gavin, the earl?"

Mapon bowed his head politely. "He is the friend. But he is not the thief. It is the younger son, the one with the eyes and manners of a wildcat, who steals the queen's cattle from beneath her nose."

Guinevere closed her eyes. She had seen it coming, but hearing the words spoken aloud made her blood run cold. Of course it would be Sir Darric, stealing King Pellinore's cattle while he flirted with the queen to keep her attention elsewhere. If it was true, Queen Alyse would never believe it, could not afford to believe it. She would certainly never believe it even for an instant if she heard it from Guinevere's lips.

Mapon seemed to read her thoughts. "Will you tell the

queen who the thief is? This we ask of you in order to prevent war."

Guinevere sought desperately for some alternative. "King Pellinore will be home by Beltane. He has the power to settle everything."

"But the troops are coming tonight."

Guinevere drew a long breath. "All right. I will tell her."

"Will she believe you?"

Her heart sank, but she told him the truth. "Probably not."

Mapon raised both shoulders and let them fall. "Then it is out of my hands. If they attack us, there will be war."

Something moved in the shadows. A pair of dark eyes glinted beneath the hood of the black cloak, watching.

Guinevere raised her head to Mapon. "I will do my best to see that my aunt Alyse learns the truth. But she will want proof before she believes such a tale as this."

"You mean, a tale told by hillmen."

Guinevere colored furiously, but she could not deny it.

"There is another way." Llyr spoke abruptly, and everyone turned to look at him.

Llyr addressed Mapon in his own tongue, rattling on and on in evident excitement. Mapon's stern visage softened as he listened, and when at last he turned to Guinevere to translate, he was almost smiling.

"Llyr reminds me of something I had forgotten. King Pellinore manages his herds with close attention, does he not? He counts his cattle when he brings them into the pens each autumn, and again in spring when they go out to graze?"

Guinevere nodded. "That's right. The spring counting was done just before all this trouble started."

"Then it can be known what beasts are missing. Tell the queen to look for them among the Marsh Lord's herds. They are marked, as Llyr reminds me. It should not be difficult."

"Marked?" Guinevere was out of her depth. She knew next to nothing about raising cattle. Queen Alyse's lecture to her and Elaine about their woeful ignorance of practical matters returned to her with all the force of truth.

Mapon raised his eyebrows. "You did not know? He marks his beasts with a knife at the edge of the left ear. Thus." He demonstrated by taking his dagger from his belt and scratching a baseless triangle on his forearm. "Let the queen look for such beasts in Sir Darric's pens. She will find them."

"She would believe that kind of proof," Guinevere said eagerly. "I will find a way to tell her."

"And I will find a way to avoid the Marsh Lord's son until Beltane."

Mapon rose, and everyone else rose with him except the Crone, who sat unmoving within her cloak.

Llyr, too, rose to his feet. Guinevere made a final reverence to the Crone. "Thank you, Mother," she said. "You are a very wise woman."

The old woman gave no sign that she had heard. She had retreated into the fastness of her cloak, and her eyes, half closed, were as dull as the eyes of the blind.

Mapon raised a hand in formal salute. "Light with thee walk."

Llyr raised his own hand in response. "Dark from thee flee." He reached for Guinevere's hand and led her out of the cave.

CHAPTER NINETEEN

Traveling Companions

They rode downhill together, Llyr sitting light and wary behind her. He had a knife in his belt, a bow slung over one shoulder, a quiver of arrows over the other, and a spear in his hand. His eyes never left the forest shadows. Clouds had sunk lower over the mountains until they bathed the forest in heavy mist. Still, it did not rain. It was difficult to tell the hour of day, it was so dim, and Guinevere was oppressed by the need for hurry. So much had happened in the cave that it seemed like days since she had last been outside. She wondered if Sir Darric had returned from the Longmeadow Marshes with his men. She wondered how she was ever going to tell Queen Alyse the truth. The queen would certainly not want to believe that Sir Darric had fooled her. But King Pellinore was due home soon, and if a dispute arose with Sir

Darric, Guinevere knew Queen Alyse would want to settle it herself.

They came to a fork in the path, which Guinevere recognized. "I know this place, Llyr. I can get home from here."

But Llyr refused to go. He wanted to wait until they came to an intersection with one of the wider, more traveled paths through the forest. Guinevere thought she knew the place he meant. They had passed it on their way up into the foothills: a huge pine tree in a thin hardwood copse marking the crossing of two paths.

"But that's half a league from here," she objected. "The light is failing, and you don't have a horse for the journey back."

"Back? I am not going back," Llyr said. They traveled on in silence as the mist grew heavier and the fitful breeze died away. Moment by moment, the forest grew dimmer, colder, and damper. Gradually, the hardwoods began to thin, until a hundred paces ahead, they could just make out the dark green skirts of a giant pine, its upper branches swallowed by the mist.

"There it is. I can do it from here, Llyr. I know what signs to look for."

"Wait. Go slow." He reached for the reins to pull the horse to a halt. "Listen."

His arm around her waist tightened as Peleth's head whipped up. A moment later, they heard voices. Following the direction of Peleth's ears, Guinevere stared into the dim depths of the forest. She could see nothing. Behind her, Llyr's bow slipped from his shoulder into his hand. They waited in the misty shadows as the voices neared.

"This should do it. I think they've got a hideout some-where hereabouts. Post three men here along this path."

"Yes, my lord." A bridle jingled, and a horse moved roughly through the underbrush.

Guinevere swallowed. She recognized the arrogant male voice that spoke with such assurance.

"Light with thee walk," a whisper sounded in her ear. The pressure about her waist vanished as Llyr slid silently to the ground and disappeared into the trees.

"Dark from thee flee," she whispered back, chin on shoul-der to watch him go.

Peleth raised his head and whinnied.

"Ho!" a voice cried. Guinevere heard the slither of metal as swords left their scabbards. "Who goes there?"

For a moment she froze, too furious with herself to speak. It was too late now to keep her wits about her and avoid dis-covery. The horsemen were already coming down the path.

She cleared her throat and pushed Peleth forward. "O-only me, my lord."

Two figures broke from the mist. Foremost rode Sir Dar-ric's minion Jordan, and behind him the owner of the arrogant voice, Sir Darric himself.

"Well, well, what have we got here?" Jordan sheathed his sword and grinned.

Guinevere frowned at the insolent tone of his voice, but she did not reply. Silence was safest while she invented some tale to tell them.

"Here's a lass who's lost her way," Jordan called to his leader.

"Bring her here and let's have a look."

Guinevere rode up to Sir Darric, ignoring Jordan. She was glad for the thick soldier's cloak that encased her. Now it felt like a suit of mail. Sir Darric leaned across the curving neck of his chestnut stallion and pushed her hood back from her face.

"What are *you* doing here, all alone in this weather and unescorted?"

Jordan rode up on her other side and peered at her. "I remember this one. From the banquet."

"Yes," Darric mused, his eyes still on her bowed head with its halo of white-gold hair, bright as a beacon against the inner darkness of her hood. "It's Guinevere, isn't it? Alyse's niece?"

"Ward," Jordan corrected, his voice full of scorn. "The hard-luck orphan. No family. Lives by the queen's sufferance. My lord, she's unimportant."

"How old are you?" Sir Darric asked softly, his wildcat eyes looking her over from hooded head to booted foot. "Fourteen? Fifteen?"

"Thirteen on Beltane, my lord."

"Thirteen," he breathed. "Amazing."

A tingle of fear slid up Guinevere's spine. There was a casual menace in Sir Darric's eyes that struck cold inside her. Jordan, too, sensed something in the air. He pushed his horse closer and stared at her with chilling intensity. Peleth jibbed and danced at her grip on the reins, and Guinevere fought for calm. She knew with certainty that Llyr watched from behind the trees and even now had notched an arrow to his bow. She slid her hand behind her back and signaled him to wait, praying he could see that far in the misty dimness.

"My lord," she said, dismayed to hear the tremor in her voice, "I am so glad I found you. I've been looking for you half the afternoon."

Jordan grinned, and his stallion shuffled as the pressure on mouth and ribs increased.

Guinevere held Sir Darric's eyes and prayed that Llyr would not let his arrow fly. "I come on behalf of Princess Elaine, my lord. I have a message for you."

A large raindrop splattered on her hand, another on her knee, then on her nose, her hood. At last, at long last, the skies opened, and a hard, soaking rain poured down through the new leaves overhead. Jordan swore aloud, and Sir Darric grinned, taking his eyes off the girl for the first time.

"The voice of heaven speaks," he said dryly. "Jordan, wait here for Drako. Once he's got the men posted, you can follow us down together. I will escort Princess Guinevere back to the castle."

Jordan scowled, and his stallion began to paw the ground. Sir Darric backed his own horse off the path and gestured to Guinevere. "After you."

Halfway down the slope, as they neared the upper meadows and the jumping field, the path widened enough to allow Sir Darric to ride at her side. Even through the rain, she felt his eyes on her, and she kept her hood well forward to hide her face.

"What's your real reason for riding out alone?" Sir Darric

asked, his voice light and casual. "It can't have been just to seek me out, not in this weather."

"My cousin—Princess Elaine—sent me with a message for you, my lord."

Sir Darric snorted. "A thin disguise. You would not have come alone and unescorted if you were bringing a message from your cousin. You'd have waited until I returned to the castle, where it's warm and dry." His full lips twisted in a mocking smile. "Of course, the castle is a crowded place. It's so much easier to be alone and unobserved in a forest."

"I bring you a message from my cousin Elaine," Guinevere repeated firmly. "She asked me this morning to get a message to you. She wants a meeting with you. If you would only see her, my lord, you may verify it for yourself."

For a moment, the smile vanished from Sir Darric's face. Then he broke into laughter. "I remember now. The little wench in the tight bodice? That's Alyse's daughter?"

Guinevere winced inwardly for Elaine. "Yes, my lord."

"She's pretty enough, I suppose," he mused. "But she'll never be a beauty. You, on the other hand, have the makings."

Guinevere kept her gaze on the space between Peleth's ears. At this pace, they would not reach the stables until lamplighting. She did not think her skill at conversation would last that long, and she certainly did not want to be found by Queen Alyse riding home with Sir Darric.

"Please, my lord, be good enough to acknowledge that the queen's daughter has asked a favor of you."

"And you came out without an escort because the daughter's plans must be kept secret from the mother?"

She nodded, staring straight ahead. He wasn't unintelligent after all. But, then, he probably had experience with assignations. He could not be as uninterested as he seemed in this one. Elaine was the king's daughter, and Sir Darric was only the younger son of one of the king's men. The most he could ever hope for was sole possession of his father's lands—if his elder brother died—while everyone knew Queen Alyse was grooming her daughter for a position of power, wealth, and influence. If Sir Darric were at all ambitious, he would jump at the chance to win Elaine for himself.

Sir Darric's voice, stripped of its arrogance, interrupted her thoughts. "Is it true what Jordan said about you, Guinevere? Are you an orphan? Have you no family living?"

She stiffened but could hear no threat in his voice. He made it sound like the least important question in the world. "Both my parents are dead, my lord. King Pellinore is my guardian."

"But King Pellinore has a daughter of his own."

"My half brother is the king of Northgallis. I still have family there."

He considered this. "Do you have something coming to you, then? When you marry?"

Color rushed to Guinevere's face, which she kept hidden deep within her hood. "No, my lord. I have no rights in Northgallis. I do live on the queen's sufferance. And the king's."

She heard him grunt and shift in the saddle. "That's a damned shame. Still, it's a great boon to those of us who'll never be kings."

Guinevere's hands tightened on the reins, and her legs tensed against Peleth's sides. The horse immediately increased his pace.

Sir Darric laughed. "Come, now, princess, don't set your sights too high. You could do a lot worse than an earl's son." He rode up beside her. "You'll have little choice, you know, unless you run away to someone. Alyse will arrange it all to her own satisfaction. What a shame it would be if she chose someone old, infirm, or ugly."

She turned to stare at him. He was jesting with her, he must be, pretending to spurn Elaine and hinting at an interest in herself. Or he was completely mad. Or he was a cruel man who enjoyed making others squirm.

He did not look mad. He looked glossy with rain, strong, handsome, his white teeth gleaming in a wicked smile. If not mad, he was at the very least a cruel villain, a liar and a thief. She wanted nothing to do with him.

On the thought, he reached out an arm to grab her reins. Guinevere pressed her legs against Peleth's sides and gave him his head. The horse bolted.

CHAPTER TWENTY

A Dangerous Ride

She heard a shout of laughter behind her and then the pounding of the stallion's hooves. Guinevere knew that if she stayed on the main ride, the quickest route back, Sir Darric was sure to catch her up. His stallion was younger, stronger, and faster than Peleth.

A short distance ahead, the way forked, the main ride descending around a hill in a long, gentle sweep to the stable courtyard, the other, narrower path heading in a series of steep zigzags and straightaways down the slope to the back paddocks. This was an old path that the newer, broader ride had been built to replace, and because no one used it anymore, she had made it her own. She had built obstacles along it, piling brush over downed trees that had fallen across it here and there. It gave her and Peleth a good long gallop and a series of jumps to negotiate on the way home. It was her favorite ride down to the castle, and she knew it like the back of her hand.

Peleth took the narrower path as a matter of course, ears pricked in anticipation. Guinevere hoped Sir Darric would opt for the easier route, but she did not expect it. Even if he could not see them in the misty gloom, he could easily follow their tracks.

Down they ran, flying around the first turn of the zigzag. She collected Peleth and steadied him, for the first hurdle lay close ahead. It was even darker under the crowding trees, and the way was difficult to see. She slowed the horse to a sharp canter and peered ahead through the gloom. For anyone who did not know where the obstacles were, this was a dangerous ride.

Peleth shortened his stride as the first barrier came in sight, a fallen pine tree whose sharp, broken branches stuck out from the trunk like spikes. Guinevere bent over his neck and squeezed his sides with her legs. Up he rose, up and over with room to spare. She praised him and patted him, and drew him into a slower canter as they neared the next turn of the zigzag.

Beneath a tangled canopy of oak, poplar, and pine, she pulled him up. They were all but invisible in the dimness, and she needed to learn whether Sir Darric or his stallion would see the obstacle in time. When she had bolted, her only thought had been to escape. She had not stopped to consider that, in these conditions, the trap she had set them might be fatal to Sir Darric or his horse. She shivered at the thought and reminded herself that Sir Darric was a skilled rider and his horse a trained war stallion. If they could not take a fallen tree in their stride . . .

Rain fell in a noisy splatter on the canopy above, but little of it reached her and Peleth. The footing so far had been firm and dry. If Sir Darric were going carefully, he would see the fallen tree in time. He would either pull up and go back the way he had come, or get his horse over it. Once over, he was committed to all five of the obstacles she had built across the ride, for there was no way around them except on foot through the impassable forest undergrowth.

Peleth's ears flicked forward, and a moment later, Guinevere, too, heard the eager thud of galloping hooves. Her hand crept to the crucifix at her throat. The stallion's scream rang out through the forest. She held her breath and waited for the sounds she dreaded, the crashing of broken branches, the wail of pain, the shout of anger. They did not come. The only sound was the steady drumming of the rain all about her. Even as she released her breath, her fear returned. If Sir Darric wasn't dead or injured, he would be after her again. His conceit would demand it. She spun Peleth on his haunches and put him into a hard gallop downhill.

In the stable courtyard, Guinevere slid from Peleth's back and ran for the side door between the paddocks. It opened in her face. Stannic stood there, torch in hand, frowning darkly.

"Oh, Stannic! How glad I am to see you!"

The stablemaster's face softened as he replaced the torch in its sconce and took the gelding's reins. "Where the devil have you been, m'lady? Ailsa's been down here thrice looking for you."

"Why? Has the queen missed me?"

At the anxious look in her eyes, Stannic's disapproval melted. He smiled reassuringly as he tied the gelding to a post and picked up a straw twist to rub his streaming coat.

"Not so far as I know. Ailsa said something about trimming a gown for a feast tonight. I think it was just an excuse to see if you'd got safely back. You'd best make haste to the castle. If you've been out in the rain all day, you'll need a rubdown, too."

Guinevere shrugged free of the soldier's cloak. "I'm pretty dry, really. The cloak was marvelous. Thank you, Stannic. I'd have been soaked without it." She paused as he took it from her. "Why is there a feast tonight? Is King Pellinore home?"

"No, alas. Not yet. But Sir Darric is back from the Longmeadow Marshes with a troop of men, and they must be fed." He gestured at the long row of rumps receding into the dimness of the stable. "And their horses, too."

Guinevere saw the new horses and frowned. "How many men did he bring? He's posted a dozen or so in the heights already."

Stannic paused. "Did you come across Sir Darric in the heights, princess?"

She nodded, shivering. "I threw him off my trail, I think, but I don't know for how long."

Stannic straightened from his task. "Was he chasing you?"

"Not exactly." She avoided his eyes. "I didn't like being near him."

"There's an easy way to avoid that," Stannic said gently. "Take an escort with you whenever you ride out."

Tears welled in the dark blue eyes, and Stannic sighed. "Listen, lass, no boon lasts forever. You will have to get used to escorts, and litters, too, in time. No highborn lady travels without an escort of armed men. It isn't safe. We've a good King now, and a bonny fine fighter he is, but he's young yet and concentrates his efforts on the Saxons. There are plenty of lawless men in the hills of Wales, aye, and in the valleys, too, who'd just as soon slit your throat as let you pass by unharmed. There, I've said my piece. Dry those pretty eyes and run off to Ailsa. You'll need a warm drink and a hot soak before the banquet."

Guinevere wiped her eyes and shook her head vigorously. "I'm not going to the banquet. I'll take to bed with a chill if I have to. Oh, Stannic, I don't want to grow up if it means being looked after all the time, even when I'm riding. Is there no other choice? Will I always have to be under someone's thumb?"

Stannic smiled. "Under someone's protection, certainly. If he's a good man, it won't feel much like a thumb. You might even have a good deal of freedom. Look at Queen Alyse. She does what she wills, as anyone can see, but she doesn't travel about without an escort."

Guinevere bowed her head. "But riding out is the only way I can be alone."

No sooner had she spoken the words than she remembered the Old Ones and their patient guardianship of nearly thirteen years. Her privacy had always been illusion. All those times she had pounded through the hills on horseback, even in Northgallis, to release pent-up anger, frustration, disappointment, or to puzzle out the answer to a problem, she had never been alone.

Stannic smiled as if he read her thoughts. "Best get back to your chambers now. Here, take your mantle. Ailsa will be right frantic by this time, and you don't want to run into Sir Darric on his way back." He tilted his head to see her better. "Come to think on it, he ought to be back by now. I wonder what's delayed him."

Guinevere drew away and pulled her mantle across her shoulders, eyes dancing. "He may be a little while. I came home along the lower ridge trail."

Stannic hooted. "With your obstacles along the straightaways? He'll never make all five, I'll wager a bronze coin on that."

Guinevere grinned. "I bet he didn't make it past the first one."

Stannic stood at the stable door and watched the girl dart between the outbuildings. She was headed, he saw, toward the queen's garden and the back stairs to the women's quarters. A smart little thing she was, and with a grace about her that reminded him forcibly of her mother. He remembered Lady Elen well. No one had been better loved in all Gwynedd. He had wept when he learned of her death. But he had not grieved once for her since Guinevere had come to Gwynedd.

The child was so much like her mother it was almost like having Lady Elen back among them.

He sighed as he led Peleth to his place and tied his halter rope to an iron ring in the wall. God grant the girl a long life, an easy death, and a husband who cared for her.

CHAPTER TWENTY-ONE

By the Garden Door

Marcus huddled under the bower in the queen's garden as the rain slashed down. He was blue with cold. It had taken him half the day to make his way unseen from the outskirts of the forest to the grounds of Pellinore's castle. The place was crawling with troops. He'd been only thirty feet away, hiding in the branches of an oak, when Sir Darric and his men had ridden in. Half of them had gone on to the stables and the barracks, but the other half Sir Darric had stationed in the hills.

The presence of so many armed men had slowed his progress considerably—that and the weight of the canvas sack he carried slung over his shoulder. It grew heavier with each step, and it stank like a week-old corpse. He half expected to see a cloud of vultures trailing along behind him.

He had reached the castle outskirts at lamplighting but

had not been able to find a way inside. As a lieutenant in the house guard, he was himself largely responsible for the vigilance of the sentries that now made his own entry so difficult. On the other hand, if anyone knew the castle's weaknesses, he did. So here he was at nightfall in the queen's garden, bedraggled with wet, sheltering under a bower, and waiting for the old porter inside the door to desert his post for his wineskin, as he usually did several times a night. It was a habit neither he nor Regis had been able to break. The old man could not be dismissed, for King Pellinore loved him, so he was put on the door to the women's quarters, where he would be least in the way.

Marcus could see the telltale flicker of candlelight through the narrow window beside the door and knew that Old Cam was still there. When the light disappeared, he would force the door and slip upstairs. He would have to leave his wretched bundle behind, but that was no hardship. He could hide it here in the garden until it was needed.

He had just finished burying it under a hedge when he heard footsteps, running footsteps, soft on the wet grass and coming closer. The torch by the door smoked and spat in the rain, shedding little light. Someone ran by him in the darkness. He had the impression of swift boots and a flowing mantle. He moved forward, dagger in hand. A shadow swept across the torchlight. A soft knock sounded on the door. Aghast, he watched the door swing open without a single password given and a slim figure dart inside to safety. He caught a fleeting glimpse of white-gold hair and soft doeskin boots.

The queen's ward! He had reached the door when

recognition struck, and in his astonishment, he almost let it close in his face. Had the girl been out all this time? Doing what? He thrust his dagger blade across the threshold just in time.

"Saints be praised!" a woman's voice cried softly. "You're safe!"

"Not yet—where's Cam?"

"Taking his refreshment. I told him I'd stand his watch until you came in. The candle's burned almost to the hour mark. Oh, Gwen, where have you been?"

"Has anyone missed me? I mean, anyone but you?"

Marcus pried open the door a little farther as the nurse hurried to replace the candle on the table in the porter's cell. The girl went to the foot of the stairs and paused. She was a cool one, he thought, traipsing about outside in the dark without the queen's knowledge, yet calm enough to wait on the stairs for her nurse.

"If you mean the queen, yes," came the nurse's voice. "But only just. Sir Darric returned with troops this afternoon, and that kept her busy. He went off again, but he'll be back tonight. She's planning another feast."

Without the candle, the entranceway was dim enough. Marcus slipped inside as the nurse followed Guinevere up the stairs, talking on without a pause.

"That's what made her search for you and Elaine. She wanted to talk about gowns and such. She found Elaine in bed, pretending to be sick. Elaine told her you'd gone off with your green gown to work in some quiet corner." She paused. "It sounded almost like she was covering for you."

A torch at the top of the stairs shed a flickering light down the stairwell. Marcus climbed up after the women, but slowly, making sure to keep in the shadows. The girl's voice floated down to him, hollow as an echo.

"Actually, she was. We have a—a sort of bargain. But couldn't she think of anything better than that? My needle-work basket's in the queen's workroom. She's sure to find it."

"Not in her workroom, she won't. Elaine's got it under her bed." Ailsa paused for breath. "Dear heaven. What is that awful smell?"

Marcus fell into a crouch and froze. In the last twelve hours, he had become so accustomed to the stench of putre-faction that he hardly noticed it anymore. It had not occurred to him, fool that he was, that others would smell it on *him*. He glanced up the curve of the stair where the women's shoes were disappearing. Even if he stayed hidden in the shadows, they would be able to find him by the stink alone.

The girl's clear voice replied. "It's probably just the evening dankness from the garden. It must have come in with me when you opened the door."

The ward continued upward, but the nurse paused on the stair. He could see her still shadow against the curve of the wall. "Dank it is," he heard her mutter. "But that's no garden scent. That's dead, that is."

Her shadow moved, descended a step or two, and stopped again. Marcus stayed perfectly still and held his breath. For ten long heartbeats, the shadow stayed as still as he was, lis-tening, watching, scenting.

"Oh, hurry, Ailsa, do! What does it matter? I've got to get

back before I'm seen!" At last, the nurse's shadow moved away. Marcus exhaled slowly. He should get back outside before Cam returned, for clearly he could not see the queen until he had changed out of these filthy garments and washed the stink from his skin and hair. But there had been fear in the girl's voice, and he wondered why.

Very slowly, he climbed the stairs. He could not hear their voices now, but whether that was because they had gone down the corridor or because they were no longer talking, he could not tell. With held breath, he rounded the curve of the stair that brought him full into the torchlight. To his relief, the stairwell was empty. He crept up to the landing, his back against the wall, and peered cautiously around the corner.

An oil lamp burned bright in its bracket halfway down the corridor, and by its light, he could see the girl and her nurse hurrying away from him. The light by the door to Princess Elaine's chamber was out—had some fool forgotten to fill the lamp with oil before he lit it?—and the farther end of the passage was in shadow.

The girl glanced over her shoulder at the huffing nurse. "Come, Ailsa, quickly! Pick up your skirts and run! I've got to get out of these clothes before Aunt Alyse finds me."

"My lady!" Ailsa gasped, and half stumbled into a curtsy.

Queen Alyse stepped out of the shadows, eyes blazing, with a candlesnuffer in her hand. For one long, paralyzing moment, all motion ceased. The three women stared at one another.

The queen's thin nostrils flared. "So. This is how you

repay me." She came forward, her body stiff with anger. "You have not been stitching in a corner. Your mantle's wet, and you stink of horses—and worse. You have been outside. Without permission and against orders. Haven't you?"

No one spoke. The girl stood stiffly; the nurse was on her knees. The queen approached.

"You've been riding. After I expressly forbade you the stables."

The ward's voice shook. "But I—"

Queen Alyse cut her off. "I will hear no excuses. What must I do to exact obedience from you? Have you horse-whipped like a common slave?"

"But—"

"Silence!" The queen breathed forcibly through a pinched nose. "I won't have it, Guinevere. I've told you so before. And you, Ailsa, what on earth do you think you're doing, trailing about after the girl and abetting her every whim? You're supposed to be a restraining hand. You're supposed to see to it that my orders are obeyed. If you won't act like a nurse to the child, I shall find someone who will."

"I beg your pardon, my lady." The nurse's voice shook worse than the ward's. Marcus didn't blame them. Queen Alyse's anger could strike fear into the breast of every soldier her husband employed, including himself.

Guinevere slid to the floor and raised clasped hands in supplication. "But, Aunt Alyse, it's all my fault. Ailsa didn't know I was going out. I didn't tell her—I knew she'd try to stop me. Please, please don't punish Ailsa—"

"Punish you instead? But I have already tried that. You disregard my punishments. You disobey me consistently. You forced Elaine to lie for you, and you rode out alone into the hills. Can you deny it?"

The ward did not deny it. Marcus found himself admiring her straight back every bit as much as he condemned her behavior.

"I didn't mean to involve Elaine," she said finally with lowered eyes. "But I did ride out. I went to find out who has been stealing your cattle." Her eyes lifted briefly to the queen's. "And I did."

Marcus started. He pressed himself flat against the wall and fought to still the racing of his heart. What could the child have learned? He had to know. Crouching low, he peered around the corner once more.

Queen Alyse's voice was cold. "Indeed? You ran across the villains themselves, I suppose? They confessed their sins and then let you get away? Foolish fellows." Her lips curled into a scornful smile. "What oafs we were to patrol the hills when all we had to do was send one witless child out alone."

The girl mumbled something indistinguishable. The nurse gasped and crossed herself.

The queen stiffened. "*What* did you say?"

"Sir Darric is the thief, Aunt Alyse. And his men, Jordan and Drako and the rest. They were seen."

"By whom?"

The sharp words fell into utter silence. The ward was shaking badly now; he could see it from where he crouched at the top of the stair. She bowed her head in a submissive gesture, but she said nothing. Marcus watched, fascinated. One did not take such a tale to the queen without solid proof. One did not give her information from a source one had to protect. The child had courage; he had to give her that. He glanced at the queen's face and felt a twinge of pity for such wasted bravery.

"You can't answer, or you won't? . . . This is the last straw, Guinevere. How dare you come to me with unfounded insults and accusations? I won't have it. It's utter nonsense. Sir Darric is a nobleman's son and a guest in this house. To accuse him of such base behavior is offensive. Demeaning. Insufferable. I expected more intelligence from you, even in your lies."

The queen approached the girl and lifted her head with a firm hand under her chin. "From now on, you will obey me in everything—in *everything*, do you hear me? Or I will send Ailsa back to Northgallis. You will not ride. You will not even walk out without my permission. You will not stir outside this castle without an escort. You will take off those ridiculous boy's clothes and leave them outside the door. I will see they are cleaned and given to the village poor. You will wear a gown from now on or nothing at all. I hope I make myself clear?"

The ward made no movement that Marcus could see, but apparently she assented, for the queen released her grip on the girl's chin and turned to the kneeling nurse.

"Get up," she snapped. "Get her into her chamber and see that she stays there. Neither of you will attend the feast tonight. You will stay in your chamber, Guinevere, until I give you permission to leave it. And as for this ridiculous tale you've brought me—"

She stopped in midsentence and raised her head, sniffing the air. "What—is—that—*smell?*"

Marcus vanished silently down the stairs. He had heard enough. Queen Alyse was not in league with Sir Darric. She had been more incensed at the girl's disobedience than at the suggestion of Sir Darric's complicity, which she had manifestly disbelieved. And now that she'd been warned, she would be on her guard or she was not the queen he thought she was. He grinned to himself. That was a sight, that was, her standing there before the two transgressors, magnificent in her regal rage, clutching the candlesnuffer in her hand as if it were a dagger. He would not have missed that for anything.

CHAPTER TWENTY-TWO

Plans for a Princess

A shout in the courtyard brought Stannic hurrying to the doors. It was still raining hard, and the spitting torches shed little light, but he could see enough to know it was Sir Darric, wet to the skin and in an evil temper.

"Has that wretched girl come back?" the nobleman called down from the back of Jordan's roan.

"What girl is that, my lord?"

"You know which one. The one who rides. The ward."

Stannic said stiffly, "The princess Guinevere rode in at lamplighting, my lord."

Sir Darric swore under his breath and slid off the horse. Stannic advanced into the downpour to catch the reins thrown at him.

"A daredevil, that one," the young man muttered, striding

into the light and warmth of the stable. "I was escorting her home when my horse stumbled and went lame—Jordan's walking him back—and I had to send her on alone. The little ninny took off like all the furies of hell were after her. I'm relieved to know she made it back in one piece."

He glanced at Stannic, but the stablemaster was bent over the roan's feet, his face invisible. Sir Darric doffed his wet cloak and shook it out, spraying the swept floor with water. "Girl rides like the wind. She's got spirit, I'll give her that. . . . Any suitors yet, do you know?"

Stannic's head appeared over the horse's flank. "I beg your pardon, my lord?"

Darric shot him a swift glance. "You heard me."

"I wouldn't know, my lord."

Sir Darric grunted. "Well, I'm glad she came to no harm. Although what she was doing riding about the woods without an escort and with a storm coming on, I'd like to know. I'm amazed the queen allows it. Unless she and Pellinore don't much care what happens to the child?"

Stannic lifted the saddle from the roan with a twisted smile. "I've reason to know, my lord, that King Pellinore and Queen Alyse care very much what happens to that girl."

"Do they? Good. Good. I'm relieved to hear it."

"She's the daughter of Queen Alyse's elder sister," Stannic continued, handing the saddle to a groom. "Her parents may be dead, but she's not without family or protection. King Pellinore's especially fond of her."

Sir Darric's petulant expression grew thoughtful. "That

sister of Alyse's, the girl's mother, that was Elen of Gwynedd, wasn't it? The beauty?"

"Aye, my lord," Stannic said, rubbing the roan with stolid concentration. "Queen Alyse had only one sister." He glanced up, curious at the young man's sudden change in manner. Gone was the arrogance and bluster. Darric of Longmeadow stood under the oil lantern, damp and disheveled, with his sodden cloak over his arm and a wistful expression on his face.

"My father was besotted with Elen of Gwynedd." Sir Darric spoke half to himself, staring at the roan's flank with unseeing eyes. "When he was my age. He tells the tale himself whenever he's in his cups. She was so beautiful she drove him wild. He nearly lost his wits when she married and went away, even though he had a wife of his own by then and two growing sons. I thought it might be a sort of justice if I could—" He broke off and sighed wearily, rubbing the bridge of his nose with finger and thumb. "Well, never mind. Damn my luck, things never fall out my way."

Stannic watched openmouthed as Sir Darric settled his wet cloak across his shoulders and strode out into the blowing night.

Queen Alyse paced furiously up and down her chamber. Cissa and Leonora flattened themselves against the wall and watched. They knew better than to attract the queen's notice when she was in a temper. She had already canceled the feast. They would have to scrounge for leftovers from the kitchens once they were dismissed. The lavish little supper laid out in the antechamber was not for them. In the meantime, they kept their eyes lowered, their mouths shut, and waited with grumbling stomachs for the queen's dinner guest to arrive.

Queen Alyse turned sharply at one end of the chamber and started back the other way. What was she to do about Guinevere? The girl's disobedience was infuriating. If it was the last thing she did, she would hammer sense into that obstinate golden head. Unlike Elaine, the child never stormed against the strictures laid upon her. She accepted them with deceptive meekness and then did exactly as she pleased. If that wasn't Elen all over again! It was astonishing, truly unbelievable, how much the girl reminded Alyse of Elen. Everything she did, she did well, from book learning and writing to stitching to riding horseback. If only she would obey, Alyse might make something of her, might find her a husband worthy of the family name. As it was, she would be lucky to marry her off at all.

She found herself standing before the wall, wringing her hands. She told herself not to be ridiculous as she whirled and started back. Of course she would find a husband for the child. Once Elaine's future was settled, once Arthur had a court, Pellinore's family would be counted among the first in Britain, and she could marry off Elen's daughter to any lord she chose.

This thought cheered her considerably, and she paused in her pacing to examine the antechamber for the twentieth time. The tables were laden with platters of roast fowl and lamb, fish grilled with pine nuts and wild onion, steamed apples swimming in cream, bowls of raisins, walnuts and honey, a clay pitcher of mead up from the cellars, and a basket of new-baked bread. She gazed at it all with approval but without much satisfaction. It was the best she could manage with the stores she had, so early in spring, but it would do. It was a feast put on for one man alone. He was no fool. He would get the message.

She turned in the doorway and smiled at her women. "Come, Cissa, Leonora. It is time to dress."

CHAPTER TWENTY-THREE

Only an Earl's Son

Elaine grabbed Guinevere's arm and dragged her into the bed-chamber. The two girls were finally alone, Ailsa and Grannic having just returned to the kitchens to take their evening meal with the rest of the household. The food they had brought up for the girls and carefully set out in the antechamber had barely been touched. Guinevere had been too silent and withdrawn to eat, and Elaine had been too excited.

"For heaven's sake, Gwen, forget about Mother's threat. I know what she said, I had my ear to the door, but she didn't mean it. She's had a rotten day."

Guinevere sat down glumly on the edge of the big bed they shared. She shivered, but not from cold. Ailsa had taken great pains to warm her and dry her when they had first come in, stripping off her damp clothes, rubbing her body with towels and then with balm, and putting hot bricks to her feet. She was warm enough now, and the shock of the queen's tongue-lashing was beginning to wear off, but still she could not control her trembling.

She listened as Elaine rattled on about all she had missed while she was out. Maelgon and Peredur had had a fight. Maelgon began it when he stabbed Peredur with his wooden sword during a mock swordfight. Peredur had lunged for him and pulled out a fistful of Maelgon's hair. After that, it had taken Queen Alyse *and* two of the house guards to separate the boys. Later, during Maelgon's riding lesson, Peredur stole his brother's toy sword and threw it down the well. In revenge, Maelgon pushed Peredur down the kitchen stairs. With the household in an uproar and Queen Alyse in a panic, the senseless lad had been put to bed.

"He's lucky he wasn't killed. Mother wept all afternoon, fearing he'd broken his wrist and would never wield a sword, but the physician eventually decided it was only a sprain and will mend in time. Maelgon's in disgrace, of course, the undeserving little brat, and not allowed to leave his chamber for a week. His nurse has been discharged. Poor Yvonet has to give up guard duty and tend him night and day until a replacement can be found."

"I'm sorry for the boys," Guinevere said unhappily. "No one told me about the fight. But I saw your mother's face, Elaine. She always means what she says in that tone of voice." Tears rose to her eyes, and she fought them back. "She has no right to take Ailsa from me. Ailsa's not one of her belongings, to be made use of and discarded on a whim. It isn't fair."

Elaine sat down beside her and patted Guinevere's hand. "I tell you, Gwen, she won't let Ailsa go. Think of the trouble it would cause her, the inconvenience. She'd have to find someone else to take her place, and now she's got Maelgon's nurse to worry about. She'd have to train her, too. And if the new nurse didn't do exactly as she said, she'd have no one to blame but herself. No, Gwen, Ailsa saves her time and annoyance, and she's an easy scapegoat. Mother would never let her go. It's an empty threat."

"I wouldn't let it happen. I'd run away first and take Ailsa with me."

Elaine's eyes widened. "Where would you go?"

Guinevere shrugged. "Out of Wales. Beyond her reach."

Elaine shook her head. It was sheer lunacy to value the services of a nurse, who could be replaced, above the privileges of birth, which could not. She certainly felt no such attachment to Grannic.

"Oh, I feel like running away all the time. But it would be suicidal to leave Gwynedd. Outside of Wales, you'd have no rank and no protection. Anything could happen. You're much better off here. Mother's temper will pass, and she'll be sorry she said such mean things to you. You might even get a guilt gift out of it."

Guinevere did not want any more gifts from Queen Alyse. Ailsa was deeply frightened. Her dear nurse, normally chatty and voluble, had hardly spoken a word all evening, undressing and redressing her charge in a meek silence so unlike her that Guinevere had known at once the depth of her distress. She had not chided Guinevere for her tardiness or demanded to know where she had been. She had asked no questions at all. Her outgoing nature had retreated to some inner fastness, where she waited, helpless and accepting, for whatever was coming next. The knowledge that she, Guinevere, was responsible for this suffering filled her with remorse. She had no idea how to alleviate it except by granting the queen what she asked for: perfect obedience to her commands.

Elaine jumped up from the bed and threw open the lid of her clothes chest. To Guinevere's astonishment, she lifted out a fresh gown, eyed it carefully at arm's length, and flung it on the bed.

"Come and help me change now, Gwen, and then I'll help you. We haven't much time. Grannic and Ailsa will be back soon, and we've got to be safely in bed when they come."

Guinevere blinked. "What?"

Elaine put her hands on her hips and frowned. "You can't have forgotten. It's why you went into the forest in the first place. We're going to meet Sir Darric, of course, while Ailsa and Grannic are asleep. He did agree to it, didn't he?"

With a monumental effort, Guinevere dragged her mind back to earlier in the day when she had raced out of the castle to meet Llyr, and when Elaine had thought she was racing out to intercept Sir Darric. It seemed a lifetime ago.

"He . . . was open to suggestions," she managed.

Elaine grinned. "Of course he was. But I've no way to get a message to him without Grannic and Ailsa knowing. We'll have to go ourselves. We'll dress now and slip our night-robes over our gowns and be under the covers, innocent as babes, when they come to check on us. Once they're asleep, we'll sneak out. Why do you look like that? We've done it a thousand times."

Guinevere found herself on her feet without willing the movement. "Not tonight! No, Elaine, you're mad even to think it! No power on earth could persuade me to disobey your mother thrice."

"You can't go back on your word, Gwen!" Elaine cried. "You promised to go with me. We won't get caught—we never have."

"It's as much as my life is worth to try it! Your mother is already furious with me. Just imagine what she'll do if she finds me sneaking about the castle in search of . . . of *him*. It's not like going out on the battlement to eavesdrop on the king's councils. This is different. It's personal. Sir Darric is out of bounds."

"But I've told you already that Mother didn't mean it. She's frightened you, which is just what she wants. She's good at cowing people. You can't let it stand in the way of your promise, Gwen, *you can't*."

"Elaine, I'm not allowed outside this chamber without your mother's permission. You heard her say so. Besides, Sir Darric can mean nothing to you, he's—"

"You promised!" shrieked Elaine. "We made a bargain, and you agreed! Forget about Mother—I told you already she didn't mean it. You promised you'd come with me, and you *will*. Because if you don't," she added, her voice hard and furious, "I'll tell Mother everything I know about your riding out, and some besides. I'll say you rode up into the hills after Sir Darric because you fancied him yourself. I'll say you made me cover for you. I'll say that Ailsa encouraged you, that it was her idea in the first place."

Guinevere gripped the bedpost. "That's not fair!"

"Neither is breaking your promise."

Guinevere shut her eyes to focus her whirling thoughts. If she disobeyed Alyse again, the queen might carry out her threat to send Ailsa to Northgallis. On the other hand, if Elaine even hinted to her mother that Guinevere had been out in the woods with Sir Darric, *unescorted,* Ailsa would be lucky to escape Gwynedd without a whipping. And if Queen Alyse thought Guinevere had gone to meet him *intentionally* . . .

She fought down rising panic and faced Elaine. "Why do you want to see him? Do you really think he's interested in you after three days of paying court to your mother?"

Elaine snorted. "For God's sake, Gwen, he's flattering her, that's all. He's not in love with her. I don't think he even likes her. He's got to be nice to her or she won't let him stay. The one he's been looking at is me."

"But, Laine, you're not interested in Sir Darric, are you? As a husband?"

"No, but—"

"Then *why* must you see him? And why tonight?"

"Because I want to. He's the handsomest man in Wales and he likes me. I want to see him alone, just for a few moments of private speech."

Guinevere drew a deep and patient breath. "He'll tell you lies. He's not an honest man, he's a thief. He's been stealing your father's cattle from under your mother's nose."

Elaine lifted her chin. "I heard you say that but I don't believe it. He wouldn't dare come here if that were so."

"But it *is* so. I've talked to people who've seen him at it."

"Who?"

Guinevere hesitated. If Elaine learned about Llyr and the Old Ones, she would not keep the knowledge to herself for long.

"You won't tell me, either? Then how do I know you didn't just make it up to rile Mother?"

"As if I would! Just take my word for it."

Elaine shook her head stubbornly. "Whoever told you that could have been lying. You didn't see anything yourself, did you? No, of course not. Because it didn't happen. The very idea, a man as handsome as that resorting to thievery . . . it's madness."

Guinevere sank down on the bed. "What has beauty got to do with it? He's a villain, Elaine. He's planning evil things and he won't thank you for interfering. He may even refuse to see you."

"He won't refuse me," Elaine snapped. "I'm the king's daughter and he's a guest in my father's house."

"But—"

"I'm going, Gwen. I've made up my mind, and if you want to save Ailsa, you'll go with me."

Guinevere stared down at her trembling hands. She wasn't going to be able to talk Elaine out of this one. Of all the escapades Elaine had dreamed up over the years, this was the worst. It was the most dangerous, had the most at stake, and was by far the least likely to succeed. She reached for the carving of Rhiannon in her pouch and fingered its smooth surface. What would her mother have done in her place, she wondered. She knew the answer at once. She would have done what honor required and faced the consequences as they arose. Even if it meant escaping with Ailsa across the mountains to Northgallis.

"All right, Elaine. I'll keep my promise and come with you."

Elaine tossed her the gray gown. "I knew you would. But it always takes so much persuasion. I wish you weren't such a mouse, Gwen."

"I have more to lose than you do. And nothing at all to gain."

"Nothing to gain?" Elaine laughed, pulling the yellow gown on over her head. "Why, you'll be spending the midnight hour with the handsomest man in the kingdoms—even if he is only an earl's son."

Guinevere slipped into her gray gown, which fit her straight frame like a second skin. "He may be only an earl's son," she said, "but he's not without weapons. See you remember it."

CHAPTER TWENTY-FOUR

Orders from Regis Himself

Marcus hurried down the path to the village as fast as he dared in the dark. He cursed himself roundly as he stumbled over unseen rocks and into unseen branches. How stupid he had been! He had got out of the castle all right, thanks to Old Cam's sleeping at his post. But dodging past the outbuildings on his way out of the grounds, he had been spotted by a guard—by Brychan of all people, Regis's tame, servile thug. He was sure that Brychan had raced to take his commander the news. Whether Regis would be surprised, Marcus did not know, but that he would be furious he had no doubt. Most likely, he would send Brychan or Clevis, or both, to Old Argus's cottage to catch Marcus out. It was essential to get home first, bury his clothes, wash the stink off, and warn Old Argus.

He slithered down the last descent of the muddy path and dodged behind the scattered cottages at the edge of the village. The rain was a blessing. Even if they came on horseback, they could not go much faster than he could on foot. What with the mist, the steady rain, the mud, and the general gloom of a starless night, he might just have time. He hoped Old Argus had followed his instructions. Lately, the old man had begun to forget things. If Marcus did not have a sickroom to return to, all this hurry was pointless.

Light-footed in spite of his fatigue, he leaped over a ditch, negotiated the barrier of brambles, ran up the path between the gardens, and jumped the rail fence into the sties. Within seconds, he had stripped off his clothes and buried them in the churned mud around the trough. Fat Fiona, the great sow, watched him with uncurious eyes from the shelter of her shed. Thanks to her pregnancy, she lay placid and comfortable on her thick bed of straw. Once she had piglets to protect, she'd turn as ferocious as a she-boar, and Marcus regarded her unnatural calm as his second piece of luck.

Naked, he pushed open the back door and slipped inside the cottage. He exhaled in relief. Opposite the stored jars of oil, wine, and vinegar; the stacked turfs; the pile of coal; and the sacks of wool and millet, he saw his pallet in the corner. The mussed bedding looked as if its occupant had risen in haste for a trip outside to the midden. There was a stub of burning candle beside it and a bucket for vomiting, foul with slime, near the dank pillow. A small bowl of medicinal gruel and a horn cup of water lay within easy reach of the makeshift bed. Marcus was pleased to see that the gruel was fresh and the cup half full. His sword hung from a nail in the wall above the bed. Even better, his boots stood in the corner, cleaned and polished to a dull shine. The old man had remembered everything.

Marcus parted the curtain and peered into the main room. Old Argus sat in his chair by the brazier, fast asleep, his feet outstretched toward the heat. The room looked neat and orderly. Old Argus must have already had his supper and tidied up afterward. His wooden eating bowl was in its place on the shelf above the table, still damp from recent washing. On the table, a carved platter of polished elm wood, as fine as any in the king's house, held a handful of mealcakes. There was not a loose crumb anywhere. The hard-packed dirt floor had been recently swept of prints. Marcus gazed at his father with affection. He had not forgotten a single thing.

"Father! Pssst! Argus!"

The old man started awake, glancing first toward the door and then toward the curtain. "Son? Is that you?"

"I'm sorry to wake you, Father. The king's guards are coming for me. Stall them as long as you can."

Old Argus rose from his chair, heavy-lidded with sleep. "And the queen? Have you seen the queen?"

"Not yet. Where's my night-robe? You haven't washed it, have you?"

"No. Look under the pallet. . . . I think I put it there, I can't remember. . . . What's that stink?"

"I'll explain later. Look sharp, now. They're not far behind me."

Marcus darted back outside and made for the rain barrel to sluice himself down. Old Argus hobbled to the fire and lifted the wineskin from its sling above the flames. With a trembling hand, he poured himself a meager cup of thin wine.

When the door burst open and two men strode into the room, swords raised, he was back in his chair again, eyes closed, head thrown back, and snoring gently.

"This is the place," said the larger of the men. He gestured toward the curtain. "Take a look back there."

Old Argus sat up and blinked. "Who's there? What's the meaning of this? Who are you?"

The younger man paused on his way to the curtain. "Never you mind, old man. We're king's men, and we're after a fugitive."

Old Argus pushed himself to his feet. "No one's been here except me and my son."

"Easy now, Grandfather," the bigger man said with a grin. "Your son's the very one we've come to see. Go on, Clevis, see if he's back there."

"I'm here, Brychan." Marcus pulled aside the curtain and stepped into the room. He wore a stained woolen night-robe, and his face was pale beneath damp, tangled hair. His legs and feet were bare. "Put up, man. Where do you think you are?"

Brychan's mouth hardened at this reminder that Marcus outranked him. "I've got orders . . . sir. I've got to search this house."

"For what?"

"A thief was seen running from the castle tonight. He came this way." He shoved Clevis forward. "Go on. Search behind the curtain. Look for mud on his boots."

Marcus stood firmly in the way. "Put up your swords. We're not armed. I can assure you no thief came in here. We would have seen him."

Clevis sheathed his sword, but Brychan clutched the hilt of his until his knuckles whitened. "Nevertheless . . . sir . . . we've got orders from Regis himself to search this place."

Orders from Regis himself. Marcus hid a smile. That was certainly more than Regis would want revealed. "This place? No other?"

"This place," Brychan repeated firmly, and gave Clevis another shove.

With a small smile, Marcus moved aside and swept back the curtain. "Go ahead. Look at anything you want."

He watched them take in the rumpled sickbed, the candle stub, the bucket, the spotless boots. Clevis glanced at Brychan nervously. "It looks all right to me."

"It stinks." The big man sniffed the air in obvious disgust and pushed open the back door. He trod through the mud of the yard, peering into the gloom and sniffing. When he saw the sow, he grunted, swore under his breath, and sheathed his sword.

"You're not out of this yet," he said, pushing past Marcus into the front room. "You're supposed to be sick with fever, and, by God, you're not."

"The fever broke this morning," Marcus said evenly. "I'm

sorry you weren't here to see it. I've been getting myself ready to report back for duty."

"I don't believe you. You're lying."

"You will not call my son a liar in my house!" Old Argus barked.

Brychan whirled, his hand dropping to his sword hilt, but found the point of the old man's sword already at his throat. "I'm a king's man!" he gasped. "Put up!"

"All right, Father," Marcus said coolly, and the sword point retreated a few inches. "You're Regis's man, not Pellinore's," he said to Brychan. "There's a difference. Now get out, both of you. And tell Regis I want speech with him tonight."

When they had gone, Marcus closed the door, leaned against it, and smiled at his father. "That was close. Thank you, Father. You did splendidly."

The old man was leaning against the table. The sword in his hand shook violently. "I'm a king's man myself. I don't like telling lies to soldiers. Not even to the house guard."

Gently, Marcus took the sword from his hand. "It was necessary. You know that. There is treachery in the house guard. It was necessary to deceive. But I won't ask it of you again."

"Treachery in the house guard," Old Argus whispered as Marcus settled him into his chair. "What is the world coming to?"

Marcus arranged a cushion behind his head, pulled his sheepskin blanket over his knees, and refilled his cup. The sword he replaced in its hanger on the wall behind the old man's chair. "I'm going to dress now, Father, and go up to the castle. Your sword is here within your reach."

The old man looked up at him with pale, watery eyes. "Will you be back tonight?"

Marcus shrugged. "By dawn, surely. But don't wait up."

Old Argus sighed and stretched out his legs toward the brazier. "Go with God, my son."

CHAPTER TWENTY-FIVE

A Private Supper

The queen stood framed in the inner antechamber doorway, waiting for Sir Darric to arrive. Cissa and Leonora had gone to their dinners, and she was alone at last. The lamps were lit behind the Roman couches, an applewood fire blazed in the brazier, and flagons of warmed wine stood ready to hand.

She had taken particular care in her dressing. She wore an ice blue gown with silver lacings in the bodice and ice blue gems at throat and ears. A silver band encircled her brow, and a net of silver threads encased her hair. She had stood before her polished bronze and knew what she looked like: lovely, cold, and unapproachable.

She heard him coming, heard his boots on the stone, heard the low murmur of voices as he exchanged pleasantries with Bredon, the guard at her door, heard Bredon's quiet knock and Sir Darric's musical voice raised in greeting.

"My lady queen. A private supper. How gracious of you."

He bowed low. He was simply dressed in a long green velvet robe. He wore no ornaments, no wristbands, no torques or rings, only a leather belt slung low on his hips to hold a jeweled dagger in its jeweled sheath. Loose though it was, the velvet robe did little to hide the suppleness of his body.

She was aware of his gaze, taking in her gown, her jewels, the neutrality of her expression, assembling their meaning, harvesting information for the swift calculations to come. She could see through him now, as clearly as through glass. His youth, his beauty, his physical appeal no longer masked his soul.

"It was good of you to come."

"I am yours to command, my dear Alyse."

She smiled and took her first step into the room. "Are you, my dear Darric?"

He took her proffered hand but, instead of kissing her fingers, turned her wrist and pressed her smooth palm to his lips. "Command me, then. I will prove it to you."

Queen Alyse let heat rise to her face. She was the first to look away. "I look forward to it," she said almost demurely. "But not on an empty stomach."

Sir Darric's hand slid up her arm to cup her shoulder. She did not pull away from his touch but turned smoothly toward the supper board and reached for a flagon of warmed wine.

* * *

Queen Alyse reclined on the Roman couch and poured Sir Darric another cup of wine. She peered into the silver flagon and saw with some astonishment that it was empty again. That was the fifth he'd emptied, and still his speech was clear. He must be very used to such indulgence; Pellinore would have been fast asleep long ago. She wondered that Sir Gavin allowed such dissolute habits in his house. How could he afford it? His vineyards might be larger than Pellinore's, but this one son drank more in a day than Pellinore's entire household.

She glanced down at Sir Darric, who sat on the floor at her feet, having slid off his seat on the couch some time ago. At least his amorous advances had come to an end. After the first flagon of wine, and during most of the second, he had cajoled her with whispered promises sweet enough to melt the coldest heart.

The third flagon had soothed his injured pride, or perhaps it had merely cooled his ardor, for his sweet talk had turned into a steady torrent of abuse against Mathowen. His elder brother was his father's favorite, God knew why; he could not do anything half so well as Darric could. Whenever Sir Gavin was summoned to fight, it was Mathowen he took with him. Darric was left behind to manage the house guard. Even though Mathowen had been badly marked by pox, his bride-to-be was the prettiest girl in the Marshes and loved him despite his looks.

This seemed to rankle Darric most, Queen Alyse observed. He must seldom have met a woman he could not have for the asking, and she wondered if his brother's bride had been one of few who had refused him. He was certainly deeply jealous of Mathowen—she understood that part of it perfectly—but she sensed that there was more behind it than a girl.

The fourth flagon proved her right. The floodgates of resentment opened wide, and a rush of venom spewed forth, all directed at Sir Gavin, at his meanness, his primness, his positively Spartan sense of discipline, his ridiculous scruples, and his unfair prejudice against his younger son. Queen Alyse listened with very little sympathy. Beauty, cleverness, and a liquid tongue were not enough for this bored and energetic young man. He wanted more. He thirsted for glory, for power, for recognition. Or perhaps he simply longed for love. He had learned, in his short and busy life, how to take. But he had never learned how to give. No wonder he could find no one to love him.

The queen looked askance at the empty fifth flagon and decided it was time to take control of the conversation.

"Darric, my pet, are you as sober as you sound?"

He leaned his head back against the edge of the couch and gazed up at her. "Alyse, my sweet," he said, mimicking her voice, "are you deaf? I've been telling you my life story, and you haven't been listening."

"I've heard every word, but I haven't an ounce of pity for you. No one pities a man as handsome as you are. For that, you should have been born with a different face."

He flashed her a smile. "You've been remarkably unmoved. I must be losing my touch." He reached for her hand and pressed her palm against his cheek. "Beautiful Alyse, tell me the secret. Give me the key."

She did not think his ardor was feigned, which was flattering, but his nerve astonished her. "Perhaps I might, if you can tell me something I want very much to know."

"Only ask," he murmured. "I can deny you nothing."

"You say your father left you to guard the Longmeadow Marshes. Why, then, my dear Darric, are you here?"

There was a fractional pause, only a heartbeat long. "Why, to spend a pleasant evening in your presence, possibly a splendid one."

"Nonsense. For that, you'd hardly have brought thirty men."

He straightened. The look in his eye was cold and clear and sober. "You invited them yourself, if you remember. To rid your hills of thieving vermin."

"At your instigation. If you remember."

"Was it? I thought it was your idea."

"It was your idea that the thieves were hillmen," she said, toying with the hilt of the little jeweled dagger he had given her during his amorous stage. "I've been wondering if that is true. It has occurred to me that perhaps you came here to distract me with your attentions while your men stole my cattle behind my back. I heard a whisper somewhere that you had."

She was watching his face as she spoke and saw the quick flinch of surprise, swiftly masked, and the briefest paling of the skin beneath his eyes. More telling than that was his sudden stillness. When he spoke again, all his ardor had vanished.

"These are lies—but you are quick to believe them. Who accused me?"

Queen Alyse shrugged gracefully and drew the little dagger from its sheath. "It would explain why you brought so many men, and half of them boys. Your trained troops have surely gone with your father and brother. But one doesn't need trained troops for cattle stealing."

Sir Darric shot to his feet. His eyes blazed. "I came for you. Alyse of Gwynedd, the ice queen. As beautiful as a winter dawning and with a heart as cold. That's your reputation—did you know it?—all over Wales. I came to melt you down, layer by layer—" He stopped and shrugged. "I should have known better."

Trembling, Queen Alyse rose and faced him. "I'm not a fool, Darric. And I will not be used. Tomorrow you will take your men back to the Longmeadow Marshes and stay there until you are sent for."

His lip lifted in a sneer. "You had the chance to command me. You passed it by. I will give no such order."

"Then I will."

He shook his head very slowly and held her eyes. "You can't make them leave. They take orders only from me."

"I am your queen."

He laughed. "Are you? My men outnumber yours." Then his insidious smile reappeared, and the smooth, seductive note returned to his voice. "Of course, there is a way out of this without violence."

She waited, her fist clenched around the dagger's hilt. She wished fervently it were a bigger weapon that could inflict more than scratches. Then she might use it.

His eyes met hers. "Perhaps if you allowed me to marry into your family . . ."

"Don't be ridiculous!" the queen gasped. "It's out of the question."

"Is it? I suppose I'm not good enough, just as my father wasn't good enough for your sister. Is that it?"

She had forgotten that. Gavin of the Longmeadow Marshes used to wear a rut in the road to the castle gates to look at Elen. "Marriage is more a matter of land than of liking," she said coldly. "Do you think my sister and I were free to marry any man we chose? Our choices were limited to men whose lands could be annexed to Gwynedd upon the death of their fathers. These things are political decisions."

Sir Darric nodded easily. "Of course. But I'm not asking for your daughter, Alyse. I don't want to be outranked for the rest of my life. I'll take the ward. The stray lamb. She's a landless orphan, I've been told, with nothing to recommend her in the way of political attractions."

Queen Alyse stiffened. The impudent scoundrel! How did he dare? "You must be jesting. She's still a child, all bone and sinew."

"She'll be a beauty, though. You see it as clearly as I do. She'll be famous for it one day . . . like her mother."

The queen's hands bunched into fists. "She's too young for marriage."

"She's thirteen. Older than your daughter."

"But not yet eligible." Queen Alyse spoke firmly and saw Sir Darric's eyes widen in surprise.

He shrugged and smiled. "A late bloomer? Makes no difference to me. I don't want her for the sons she'll bear me. I want the girl for what she'll be herself, Alyse."

"She has no patrimony," the queen spluttered. "No dowry but what I give her."

He lifted a shoulder and let it fall. "So give her half your daughter's dowry. It would content me."

Half! The notion nauseated her. This greedy upstart to take half Elaine's dowry? Guinevere's dowry to be equal to Elaine's? She and Pellinore to be permanently allied to Darric of the Longmeadow Marshes? She turned on her heel and strode across the chamber, trying to force her mind to think amid the tumult of her emotions.

"Come, Alyse, don't let your pride get in your way. I'm doing you a favor, taking the girl off your hands. She's nothing to you, just another mouth to feed, another dependent to marry off. Give her to me and I'll go home quietly."

His tone was smooth and persuasive, but his words struck chill into Queen Alyse's heart. He had the nerve to try to blackmail her, his sovereign queen. As outraged as she was at such presumption, part of her nevertheless weighed the offer. Here was an easy way to bury Guinevere in obscurity and foil the dreadful prophecy. Here was an end to sleepless nights and arguments with Pellinore over the girl's future. She ought to rejoice at the chance to rid herself of all that fear and worry; instead, her blood ran cold at the thought.

Was it because the child carried the blood of the royal house of Gwynedd? Or was it because Queen Alyse had seen in her, from time to time, flashes of intelligence, courage, a patience she had often wished Elaine might learn, and a loyalty that, despite her repeated disobedience, inspired trust? For all these reasons, and perhaps also because she recognized in herself a burgeoning admiration for the girl, Queen Alyse knew that she could not do less than her best for Guinevere.

She turned and faced Sir Darric. "Why Guinevere? Tell me that."

He smiled. "Let's say I have an old score to settle." His voice softened to a purr as he came closer. "You know as well as I do that the girl will be someone someday. Her beauty, like her mother's, will melt my father's heart; he'll forgive me anything for her sake. I'll be the envy of Mathowen and every other man in Wales. She'll be my stepping-stone to power and influence. With a wife like that, I can go anywhere." His hands clasped her shaking shoulders. "You know I'm right, don't you, Alyse? You know that girl has power—Lady Elen's power—although she doesn't yet guess at it herself."

Queen Alyse shuddered and shrank from his touch. Next week, when Pellinore came home, she would see Sir Darric's handsome head impaled upon a spike above the entrance gates, if it was the last thing she did. . . .

"You're talking nonsense," she said stiffly. "I refuse to consider it."

Sir Darric backed away, the smile gone. "Have it your way, then. I'll take the castle and the girl with it. When I'm king of Gwynedd, there'll be no one to deny me."

"Your arrogance is insulting. Thirty men are not enough. The house guard are loyal to a man."

"Are they?"

It was the mischief in his eyes that frightened her most. He was enjoying himself too much, and he was not afraid. He must know something she didn't about the house guard. She wondered suddenly where Marcus was.

"It would take a battle. Men would die. You would cross the line into treason, Darric. With King Pellinore only days away, are you willing to risk the whole of your life on the chance?"

Something flickered behind his eyes, some flash of uncertainty, and Queen Alyse clutched at hope. "In any event, I can't respond to your threats tonight. There is too much to consider. I must think what Pellinore would say."

Sir Darric raised his eyebrows in mock surprise. "Have to run it by the king, do you? Why? You're the daughter of the king of Gwynedd. Pellinore's only the man who had the largest patrimony fifteen years ago."

Blood rushed to the queen's face, and Sir Darric laughed. "Give me the girl, Alyse."

Queen Alyse walked to the door and pulled it open. "Bredon," she said to the guard outside, "Sir Darric is ready to retire. Escort him to his chamber."

Sir Darric made no move to leave. He watched her with narrowed eyes, as if weighing up her strength or her resolve. Finally, he shrugged and went to the door, his robe of green velvet sighing as he passed. "You have until dawn," he said. "I'll give you that long to decide. But what a shame to waste the night."

She watched him out of sight, closed the door, and

dropped the bar across it. Her heart was racing so fast she thought she might choke. She hurried into the inner chamber to find her women. Cissa and Leonora were both there, looking pale and frightened. And rising from a chair between them was, at long last, Marcus.

CHAPTER TWENTY-SIX

Discovery

It was not hard to fool Grannic and Ailsa. The two nurses slept so soundly that the girls had made it a regular practice to slip past them late at night and go where they pleased about the castle. They took great care to avoid the guards' notice. This required careful scouting of rooms and passageways and a thorough knowledge of the guard postings and the changes of watch. Consequently, there was not much about the nightly running of the castle that Elaine and Guinevere did not know. They were able to make their way out of the women's quarters, down a stair, through several passageways, up another stair, and into the men's quarters without once being seen.

Elaine came to a halt in the shadow of a window embrasure and clutched Guinevere's hand. "That door there, under the lamp ahead, that's where the best guests are housed. Lucius is standing guard. Let's wait until the watch changes. It's Darnal's night, and he's much more likely to be lenient. He owes a gambling debt to my uncle Melleas."

They waited in the narrow window niche until they heard the scrape of boots on stone that signaled the approaching change of watch. They looked on as passwords were given and received, salutes were exchanged, and Darnal replaced Lucius outside Sir Darric's door.

Elaine drew a deep breath. "Well," she said, "here we go."

"Wait." Guinevere touched her arm. "Someone else is coming."

A moment later, two men rounded the far corner and came down the corridor toward them.

"It's Sir Darric," Elaine whispered. "With Bredon as escort. He must have been to see Mother."

The men stopped before the door under the oil lamp. Bredon saluted and went back the way he had come. Sir Darric, a little unsteady on his feet, braced an arm against the wall and waited until Bredon had disappeared back around the corner.

He leaned toward the guard. "He's not one of us, I'm guessing?"

"No, my lord," Darnal replied. "Do you need a hand?"

Sir Darric laughed. "You think I'm drunk? This is nothing. I'm still standing. Where's Regis?"

"Here, my lord." Regis appeared at the head of the stair and glanced quickly around him. "Is all well?"

Sir Darric leaned against the wall and folded his arms across his chest. "Report."

Regis saluted smartly. "Sir. The watch has changed. I've

just made the rounds. Every guard on duty is one of my hand-picked men."

"Don't you mean one of *our* handpicked men?" Sir Darric's voice went dangerously soft, almost sleepy.

Regis hastened to correct his error. "Of course, my lord. One of our men. At every door except the queen's."

A shiver ran up Guinevere's spine, and she gripped Elaine's arm. "Be very still," she breathed into Elaine's ear. "There's something going on."

"Everything's ready," Regis said. "We await your command."

"They've changed the guards?" Elaine wondered. "What for? And what is Regis doing saluting one of Mother's guests?"

"We have until dawn," Sir Darric said. "If I choose to wait that long. Perhaps I won't. But I need to get out of this useless garment"—he flicked the green velvet robe with a casual finger—"and into battle dress. Come in while I change. We'll go over the details."

He pushed at the door, which refused to open until Regis reached past him and lifted the latch. Sir Darric staggered into the jamb and righted himself with difficulty.

"Cold bitch filled me with wine. Thought she'd get something out of me. Women." Sir Darric swayed on his feet and grinned at Regis. "More beauty than brains, all of 'em."

"Who's he calling names?" Elaine gasped. "Why, the traitorous dog! How does he dare?"

"Shhh," Guinevere pleaded. "They'll hear us."

Sir Darric made it into his chamber and turned to wave

Regis in after him. "Who's on the door of the armory? What about the stables? Have we got enough blades for the men coming in from patrol?"

"Just one moment, my lord." Regis signaled to Darnal. Without a word, both men drew their swords and began to move silently down the corridor, one against each wall.

"Oh my God!" Elaine squeaked. "They're coming for us!"

The girls flattened themselves against the shallow curve of the embrasure and waited, breathless, for discovery. There was no possibility of escape. Their hiding place had become a trap.

Regis and Darnal came to a halt, one on either side of the embrasure, a sword's length away. "Drop your weapons and come out," Regis ordered, leveling his blade. "Now."

Elaine drew herself up to her full height and stepped forward into the light. Regis's jaw dropped. "Struth! It's the princess."

"And the ward," Darnal added, slamming his weapon home to its scabbard.

"What's the meaning of this?" Elaine demanded in her haughtiest manner. "What are you up to, Regis? Why did you salute Sir Darric?"

Guinevere tugged hard at Elaine's gown, but it was too late. Regis scowled at them both.

"If you've seen that, princess, you've seen too much. Come along, now. Sir Darric will have to deal with you."

"You will address me as 'my lady,' " Elaine returned, in her best imitation of Alyse's superior manner. "And you will take me to see Sir Darric at once. That's why I've come."

"Is it, indeed?" Regis sneered. "That suits me fine. Just you march on ahead, princess, and I'll announce you."

Guinevere followed Elaine down the corridor, her heart pounding in her ears. Something was very wrong. These men were not behaving normally. All her senses had grown suddenly alert, as if danger lurked just out of sight in the dark. Gooseflesh crept up her arms and raised the hair on the back of her neck. She hoped very much that Queen Alyse had not retired for the night.

Sir Darric's antechamber was empty when Regis ushered them in. Singing came from the bedchamber, a rough soldier's ditty sung in a slurred and bleary tenor. Regis smothered a sigh of impatience.

"Stay here," he ordered the girls. "I'll be right back. Darnal, guard the door outside." He tapped lightly on the bedchamber door and entered without waiting for a response.

Guinevere glanced around the antechamber as the door closed behind Darnal and left them alone. "I don't like this. They're planning something. This isn't the time to visit Sir Darric, Laine. Just make some excuse—say we have to get back before our nurses miss us or something—but let's get out of here as fast as we can."

Elaine, who had been straightening her gown, spoke soothingly. "Nonsense. There's nothing to fret about. Regis is an insolent fool and always has been. The important thing is that Sir Darric will see us."

"I wish he wouldn't," Guinevere said under her breath.

Elaine almost smiled. "You're such a little rabbit sometimes.

He can't do anything to harm us. Mother would have his head on a spike if he tried."

Guinevere's voice fell even lower. "Your mother isn't here."

Elaine patted her cousin's arm reassuringly. "Be brave, Gwen. Everything will turn out all right."

CHAPTER TWENTY-SEVEN

In the Lion's Den

The bedchamber door flew open. Sir Darric stood on the threshold, bug-eyed, half dressed in boots and leggings, a look of astonishment on his face. "Well, I'll be damned." His gaze rested on Guinevere. "I don't believe it."

Behind him, Regis smirked, and behind Regis, the chamberlain loitered anxiously with Sir Darric's tunic, mantle, armor, and weapons.

Elaine looked pointedly at Guinevere, who made a quick curtsy. "My lord, please take no offense. If you remember from our . . . our conversation in the forest, the princess Elaine wished an audience with you. You . . . you had no objections at the time."

"Ha!" Sir Darric barked. "That's good, that is. Our

conversation in the forest." He staggered forward into the room, eyes boring into Guinevere. "Why did you run away? Did you lead me down that trail on purpose, you little hellion? Nearly killed my horse. Got a splinter in his chest that long." He held up his hands to demonstrate, swayed dangerously, and was quickly steadied by Regis with a hand on his arm.

Guinevere lowered her eyes. "I meant no harm to your horse, my lord."

Sir Darric laughed. "So it was me you meant to kill? Who set that trap for you? Who built it?"

Elaine turned to Guinevere. "What trap? What's he talking about, Gwen?"

Sir Darric shrugged off Regis's arm. "You sent me down that trail on purpose. Confess it."

"Gwen?" Elaine poked her. "What did you do to Sir Darric?"

Reluctantly, Guinevere met his taunting eyes. "I take that way home at least twice a week, my lord. It's not a trap. It's only a matter of practice."

Sir Darric reddened. "That be damned for a tale!"

Regis grabbed his arm again. "My lord," he murmured, speaking slowly and enunciating clearly. "Remember our conversation about the princes? Maelgon and his brother?"

Elaine scowled at Guinevere. "One of your stupid obstacles?"

Sir Darric swayed in Regis's grasp. "Nearly killed me."

"My lord," Regis said patiently. "Remember our conversation. *Princess Elaine is here.*"

Silence followed this pronouncement. Guinevere saw Sir Darric's anger cool and a malicious light enter his eyes. He straightened and shrugged Regis off.

"Yes," he said. "Let's not forget the point." He bowed to Elaine. "Princess, forgive me."

Elaine raised her chin and spoke in her most superior manner. "Sir Darric. I have done you the honor of paying you a private visit. Pray, take a moment to make yourself presentable. I will not take up much of your time."

Sir Darric frowned, confused. Following her gaze, he looked down at himself and saw that he was only half dressed. "Well, I'll be damned." When he looked up, he was smiling.

Guinevere moved swiftly to Elaine's side, grabbed her sleeve, and pulled her away. "We will leave you now, my lord. We can see this is not a convenient time."

"On the contrary, it's perfect timing." If he had been drunk before, he was sober now. His eyes glittered with malice as he gestured to the couch behind them. "What's your hurry, now you're here? Make yourselves comfortable."

"No," Guinevere said quickly. She recognized that tone of voice. It had driven her down the lower ridge trail like an arrow flying. "We must be going."

Sir Darric, too, was firm. "I insist."

"Are you mad, Gwen? Let go." Elaine shrugged off the restraining hand and faced Sir Darric. "We will wait until you have dressed, my lord. Then we should like a few words with you."

Sir Darric's smile widened. "Should you, indeed? How like your mother you are." He turned to Regis. "Send Jordan and

Drako to me. Now. Then pass the word among the guards. Tonight's the night, and I'll not wait for dawn, after all."

Regis saluted and made for the door.

"Wait." Sir Darric rubbed his forehead as if trying to clear his mind. "Do the numbers three-five-seven mean anything to you?"

Regis stared at him. "No, my lord. Should they?"

Sir Darric drew a long breath. "I sent you a message, but the messenger must have been a spy. I'd like to know whose. Never mind. Go get Jordan and Drako."

Regis went.

"I don't want Jordan and Drako," Elaine objected. "Gwen is chaperone enough."

Guinevere made a reverence to the ground. With a tremor in her voice, she said, "My lord, we pose no danger to you. Please let us go."

Sir Darric snapped his fingers, and the chamberlain came running. "Not now. Had you stayed abed where you belong, I'd have left you alone. But you've stumbled into the middle of things, and now the matter is out of my hands."

He donned his tunic and his armored corselet, while Guinevere pulled Elaine behind the couch. "Say nothing to him," she begged Elaine in a fierce whisper. "He's planning something. He means us ill."

"Nonsense," Elaine retorted. "Men don't don armor to fight women."

"Exactly," Guinevere said. "Something bigger is afoot."

Sir Darric raised his arms as the chamberlain buckled the sword belt around his hips. He looked at Guinevere over the servant's head. "How right you are, princess. Prepare yourself for a change. By morning, I will be king."

Elaine gasped. Guinevere swallowed hard. "Then let us go, my lord. We can do you no harm, and it will go easier with you later if you leave us alone."

"Yes!" Elaine burst out. "When my father, the true king, comes home!"

Sir Darric lowered his arms as the chamberlain fastened a dark green mantle over his tunic. The clip he used was gold. "He will have no kingdom to come home to. The house guard is loyal to me now."

"The house guard!" Elaine hooted. "What are they? Soldiers too old or too unskilled to go to war. My father has seasoned troops with him. You won't stand a chance."

"Seasoned troops returning from six weeks of a hard campaign with who knows how many wounded. Men whose homes and families, the king's included, will be in my hands. Even without hostages, Pellinore will never take the castle with the men he has. My men are handpicked and well trained."

"Hostages?" Elaine squeaked.

"King Pellinore's men are loyal," Guinevere said quickly, "because they honor and respect him. If the house guard is under your control, it's because you've bought them. You don't have their hearts. They'll turn as soon as they foresee defeat."

Sir Darric thrust his dagger under his belt and waved the chamberlain away. "Bought them, have I? With what? We're not rich men in the Marshes. We barely get by."

"With cattle," Guinevere replied evenly. "Stolen from

King Pellinore's pens. You bought the king's guards with his own gold. That kind of loyalty doesn't last."

Sir Darric froze. For a long moment, no one spoke.

Elaine glanced from one to the other and back again. The tension in the air raised gooseflesh on her skin. "*He* stole Father's cattle? How do you know?"

Sir Darric spoke very softly. "I'd like to know that, too."

Guinevere's hands were shaking, and she clasped them behind her back to hide them. "You were seen."

"By whom?"

Guinevere shook her head.

"What do you mean, hostages?" Elaine said into the silence. "You wouldn't dare."

Guinevere took her hand as a sudden knocking sounded at the door.

Jordan stuck his head in. "My lord?"

Sir Darric smiled. "Come in."

Jordan and Drako entered, looking hastily dressed. They glanced at each other when they saw the girls but kept their faces carefully empty of expression. Sir Darric took Elaine's arm and pulled her forward.

"Take this one to the camp," he said. "Stay there until I send for you."

"Let me go!" Elaine cried. "You filthy traitors!"

"Don't harm her," Sir Darric said sharply. "She's my guarantee of Pellinore's good conduct. Understand?"

Drako scowled, but Jordan nodded. "Yes, my lord." He glanced at Guinevere. "What about the other one?"

"She stays here."

"No!" Elaine cried, struggling against Jordan's grip.

Guinevere slid to her knees. "Please, my lord, let me go with Elaine. It is my duty to accompany her, and I have promised it."

Sir Darric reached down and raised her to her feet. "You'll stay here."

Elaine shrieked and bit Jordan's hand. "Why are you keeping Gwen? What are you going to do to her? You'll be sorry for this, Darric of Longmeadow. When my mother hears—"

Sir Darric laughed. "Your mother has her own troubles just now, and by morning, she'll be mine, too. Get going, Jordan."

Elaine screamed and began to kick, but her satin slippers made no impression on the men's booted legs and Sir Darric gagged her with a strip of sheeting torn from his bed. Jordan and Drako lifted her from the floor and carried the writhing girl away at arm's length between them as if she were a large and poisonous snake.

Sir Darric turned to Guinevere. His eyes looked hard as metal, and his smile had gone. When he spoke, his voice was gruff.

"Who saw me?"

She lowered her eyes and said nothing. Sir Darric grabbed her arm and breathed into her face. "Who told you I took the cattle? Who said they saw me?"

Dark blue eyes flashed up at him. "About fifty people."

He stared at her unbelieving.

"Your secret's out," she said, taking courage from his silence. "Getting rid of Elaine and me won't solve anything. And you can't get rid of Elaine or you'll lose your hold over King Pellinore and Queen Alyse."

"Damn your insolence." He spoke roughly, but his hands cupped her shoulders not ungently, and the corners of his mouth twitched in a smile. "You're beautiful when you're angry, by God you are."

Guinevere backed away at once, eyes cast down, but he caught her by the wrist and held her.

"There's another way," he suggested softly. "It will save Elaine's hide, if that worries you. It will save all Gwynedd without a drop of blood spilled."

She waited, eyes averted, for him to let go. Instead, he drew closer and bent his head near hers. He reeked of wine, and his breath stank of onions.

"Aren't you interested, princess?"

"No."

"Would you condemn your kinsmen to death without hearing how you might save them? Coldhearted maid. At least listen to my proposal. It will bring you an honor you'd never otherwise attain."

She waited with held breath while he touched his lips to her ear. "You can be queen," he whispered. "Marry me tonight and by morning you'll be queen of all Gwynedd."

Guinevere stared at him, speechless. Such stupendous arrogance was beyond her comprehension. She could not believe he was serious. He could not possibly think her capable of such an action, of betraying her own family for a chance to be queen. Yet, the hazel eyes that held her own were clear and steady, waiting with hope for an answer—yes, with hope! To him, it was a matter of choosing between more or less accept-able alternatives. For her, there was no choice at all. A deep shudder of disgust rose from within her and shook her body.

"I don't betray," she said. "And I wouldn't marry you if you were the last man living."

She watched him color, saw the birth of fury in his eyes, and tried to turn away. He was too quick. He caught her arm, dragged her to the bedchamber, and threw her to the floor.

"Think you're too good for me?" he snarled. "You're as bad as Alyse. Nothing to choose between you. Proud, pampered, headstrong little brat—I'll teach you a lesson you won't soon forget. I will, indeed." He grinned as he turned away. "As soon as I return."

CHAPTER TWENTY-EIGHT

Escape

The moment the door closed behind Sir Darric, Guinevere raised her head. She looked straight at the chamberlain. He was a small man, somewhere between twenty and thirty, as near as she could judge, and neatly dressed in poor, much-mended clothes.

"What's your name?"

He ducked his head and replied with downcast eyes, "Liam, m'lady." His face was impassive, but his hands wrung and twisted the hem of his tunic.

"Liam, is there another way out of here besides the guarded door?"

"No, m'lady."

Guinevere rose to her feet and went to the window. It was unglazed and narrow, but wide enough for a slim person to wiggle through. She leaned over the deep stone sill and looked down. Torches on the battlement below lit a sheer drop of thirty feet. She drew back, giddy from the sight. The person would have to be nimble, too, and not weighed down by skirts.

She turned and looked quickly about the room. She would need more than twenty feet of rope—or knotted bedding—to get down safely. There had been no guard on the battlement. Perhaps Sir Darric did not have enough men to spare one to watch below his window. Or perhaps it was an oversight that in time he would correct.

"Liam, is there any rope? Or a stout cord? In Sir Darric's baggage, perhaps?"

Dark, frightened eyes lifted to hers, then quickly looked away. "No, m'lady. There's nothing like that here."

Of course there wouldn't be. What fool would keep twenty feet of good rope in his bedchamber? It would have to be bedding, then. She wished fervently that part of her education had been devoted to the tying of knots. She had heard of people escaping this way, but she had never known anyone who had tried it. They must have been desperate. . . .

Guinevere threw back the furred coverlet on the bed and pulled at the linen bedsheet. It was soft and pliable, but old and frayed from many washings. She did not know if it would hold her weight. Leather would be stronger.

She set the bedsheet aside and knelt by the chest at the end of the bed. Ignoring Liam's gasp of protest, she lifted the lid. A man as vain as Sir Darric was sure to have brought a fine selection of garments with him. She pulled out a light gray cloak, a dark brown overmantle of fine wool with a gilded border, a pair of good leather leggings, and, she saw with satisfaction, the green velvet robe.

"This might do. If it's not long enough, we can add the bedsheet last. Come, Liam, help me knot these things together."

But the man shrank from her. "Oh no, m'lady. You can't touch those. Those are Sir Darric's things."

Guinevere looked up at him. "Didn't you hear what he said? What he threatened? I've got to get out. I've got to save Elaine."

But Liam's only reaction was a fist shoved hard against his teeth and lowered eyes that refused to meet her own. Helplessly, Guinevere recognized the withdrawal of personality, the mask of stupidity that was the poor man's only defense against the caprices of the higher born.

"King Pellinore is your lord!" she cried, as if her own need could call up courage in him. "Sir Darric is planning to betray him. He's taken Elaine. He's planning an attack against the queen. He's a traitor, and he's got to be stopped."

But Liam only shrugged. That was when Guinevere knew he would not help her. He had a set of commands to obey, and it was not his place to think beyond them. Such obstinacy made her tremble with frustration. Time and time again, she had seen this blank passivity in the faces of servants, peasants, and villagers who came face to face with an unreasonable demand. They knew nothing, they saw nothing, they were responsible for nothing. In a land run by the wealthy and the strong, noninvolvement was the only way they could survive.

She recognized that she had a choice to make. Either she could knot the clothing herself and trust the makeshift result with her very life, or she could try to enlist this man's help. But she had to do one or the other right away.

Still on her knees, she turned to him. "Liam, you live in the village, don't you?" Her voice was as gentle as she could make it, the same voice she used with a skittish horse. "I've seen you walking there with a little girl, I think."

He avoided her gaze, keeping his eyes on the floor at his feet. What she could see of his face held no expression at all. Guinevere's heart sank as she waited in vain for some response.

"A pretty little girl with dark curls and rosy cheeks. I thought she looked three or four. A little cherub."

A dull flush darkened Liam's face. "Lind," he said roughly. "My daughter."

"She's a beautiful child. She'll make you proud one day."

Liam fidgeted. For just the briefest moment, his bright eyes lifted to hers. "If she lives."

"She'll live. Gwynedd is a safe place to grow up. It's why my own father sent me here."

"Aye," Liam ventured. "I'd heard that."

"Gwynedd is a wider and wealthier land than poor North-gallis. King Pellinore's a strong king, and his kingdom is secure. King Pellinore's friendships with the other Welsh kings have kept our borders safe and strong. Even the Saxons have left us alone. As long as Pellinore is king, you and your daughter have nothing to fear."

If Liam knew where she was heading, he gave no sign of it. He merely nodded in agreement.

"What do you think makes him so strong a king?" she asked, knotting one leg of Sir Darric's leggings to a corner of the green robe. Liam said nothing. Guinevere tied the brown overmantle to the other end of the green robe. "It's not just his soldiers. Every king has those. The real reason King Pellinore is a strong king is that his people support him. They do what they can to help him keep the land safe. There are many more of us than there are of him. Without us, he has no kingdom. No king can rule for long without the support of his people. You see, Liam, in the way that matters, *we* are Gwynedd."

Liam was watching her very carefully now.

"What would happen, do you think," she said, wrestling with a corner of the thick gray cloak, "if we stopped supporting Pellinore? If we turned away, refused our tithe, and ignored his commands? We would be at the mercy of any greedy adventurer who came our way. I don't know about you, but I don't want to live under the rule of a tyrant or an arrogant hothead like Sir Darric. And I don't believe you'd want little Lind to grow up under such a rule."

Liam's eyes bored into her. At last, she had his full attention.

"I will do anything I can—no matter the cost—to keep a man like Sir Darric from taking power in Gwynedd."

The cloak was too thick to knot easily, but finally she achieved something more or less sturdy. She rose and pulled the unwieldy length of cloth toward the window. "That's why I'm going to get out of this chamber. Because, when all is said and done, King Pellinore's power lies in the hands of people like you and me."

Praying hard to whichever god was listening, Guinevere fastened Sir Darric's leggings to the foot of the bed and tossed the end of her makeshift rope out the window.

A sharp cry sounded behind her. "You're never going to trust yourself to that contraption, m'lady?"

She turned. Liam had made his decision. He strode forward, grabbed the knotted end of Sir Darric's leggings, and with a quick jerk, pulled them free. The rest of the knotted clothing slid out the window and disappeared into darkness.

"Beg pardon, m'lady, but only a fool would try to escape that way."

Guinevere turned so he could not see the tears of gratitude that had sprung to her eyes. "But I must get out."

"Aye, but not by yon window. That's death, that is. You want to go out by the door."

She drew a deep breath and let it out slowly. Silently, she thanked the listening god for Liam's anger. It was like being handed an extra weapon in a one-sided fight. "Then what shall I do?" she asked meekly.

Liam considered. "You're tall for a lass. My clothes would fit. I could ask the guard for permission to fetch you something—another blanket, perhaps, a skin of wine, or a dish from the kitchens—and then you could get out disguised as me." He glanced at her uneasily. "If you'd consent to wear these rags, m'lady."

"I would not consent," Guinevere said firmly, "because where would that leave you? If Sir Darric returned and found you here without your clothes, he'd know you'd helped me. He'd kill you. And it would be my fault." Her voice softened, and she smiled at him shyly. "But I thank you for the offer."

Liam shifted from foot to foot. He was relieved but trying to hide it. "What then, m'lady?"

"Perhaps we could disable the guard."

"But we have no weapons."

She glanced around the room again, this time looking for something that could serve as a weapon. In the corner opposite the bed, she saw the waste pot, a heavy bronze bowl with a copper lid. "Liam, is the waste pot empty?"

Startled, Liam shook his head. "Sir Darric, he's a drinking man." He grinned. "I could always empty it."

Guinevere smiled back. "There's no one on the battlement just now. Just a pile of clothes."

Smiling, Liam emptied the waste pot out the window. "Now what?"

Guinevere explained her plan. Together, they moved the bench in the antechamber to a position behind the door. She climbed up on the bench, and Liam handed her the waste pot. It was cold and very heavy, a cumbersome weapon, but a weapon nonetheless. She would have to do this part of it herself. Even for his daughter's sake, she doubted if Liam could be brought to attack an armed guard.

"Now, you stand there," she directed, "so that when he comes in, he'll stop at once. Is the bedsheet handy? Good. Ready now? Here I go." She drew a long breath, opened her mouth, and screamed.

A heavy fist pounded on the door. "My lady? My lady?"

Guinevere shrieked again. "Help! Help!"

The door flew open. Darnal ran in, almost knocking Liam down, but he stopped where she wanted him to stop. Raising the heavy pot high in the air, she brought it down with all her strength on Darnal's head. He staggered, grunted once, and fell.

"Now!" she cried.

Trembling, Liam bound the man's wrists to his ankles with the bedsheet while Guinevere grabbed the dagger from his belt. Darnal lay senseless and unmoving.

"Now get in the bedchamber, quick!" she ordered. "I'll drop the bar across the door. That way, you can't be blamed."

But Liam, his courage aroused, objected to going. It took precious moments of pleading to get him to obey. "Knock yourself on the head with something," she suggested. "Be in a faint when Sir Darric returns." He seemed pleased with this idea and finally retreated to the bedchamber. She secured the door, then raced into the hall, only just remembering to close the antechamber door behind her.

It was quiet in the corridor. She slipped down the stairs, moving cautiously at first, until she saw that all the corridors were empty of their guards. Had Sir Darric called some kind of meeting, now that all the guards on duty were his own men? So much the better. Guinevere ran to the kitchens, which were empty at night but for the cook's boys, who slept on the hearth. The quickest way to the stables was through the kitchen gardens, and to the stables, forbidden or not, she must go. If only Queen Alyse had not picked this night to rob her of her tunic and leggings!

On the thought, she made a quick detour to the fuller's quarters, hard by the kitchens. No one was about in the middle of the night, but the baskets of clothes awaiting cleaning sat just inside the door. She found her tunic and leggings in the second basket and struggled impatiently out of her gown. Time seemed to weigh her down, each moment passing like a flash while she wrestled awkwardly with laces and thongs that Ailsa daily managed with such ease. Twice she heard thunder rumbling in the distance while her fingers pulled and pushed at the fastenings of her gown. At last, she was free of the hampering skirts and dressed again in her old, comfortable riding clothes.

She grabbed an old cloak from another basket and ran light-footed across the stone-floored kitchen to the garden door. She raised the heavy bar from its housings, pushed open the door without waking the sleeping servant boys, and stepped at last out into the rainy dark. Pulling the hood of her cloak tight around her head, she fled toward the stables.

CHAPTER TWENTY-NINE

Rescue

At the edge of the stable block, she stopped. A torch gleamed dully in the rain, and by its light, she saw a guard in the courtyard, not far from the open stable door. She did not recognize him, which meant that he must be one of Sir Darric's men. She ducked back around the corner and ran to the rear door. It was barred from the inside. She wondered if she could slip in through one of the little horse windows without disturbing the animals. She had just decided to try it when a firm hand came down on her shoulder.

"Halt!" a voice behind her whispered. "And be silent."

She whirled, the stolen dagger in her hand. Her wrist was caught in a vicious grip and the dagger wrenched away. A cloaked man pushed her hard against the stable wall, dislodging her hood.

"What are you doing here, boy?" he said roughly. "Who are you?" Then, as a stray gleam of light caught a wayward strand of bright hair, he drew a sharp breath. *"Princess Guinevere?"*

At last, she recognized the voice. If the light had not been so dim, she would have known him sooner by the odd tilt of his shoulders. "M-Marcus?"

"Shhh," Marcus whispered hoarsely. "Keep your voice down. What are you doing here, my lady?"

Guinevere swallowed in a dry throat. "Did Regis send you to look for me?"

Marcus laughed softly. "No, princess. There are traitors abroad tonight, but I'm not one of them. I've just come from a conference with the queen." He looked at the dagger in his hand. "Whose weapon is this?"

"Darnal's," she said quickly. "Sir Darric imprisoned me in his chamber, and he's—he's abducted Elaine! Jordan and Drako took her. Have they come this way? Have they ridden off? Am I too late?"

Marcus stared at her. A hundred questions rose to his lips, but there was no time to ask them. He was certain the queen knew nothing of this disaster.

"They've taken Lady Elaine? Where? Not out into this storm?"

Thunder rumbled again in the mountains, and Guinevere shivered. "I don't know where they're going. To some kind of camp, Sir Darric said. I don't know where it is, but I've got to follow them. I'm sure I can track them in this soft ground. I've—I've got to save her." She raised a pale face to Marcus. "Sir Darric is taking over the castle."

Something like a growl issued from Marcus's throat. "Over my dead body. How long have they been gone?"

"I don't know. The best part of an hour perhaps."

Marcus grunted. "Time enough. Never mind. I know where the camp is."

"You do?" Guinevere cried. "Then you can lead me to her!"

Marcus shoved his hand over her mouth. "Keep your voice down. The guard will hear you." He glanced swiftly about and withdrew his hand. "Not tonight, I can't," he said apologetically. "The queen has sent me to muster as many loyal men as I can find. There's not a moment to lose. Nor can I let you ride out alone, not at night, not in this storm."

"But, Marcus," Guinevere pleaded, "how much use will your loyal men be when all Sir Darric has to do to force the queen's surrender is threaten to kill her daughter? She's his hostage. I heard him say himself that she was his promise of King Pellinore's good behavior. If we don't save Elaine, the kingdom is lost."

Marcus swore softly. "All right," he agreed. "But if I can't muster the men, someone else has to. Where's Stannic? He's a loyal man. I was coming to find him first."

"Probably at home. Sir Darric waited for the change of watch to set his plans in motion." She pointed into the darkness beyond the paddocks. "He lives yonder, in a cottage near the mares' meadow."

"I'll get him. You wait here."

Guinevere clutched at his cloak as he turned away. "Give me back the dagger first."

Marcus obliged and moments later was swallowed up by

the darkness and the pelting rain. Guinevere looked about anxiously. It was impossible to stand here in the wet and wait. Every moment that passed was a moment wasted, when she could be doing something to help Elaine. She must do what she could while Marcus was away. If she were caught, he could find Elaine without her. If she were not caught, they could be off all the sooner.

Thrusting the dagger into her belt, she hoisted herself up to the nearest of the horses' windows. The torch outside the main stable door, which was still open, shed enough light to see a wide blaze on a long bay nose. It was old Gus, thank God, and not one of the younger stallions. He threw up his head and rolled an eye at her but he made no sound as she squeezed herself through and dropped lightly to the ground. Giving old Gus a quick pat, she slipped out into the aisle between the double line of horses. It was important to keep her breathing calm and her steps casual as she made her way down the aisle to Peleth's place in the lines. Horses could sense fear more quickly even than dogs. In the wild, it was fear and speed that kept them alive.

She saw no one about. Stannic's grooms slept in a room at the end of the stable block. She could not see the room from where she stood and had no way of knowing whether the grooms were imprisoned as she had been or taken captive or left alone to sleep in innocent ignorance. If they were there, they would be up at dawn to feed the horses and would raise an alarm when they saw Peleth gone. She wished she knew how far off daybreak was.

The old gelding nickered as she approached him. She

hurried to his side and hushed him, stroking his neck and whispering endearments. She dared not fetch his bridle, for the bridles hung right next to the grooms' sleeping chamber, and she did not want to risk waking anyone up. Besides, she would have to pass the open stable door twice to get there and back, and the guard might see her.

She did not mind riding Peleth with only a halter and lead rope—she had done it often enough before—but what about Marcus? Which horse would he ride? She could not remember ever having seen Marcus on a horse. Danger beyond the castle grounds was not the business of house guards. That meant he would almost certainly need both a saddle and a bridle. She bit her lip, thinking hard. They could not risk discovery; their mission was too important. She dared not ready a horse for him when she didn't know his level of skill. Was there a chance she could persuade him to ride double with her? Stannic would know, she thought, with a great rush of relief. Stannic was coming, and Stannic would know what to do. In the meantime, she would get Peleth ready and lift the bar from the back door.

Her night sight was good now, and she walked down the aisle with something near her normal step. With infinite care, she raised the bar across the back door and went to set it down silently in the straw. But the bar was heavy, her hands were wet and slippery, and her arms, strained from the weight of holding the heavy waste pot over her head, trembled with the effort. The bar slipped from her grip and fell with a dull thud to the ground. It was not a loud noise, certainly not loud enough for the guard or the grooms to hear over the sound of pelting rain, but the horses heard it. Several of them snorted and blew, and one young stallion, backing to the end of his rope and finding he could go no farther, whinnied shrilly.

Guinevere fled down the aisle to Peleth and crouched by his head, pulling the borrowed cloak around her and the hood over her head. She waited, barely breathing, for the guard's approach.

"Who's there? Declare yourself!"

His voice, coming suddenly out of the dark, was loud, nervous, and belligerent. The horses snorted again, and the young stallion's hooves drummed on the dirt as he danced at the end of his rope. All of the animals were wide awake now and looking warily about them. Some blew, some snorted, a few whinnied uneasily. Guinevere expected the guard to light a lantern from the torch and search the aisle, for he must have seen that someone had taken the bar from the back door. But no light came down the aisle, nor any footsteps. Tentatively, she rose and peered around Peleth's haunches.

The guard was standing just inside the doorway, sword raised. Light from the torch outside fell on his face, and she saw that he was young, beardless, and frightened. All his attention was on the young stallion who was misbehaving, but he did nothing to calm the animal. He just stood there, light winking off his sword as the blade trembled, and called out again, "Is anyone there? Come forth, in the king's name!"

Guinevere heard movement outside, footsteps in puddles of water. She waited with held breath for the reinforcements that were bound to appear, for surely Sir Darric had not left the stables in the hands of this one youth alone.

A voice called from the yard: "Ho, there, you! Who are you to use the king's name so freely?" Guinevere's heart leaped. It was Marcus's voice.

The guard whirled, and his grip on the sword tightened. "Stand back! Give the password, sir. No one may enter without it."

"I'm Marcus, Regis's second-in-command. Put down the sword. I bring news from the castle."

After a moment's hesitation, the young guard moved out into the rain and beyond Guinevere's sight. At the same time, the back door opened. The young stallion screamed again and then stopped in midwhinny. The drumming of his hooves ceased, and a general air of relief and calm swept down the horse lines. Guinevere smiled and stepped out into the aisle. "Over here, Stannic."

A large, black shadow came toward her, resolving itself at last into the familiar, bearlike form of the stablemaster. For greeting, he took her in his arms and gave her a great hug. When he let her go, his voice was rough with anger.

"Well, princess, this is a fine state of affairs. Marcus says I'm to let you go with him, storm or no storm, and against the queen's orders."

"Yes, please, Stannic. Has he told you why?"

"Oh aye. I might have guessed that young scalawag was up to something. But I didn't think he had treason in him."

"None of us did," Guinevere said. "But we may yet be able to stop him."

From outside came the sudden clash of swords and then a sharp cry, broken off. Stannic turned on his heel and hurried back down the aisle, pulling a dagger from his belt. "Bring the horse," he cried over his shoulder, and disappeared out the front door.

Guinevere untied Peleth's lead rope and led him down the aisle in Stannic's wake. They reached the door just as Marcus and Stannic dragged the inert form of the young guard inside. A bump was rising on his temple, and a cut on his sword arm bled sluggishly. Stannic grunted when he saw it and went to retrieve a horse bandage from the storeroom.

"Leave it," Marcus said. "It's not a deep wound. He'll live. Just gag him and bind his hands behind him."

"Can't have him bleeding all over my stable in the meantime," Stannic replied easily. "Horses fear the smell of blood."

Guinevere turned to Marcus. "Are you ready? What horse will you ride?"

By the light of the torch, she saw him flinch, which strenghtened her suspicion that perhaps he didn't ride at all. "It will be faster if you ride with me," she said quickly, to save him the shame of admitting this dreadful shortcoming. "Peleth can carry us both, and he's ready now."

Marcus stared at the unsaddled, unbridled horse and swallowed the protest that rose to his lips. "If you're sure . . ."

She led Peleth out into the cobbled yard and leaped onto his back. Stannic came out to give Marcus a leg up.

"Put your arm around her waist and hold on tight," he said, with a twist of a smile at Marcus. "Don't think of her as a princess. She's your anchor in a storm, that's all. Now relax, and you'll balance better. That's right. You can trust her and the horse. They'll see you don't fall off."

Guinevere heard these words and knew her guess had been correct. "Which way?" she asked over her shoulder.

"Uphill," Marcus said gruffly. "Past the cattle meadows, there's a trail that heads northeast."

"We'll canter, then. It's easy, really. Like sitting in a chair that rocks."

She moved Peleth forward and then put her heels to his flanks. He picked up a canter at once. Stannic watched them fade into the gloom, torn between pride at her skill and fear for her safety, before he turned and went to wake his grooms.

CHAPTER THIRTY

The Queen's Choice

Queen Alyse wasted no time. As soon as Marcus had delivered his report and left to raise a force of loyal men, she sent a guard to fetch her sons. Leonora was dispatched to fetch Elaine and Guinevere, and Cissa went to awaken the rest of the women, whose loyalty could not be in doubt.

"Gather everyone in the hall of meeting," the queen instructed. "Bring spindles, awls, sewing needles, kitchen knives, jars of vinegar or acid—anything you can think of that might be useful as a weapon."

She collared Bredon when he returned. "I cannot hold the castle against an organized force of men, not with so many loyal soldiers away at the wars. We will gather in the hall of meeting and hold it against the traitors. There are only two doors, and one of them opens onto the kitchen stairs. Marcus has gone to the barracks to muster the men who've gone off watch, but time is short. I don't know where Sir Darric is or his men—in the armory, most likely, handing out spears—but we can't give them time to organize. Until we are all safely gathered, there are only the two of us to distract them from whatever they have planned."

"How distract them, my lady?" Bredon hurried to keep up with the queen's brisk stride.

"We shall set fire to Pellinore's rooms. After the throne itself, it's the trappings of wealth and power Sir Darric covets. We shall burn the royal apartments. That will bring him running."

Bredon had no time to protest his astonishment. The queen was already five paces ahead and reeling off instructions. They robbed the stairwells of their torches and put out every lamp in the corridors they passed. If there should be pursuers, utter darkness would slow them down.

The doors to the king's rooms were guarded by two of Sir Darric's men, who drew their swords as soon as they heard footsteps approaching. "Halt and declare yourself!"

Bredon slipped his own blade from its scabbard.

"Wait," Queen Alyse said softly. "Hold back."

She watched the two guards' faces as she neared them. One was a man of middle age, a veteran, judging by his stance and the way he held his sword. From the flush on his face and the flaccid wineskin at his side, she judged him to be a drunkard. That was probably why Sir Gavin had left him home. The other guard was a mere boy of eleven or twelve with wide, frightened eyes and a sword that trembled visibly in the torchlight. When he saw it was the queen, he lowered the weapon and bent his knee.

"Get up, Ewen!" the veteran grumbled. "Remember why you're here."

Queen Alyse smiled coldly. "You men are relieved. Bredon will stand your duty. Put up your swords."

The boy began to obey, but the veteran stopped him.

"Begging your pardon, my lady. We answer only to Sir Darric. We've got orders to guard this door."

"Against *me*?"

His face hardened. "Against all comers."

"Sir Darric's attempt to take the castle has failed," she said coolly. "I am afraid you are the last ones to learn it."

The boy Ewen gaped at her, but the veteran only grunted. "If that were true, you'd have brought more men with you."

Queen Alyse smiled. "You don't think we two are enough?" She signaled to Bredon, who stepped forward and crossed the veteran's blade.

The veteran lunged, and the fight began. Queen Alyse stood before the boy. He had raised his weapon, but it shook wildly in his hand.

"Make your decision, Ewen," she said softly. "Kill me and be dead yourself before morning, or put the weapon down and let me pass. Show yourself true of heart, and King Pellinore will reward you and your family. You can make your name bright, Ewen, by choosing loyalty over treason. Or you can die a shameful, traitor's death. Which shall it be?"

It was the gentleness of her voice that convinced him. He sank to one knee and offered up the sword. Queen Alyse took it from him, thanked him, turned, and stabbed the veteran in the back. As a stroke, it was inexpert, but it took the veteran by surprise. He staggered, giving Bredon a chance to move in close and knock the sword from his hand. Bredon bound him hand and foot while the queen led Ewen into the king's apartments and handed him a torch.

Queen Alyse was the first to set fire to Pellinore's belongings. She said a quick prayer for forgiveness under her breath and touched the flaming torch to the crimson hangings around the royal bed. She had made them herself fifteen years ago for her new husband. She watched with angry tears as Bredon and young Ewen set fire to the other chambers, the workrooms, the anterooms, to ancient furniture upholstered in silks and wool, to priceless tapestries handed down, generation to generation, from Roman times, and irreplaceable. The rooms were full of treasures, many of them gifts of kings over the years of Pellinore's reign and some inherited from Alyse's father: silver flagons, bowls, and dishes; imported mahogany boxes inlaid with mother-of-pearl; fine carpets woven in a hundred colors and imported from the deserts of the East. She made no attempt to save anything. She wanted Sir Darric in a panic.

Smoke and heat drove them back at last, and they retreated swiftly down the back stairs, taking Ewen with them. Dimly, they heard shouts and cries of warning as they made their way to the hall of meeting. Once inside the great room, they removed the oil lamps from their sconces and replaced them with torches, which, as Queen Alyse pointed out, were weapons untrained women could handle. Men were stationed at the doors. The queen descended the kitchen stairs to wake the cook's boys and enlist them, and to bar the other entrances into the kitchens and pantries. She did not know how long they might be besieged and was determined that if anyone should go hungry, it would not be the loyal folk under her command.

Having made all the preparations she could until she had more help, Queen Alyse walked to the dais at one end of the hall and sat on her carved and gilded throne next to the king's great chair. From her pouch, she withdrew her crown, a band of beaten silver inlaid with gems, and set it on her head. The sphere of her government had shrunk to a single room, but as long as she sat on her throne, it was a government still. She knew that in times of crisis, people looked to a leader. Her sitting there, gowned, crowned, and composed, would impart strength and comfort to her people when they found themselves surrounded by a hostile force greater than their own.

Her instincts were proved right. As men and women began to filter in, bleary-eyed with sleep or wide-eyed with terror, they made obeisance before the dais and were openly relieved to find their queen so calm and so certain of success. Queen Alyse gave each of them a task to perform—stoking the kitchen hearth fire to a blaze; filling jugs with water; stacking stools, chairs, tables against the doors—and they went willingly to work.

Queen Alyse watched the door to the hall of meeting with anxious eyes, waiting for her children. At all costs, she must keep them out of Sir Darric's hands. At last, Yvonet appeared with Prince Maelgon, the heir. Maelgon had taken time to dress and buckle on his dagger in its little sheath. His eyes were bright with excitement. He ignored his mother's kiss of welcome and demanded to know when the fighting would begin. In his wake came little Peredur, still in his nightshirt and half led, half carried by his nurse, Julia. Queen Alyse made much of him. She instructed Yvonet and Julia to make a place for the boys at the back of the dais, where they could sleep, if they chose, and where they could best be protected. Yvonet and Bredon were to stand guard over them. Then she returned to her chair and waited with rising anxiety for her daughter.

More people filtered in, openly nervous now, and reported that parts of the castle smelled like smoke. The kitchen doors were secured, the fire stoked, and water put to boil. Men stood at the doors; women gathered in small groups and sat on the tiled flooring with oil lamps for light. No one dared more than whispers. They waited, watching the queen. And the queen waited, watching the doors. Still her daughter did not come.

Finally, Leonora burst into the room, gasping for breath, and threw herself at Alyse's feet. "My lady! They are gone! They are taken! Oh dear God, they are lost!"

Queen Alyse could only stare at the woman, whose face, hair, and clothing were in wild disarray, and who blubbered unintelligibly in her fear. All other sound in the great hall faded into silence.

The queen rose to her feet as Ailsa and Grannic hurried into the hall and fell on their knees before her. She looked from one of them to the other. She had to force the words out. "Where is my daughter?"

Disaster and disgrace were plainly writ across their faces, but Queen Alyse could not believe the tale they told. Both girls tucked safely in bed one moment and gone the next—it was impossible, unless both nurses were drunk and incompetent. A whisper snaked around the walls as the news traveled to the rest of the company. The princesses had disappeared, and no one had seen them go. That was the whole of it, the impossible, unbelievable whole of what they knew.

Having placed herself in public view before them all, Queen Alyse could not allow herself the luxury of collapse. She wanted to scream, to strike out, to flail against this unfair fate, but she could not. All these people she had gathered together for their joint defense depended on her strength and calm. This was what it meant to be a leader, always to put their good before her own. She could not fail them. They were Gwynedd. At that moment, she would have given years off her life to see Pellinore walk in the door.

Stannic walked in, instead. With him came twenty men armed with swords and daggers and a handful of grooms armed with clubs. Tears rose to the queen's eyes as she looked at their grave, determined faces. Kneeling, Stannic told her he had come at Marcus's request, as Marcus was busy on an errand of his own. These were the men he had roused from the barracks and the stables. There were others, he was certain, who were loyal, but they lived in the village, and it would be the work of hours to get them.

"He's taken the armory," Stannic growled. "He's got

weapons enough for a hundred. But not bodies enough, until his men come down from the hills. We'll hold him."

Queen Alyse gathered her wits and forced her mind to work. "Where did Marcus go?"

Looking up, Stannic saw young Maelgon and little Peredur on the dais and knew that the queen must already have discovered the girls were missing. That explained her cold, bloodless face and the eyes wide with suffering.

"My lady, Marcus has gone with young Guinevere to rescue the princess Elaine, who was taken by Sir Darric's men."

"Taken!" Queen Alyse staggered, felt behind her for the arm of her chair, and sank into it. She listened with growing consternation as Stannic related what little he knew about the abduction of her daughter, Guinevere's determination to thwart the plan, and Marcus's decision to help her. "Is it . . . is it known where he has taken her?"

"Not to me, my lady, but Marcus knows. That's why he went with Guinevere. He's the only one who does know."

"How did it happen? How did Darric get hold of her? Did he—?"

Stannic shook his head. "I don't know any more than I've told you, my lady. You'll have to wait for Marcus to learn the rest. He'll find her, and he'll bring her back. He does what he sets out to do, does Marcus."

Queen Alyse rested her head against the cushioned back of her chair and closed her eyes. Things were going from bad to worse very swiftly. Her daughter had been abducted by traitors, and her only hope of rescue depended entirely upon a one-armed man and a miscreant child. If Elaine could not be rescued . . . Shaking, Queen Alyse forced herself to face the worst. She might have to make the excruciating choice between Elaine's life and the future of the kingdom, the inheritance of her sons, the sovereignty of Gwynedd.

She opened her eyes to find Stannic on his feet, looking at her with genuine concern. On her cheeks, she could feel the cold tracks of silent tears. "How is rescue possible when the hills are full of his men?"

"I don't know, my lady. But Marcus has brains, and so does your niece. If the thing is possible, trust them to do it."

"They will be taken themselves and add to the threat." Queen Alyse clutched the cross at her throat. She looked at Stannic, at Ailsa and Grannic, at Cissa and Leonora and all the folk gathered in the hall behind them. She could bear no more of Stannic's empty reassurances. What she needed was a miracle.

She rose to her feet and faced the silent group of frightened people. "Men and women of Gwynedd, we face a great trial. Princess Elaine has been abducted by the traitor Darric of the Longmeadow Marshes. He seeks to force our hand by holding her hostage. We must be strong. We must stand together. We must not yield to weeping and lamentation. We must be united and strong of purpose. We will hold out until King Pellinore arrives. We will not surrender."

They cheered her then, united in their admiration for her courage and her strength. Queen Alyse looked up at the narrow, unglazed windows set high in the eastern wall.

Beyond them lay the pastures and the mountains of Gwynedd, the rest of Wales, the rest of Britain.

"I lift mine eyes to the hills," she whispered, "from whence cometh my help." The people prayed with her for their deliverance, but the prayer in the queen's heart was more personal. *Dear God, I cannot choose between my daughter and my kingdom. Merciful Lord, deliver me from the choice.*

CHAPTER THIRTY-ONE

An Arrow in the Dark

Through the blowing dark, Peleth labored up the hill behind the castle. His sides were slippery with wet and his legs heavy with mud. The familiar, light weight of the girl he carried easily enough, but the stranger behind her had an uncertain seat. He had to adjust his stride at almost every step to keep the man from sliding off.

Guinevere kept a firm hold on the lead rope to help him balance, stroked his neck, and murmured to him to keep his spirits up. He'd been a warhorse once; he was trained to endure. She did not worry about Peleth or even about Marcus, bobbing like a cork behind her. His arm about her waist was tense and sometimes pressed against her hard enough to hurt, but she could not blame him for being unable to relax. No one could learn to ride by galloping uphill in the pelting rain without a saddle to cling to or light to see by. He was a stalwart enough companion, speaking seldom, and then only to direct her to the right path.

Her only worry was Elaine. She could not let them have Elaine.

All the times she had been cross with Elaine, had suffered from her bossiness, had thought ill of her in her heart, now passed before her memory and filled her with shame. Elaine had befriended her from her first day in Gwynedd. At a time when Guinevere's world had shattered around her, when she had been devastated with grief at leaving her father and her homeland forever, Elaine had accepted her instantly as a bosom companion, had taken her by the hand and led her into the busy whirl of a new life. She needn't have done it. Elaine was the queen's only daughter and might well have felt annoyed, angry, or even jealous at this unasked-for addition to the family. Instead, she had welcomed Guinevere with open arms. Ailsa and Elaine, between them, had made it possible to begin a new life in Gywnedd.

Guinevere lifted a hand to her face to wipe away tears and found her cheeks already streaming with wet. The hood of the cloak was too big and blew back into Marcus's face whenever she tried to pull it forward. That her eyes were blinded hardly mattered, since she could see next to nothing in the gloom and didn't know where they were going. She might as well let herself weep and give vent to her fears. The abduction of Elaine was too dreadful to comprehend. The injustice of it made her hot with rage. Elaine was but eleven years old.

"Pull up," Marcus said behind her. "We're near the turning."

They slowed to a walk, and the rain, which had been coming at them before, now fell straight down. Guinevere pulled her hood forward again and received a cold sluice of water down her back. Shivering, she had reached for her cloak to pull it tighter around her when a hiss of movement came out of the dark and something thudded into a tree beside them.

"Christ!" swore Marcus. "An arrow! Get down!"

He slid off the horse and drew his sword. Guinevere stared at the shaft protruding from the tree trunk at her elbow and pulled Peleth to a halt.

"Wait!" she cried, as Marcus reached for the lead rope. "It's a friend, I think."

He stared at her blankly. She turned, and from the trees on the other side of the path stepped a slender figure in a wolfskin cloak with another arrow already notched to his bow. Marcus was between them at once, sword raised. He was soldier enough to realize his disadvantage. The stranger's arrow could reach farther than his blade. Uneasily, he lowered his weapon. "Who are you, in the king's name? And what do you do here?"

Guinevere reached out to touch his shoulder. "Marcus, don't fear him. I know him."

Marcus ignored her. He knew at once that this was one of the Old Ones, a primitive people gone now from all but the highest hills. But primitive or not, this young man was armed with a weapon he was skilled at wielding. He was dangerous. "You, there. What do you want? I mean you no harm, but you must let us pass. We are on the queen's business and have no time to spare."

After a long moment, the bow sank to the young man's

side. He glanced up at Guinevere and mumbled something guttural.

"Does he not speak Welsh?" Marcus cried. "Tell him to back away!"

"He speaks Mountain Welsh," Guinevere replied. "Do you know it?"

Marcus shrugged. The language he had heard sounded nothing like the Mountain Welsh he knew.

"His name is Llyr," Guinevere continued. "He is a prince among his people. He means us no harm. Shall I ask him to put down his bow?"

"Let me try." Marcus faced the figure clad in wolf skin and fumbled for the words of a language he had not spoken since childhood. "Sir, I serve the king. Put down your weapon. I mean the princess no harm."

The odd prince glanced quickly at Guinevere for reassurance, then not only unnotched his arrow but unstrung his bow and, fixing his dark gaze on Marcus, laid it down on the sodden ground. Now Marcus had the advantage. It would take twice the time to ready the bow again as it would take to cross the path and strike a swordblow. Marcus met the challenge of those fierce, dark eyes and wondered, as he made the stranger a respectful bow and sheathed his sword, how on earth the girl had come to tame so wild a creature as this.

He waited while they spoke together, catching fewer than half the words at first, but more as the conversation continued. There was urgency in their voices, and it was clear that the young man was arguing with the princess. They must know each other well, Marcus realized, to interact so freely.

Then he remembered the girl's habit of riding about in the hills unescorted. He grinned to himself. Queen Alyse would be furious.

"Come, Marcus," Guinevere called. "It's time to go. Llyr will give you a leg up." She made a basket of her hands and demonstrated this to Llyr.

"Does he know where Sir Darric's men are stationed? We have to get past them unobserved."

"Yes," Llyr said, addressing Marcus and enunciating clearly so Marcus could understand him. "Two men on horseback rode up this trail a little past moonset. One of them carried a bundle of blankets, a bundle with yellow hair."

"Moonset!" Marcus grumbled as he trusted his foot to the young man's hands. "How can he see the moon on a night like this?" He landed more or less on the horse's wet back and slid his arm around Guinevere's waist. The Old One glared at him with fierce disapproval.

"They live so close to the heavens," Guinevere said, "they don't need to see the stars to know where they are. To them, it's like knowing left from right."

"Light with thee walk," Llyr said, saluting.

Guinevere raised her own arm in response. "Dark from thee flee."

Glancing over his shoulder, Marcus saw the young man pick up his bow, restring it in a flash, and disappear into the gloom.

"He thought it was me, you see, in the bundle, and he followed them up to a cave in the hills."

"Followed on *foot?*"

"Of course. He can track anything. When they dismounted, and he saw it wasn't me, he came back down to find me and let me know. He was going to try to get into the castle somehow, but then he heard us coming. He thought you were one of them, one of Sir Darric's men, following with me. He stopped us the only way he could."

"Damn near killed us both," Marcus muttered, but his voice was more amused than angry. He remembered the latent threat in those fierce black eyes and smiled to himself. He recognized jealousy when he saw it. "Where's he gone now?"

"Back to his clan to summon their help in rounding up Sir Darric's men."

Marcus gasped. "You've started a war?"

"No, no. I asked him not to kill them, just to tie them up and take their weapons. He tells me most of them are boys and scared of the dark. It shouldn't take the Old Ones very long."

Marcus laughed aloud. "And after that, he will come to the cave."

Guinevere looked at him over her shoulder. "Yes. How did you know?"

"That's easy. Because he's in love with you."

He felt her stiffen.

"Is that the turning ahead?" she asked coolly. "There on the left?"

"Aye. That's the road to the north and the pass to the Longmeadow Marshes."

Without any movement on her part that he could detect, the horse turned to the left and picked up a canter. Marcus abandoned any attempt at conversation and focused all his attention on staying astride the slippery, bouncing back beneath him.

When Guinevere next spoke, her words seemed to come from a great distance. "Llyr is my guardian," she said. "That is all."

Marcus smiled to himself. She sounded exactly like Queen Alyse.

CHAPTER THIRTY-TWO

The Cave

It was cold in the heights. The rain had stopped, and a small breeze trickled down from the mountaintops. Guinevere shivered. The cloak she had borrowed was not as thick and warm as the soldier's cloak Stannic had loaned her, and her clothes were thoroughly damp. There was little protection from the breeze, for at this height, the trees had not yet leafed out. This was a land of rocks, scrub, stunted evergreens, and bare-branched hardwoods, a cold and forbidding land far above the fertile valleys, home to hawks, vultures, wolves, goats, and Old Ones.

She slowed the horse to a walk, for the trail was steep, narrow, and twisted around boulders and rocky outcrops. The need for hurry oppressed her, but it was dangerous to go at a faster pace. Her only consolation was the realization that the going had been just as slow for Jordan and Drako.

"Stop here," Marcus said softly. "We're close now." He slid off the horse, landing with a grunt and a slither of loose stone. Guinevere, too, found her legs stiff with cold and difficult to manage for the first few steps. Marcus led her off the trail and into a copse of juniper. "Stay here and out of sight," he said, "while I climb up beyond those rocks and take a look around."

She protested at first, not wanting to stay behind now that they had finally come to their journey's end, but Marcus prevailed. He was going only to scout around, not to reveal himself, not to attempt any action. Jordan and Drako had two horses with them, he reminded her, and someone had to stay with Peleth and keep him quiet.

Guinevere watched him go, then shrugged off her cloak, shook the water off it, and began to rub Peleth down. He was warm from his exertions and could not be left standing barebacked in the fitful breeze to grow cold and stiff. When she had dried him as best she could, she covered his back with the cloak and nestled up against him to share his heat. Her shivering had almost stopped by the time Marcus returned.

"They're up there," he said tensely. "They've built a fire, and Princess Elaine is with them. They've got her wrapped in blankets at the back of the cave, but I can't tell whether or not she's bound. They've got their bedrolls with them and supplies. The place is a camp, of sorts. A wide cave, but shallow, no good for wolves or wildcats. They've used it before."

Guinevere stared at him. "How do you know?"

"I tracked them there last week on orders from the queen."

Whether it was the lifting clouds or the lack of a forest canopy Guinevere did not know, but she could see him much better now.

"Queen Alyse knew all the time it was Sir Darric?"

"No. But she knew that cattle and sheep leave tracks."

"But there were no tracks. That's what everyone said."

"There were tracks if you knew what to look for," he said gently. "And she knew that perfectly well. So she sent me to find them and follow them, but in secret. That's where I've been for the past five days."

The girl's wide eyes looked black in the dark. "And this cave is Sir Darric's camp? Right here in the hills above the castle? I wonder he dared!"

Marcus grunted. "He has nerve and to spare. This was a staging area. There's a makeshift pen on the hill behind the cave where they rested the animals overnight before the long trek downhill to the Marshes. I wager that's where those two scoundrels up there have put their horses. I saw no sign of them, but I didn't go around back."

"Well, I am ready for anything. Let's go."

"Bring your cloak. It's getting toward dawn, and the air is chill."

But Guinevere shook her head. "I've got to leave it on Peleth or he won't make it back down tonight. I'll be all right as long as I'm moving."

To this, Marcus objected, and no amount of argument could sway him. Finally, Guinevere consented to wear his own cloak. "It'll only be in my way in a sword fight," he said. "And you're sure to catch a chill without it. I'd rather stay in the queen's good graces, if it's all the same to you."

Guinevere grew grateful for the cloak as she climbed the twisting trail behind him. The breeze was sharper now, and Marcus's cloak was thick, warm, and fairly dry. The breeze carried smoke with it and the damp, acrid smell of wet wood, wet wool, and horses.

They came upon the cave quite suddenly around a bend in the trail. The fire at its mouth burned and spat, shedding more smoke than light. Guinevere wondered how they had managed to light one at all, since there couldn't be a dry stick left in the forest after so much rain. Perhaps they had some tinder and dry wood stored within the cave. Behind the two men in the foreground, she could dimly see the stone face at the back and a huddle of blankets piled against it, a huddle of blankets with yellow hair.

She crouched beside Marcus behind a boulder. "I see her," she whispered. "How do we get her out?"

"We've got to disarm those two first." He nodded toward Jordan and Drako, one on either side of the fire. Jordan was sitting cross-legged, whittling something with his knife and drinking steadily from a hip flask. Drako lay curled on his side, snoring, an empty wineskin in his hand. Marcus turned and considered her. "How strong a stomach do you have? Do you fear the sight of blood?"

She straightened her shoulders. "I'll be all right. But you can't just go in there, Marcus, and challenge them. It's two against one, and if they kill you, where will Elaine be then?

Where will I be? We've got to make them come out, one by one. I can help you do that. I'll be a decoy."

Aware of her intelligence, Marcus bit back the hot refusal that rose to his lips and asked her to explain her plan.

"If you show yourself," she said, "all they need do to disarm you is drag Elaine out and put a knife to her throat. So you must stay hidden. In those pines over there, perhaps? I will go far enough into the light for them to see me. I have no weapon; they won't be afraid. They'll think it's a chance to capture the queen's ward and strengthen Sir Darric's hand. One of them will probably stay with Elaine, and the other will come after me. I'll let him chase me into the pine grove, where you can cut him down. The other will likely come out when he hears the sounds of fighting, so I hope you can deal with the first one swiftly."

Marcus estimated the distance between the cave mouth and the pines. "Can you outrun him, princess? He's a young man and strong."

"Yes," she said. "I'm fast."

He remembered those flying feet going past him in the queen's garden and acknowledged the truth of it. "But once you show yourself, they'll know you're here. If I don't kill Jordan fast enough, or if he kills me, they'll both come looking for you."

Guinevere gulped. "We could try throwing stones to get their attention," she said weakly, "but they might think it was soldiers coming and try to use Elaine for protection. I don't want Elaine frightened any more than she is now. I'm . . . I'm willing to take the risk of being seen."

Marcus thought hard. It was not a risk he was willing to take for anyone else but the queen's daughter. Guinevere's plan might work for the first ruffian. Marcus was confident he could stop any man in his tracks if the fellow didn't know he was there. It was the second man he worried about. The second man would be alert to danger, would suspect an ambush, would know he was not facing a force of any size, and would have his sword drawn. But he could think of nothing better. He would prefer to charge straight in and take them by surprise, but the risks were too great. The girl was right about that. If he failed, he left her and the queen's daughter alone in the heights with two armed traitors. They needed Elaine to blackmail the queen. The gods only knew what they would do to the ward.

"All right," he said at last. "Let's get over into the pine grove and plan the ambush. Follow me."

The pine grove proved to be well suited to their purpose. A ring of trees surrounded a little clearing on the edge of a low cliff. The landslide that had created the cliff had taken a score of pines down with it, and the trees lay some forty feet below, protruding from the rubble like the spine of a giant hedgehog with their dead spikes pointing upward.

Marcus peered over the edge of the cliff and shuddered. "If I can't kill him myself, I'll push him over. That's a death trap more certain than any I could devise."

There was enough room in the clearing for a sword fight and enough space between the living branches for Guinevere to hide. All that now remained was to lead the men into it, one at a time. Guinevere looked at Marcus standing at the cliff's edge and, for the first time, saw him as a soldier might. That he was tough, wiry, brave, strong, and capable she already knew from her night's adventure, but she had forgotten that he had only one useful arm. She had forgotten, too, how short he was, how unlike a warrior in appearance. She swallowed in a dry throat. Jordan and Drako were almost twice his size.

She shivered and pulled his cloak tighter around her. It was too late now for misgivings and, after all his help, unkind to have them. A thousand things go could amiss with any plan. They could only do their best and hope it was enough. She gripped the edges of the cloak to still her trembling hands.

"I'm ready. Shall I go now?"

Marcus came over to her and put his hand on her shoulder. "You don't have to do this, princess. You're a brave girl; you've proved that to everyone. Why not let me charge straight in and take my chances? I'm not without skill, you know."

"It will endanger Elaine," she whispered. "They'll harm her to stop you."

Marcus sighed. "All right, then. I'll get in position here. You attract their notice and run in between these two trees. Hide over there. Wrapped in that cloak, you'll be invisible." He smiled gently at her. "Provided you cover that beautiful hair. Now go."

Guinevere walked alone across the stony ground to the apron of flat, grazed turf before the cave mouth. She pulled back her hood and faced the cave. But the sound of Drako's snores must have covered her approach, for Jordan did not look up from his whittling, except to raise his empty flask to his lips and then throw it from him in disgust. He leaned around the edge of the fire and grabbed Drako's wineskin. That, too, proved to be empty, and Jordan swore as he flung the wineskin at Drako's head. Three things then happened at once. Drako grunted and awoke; the breeze shifted and blew the firesmoke into Guinevere's face, making her cough; and Elaine lifted her head and cried out, "Gwen!"

Jordan jumped to his feet, a dagger in his hand.

"Oh, Gwen!" Elaine cried again. "You're alive! Thank God! Have you brought troops?"

At these words, Drako drew his sword and looked blearily about him. "Troops? Where?"

"Th-there are no troops," Guinevere stammered. "I—I came alone."

Elaine's face fell, and great, shining tears rolled down her cheeks. "No troops? But how will you get me out of here?"

Guinevere said nothing to this, and a slow smile creased Jordan's face. His stance relaxed, and he pushed his dagger back into his belt. "Yes," he said easily, "I'd like to know that, too."

Guinevere ignored him and focused only on Elaine. "I came to find out where you were so I can go down and tell the queen. Then the troops will come to save you."

Hope lit Elaine's face, followed quickly by impatience and vexation. "Then why did you show yourself and put yourself in danger?"

Jordan snickered. "And how do you propose to get back to the castle?"

For only an instant, Guinevere met his eyes. "Run," she said, and was off.

She heard a shout behind her and the pounding stride of a heavy man. Fear gave her wings, and she shot between the pine trees and into her hiding place with a gasping sob. She just had time to realize that Marcus was not there before Jordan crashed into the clearing. She heard a soft thud. Jordan staggered and drew his sword—*thud*. He staggered again, swung around, blade raised, seeking his enemy—*thud*. He staggered a third time, dropped his sword, and slowly sank, knees buckling, to the ground. A shadow appeared from the trees at the edge of the cliff. She saw Marcus bend over the bleeding man and pull his daggers out.

"What'll it be, you traitorous dog?" he growled. "A quick death or a slow one?"

A bubbling reply came from Jordan's throat. It sounded more like a curse than a plea for mercy. Marcus searched his body, removing his dagger, his sword belt, and the rings from his fingers, before dragging him to the cliff's edge and pushing him over. Guinevere heard him bounce down the slope in a shower of pebbles. A sharp cry pierced the night, and after that, there was only silence.

CHAPTER THIRTY-THREE

The Guardian

Marcus stood at the cliff's edge and crossed himself.

"Are you there, princess?" he asked quietly.

"Y-yes," she whispered.

"Stay there. The ground's slippery with blood. I'll collect his things and stack them under the trees. I'm afraid we have time enough to work up another plan. The other's not coming."

Guinevere realized with a start that this was true. When she turned her head, she could see Drako standing by the fire at the cave mouth, sword in hand, peering anxiously out into the darkness and calling Jordan's name. The darkness itself seemed to be lifting with the clouds. Dawn could not be far away.

"I didn't think of this."

"Don't be dismayed. You did beautifully. You've a head on your shoulders and a gift for doing the right thing."

She could hear the smile in his voice and was comforted. "You surprised me, Marcus. I expected a sword fight. I didn't know you were so skilled with knives."

He laughed lightly. "I prefer to fight at a distance, if I can. I'm at a disadvantage in a sword fight, with no hand to hold a shield. Besides, the man was twice my size."

Guinevere smiled. She could see his face now across the clearing.

"That's better, princess. I like your pretty smile. I wish half the men in the house guard had your courage. You came through those trees like all the Furies of hell were after you, but you did your job. I'm proud of you."

Guinevere flushed. Warmth spread through her, even to her fingertips and toes. "Thank you. I'm ashamed I didn't know what a good fighter you are."

Marcus grunted. "It may yet come to a sword fight with the other one. He's not going to budge." His voice turned suddenly sharp. "Look!"

From behind the screen of pine boughs, Guinevere saw Drako dragging Elaine to the mouth of the cave. The blankets had fallen from her, and they could see that her hands were bound behind her back. Her gown was dirty and torn in places, and her eyes were wide with terror.

Drako turned in their direction. He took Elaine by the upper arm and shook her hard. "Come out! Come out, you bloody scoundrels! Or I'll put the princess to the fire!" He pushed Elaine toward the flames.

"Let me go!" she screamed, kicking at him. "Gwen! Go for help! Go for help but don't come out!"

"Oh dear God!" Guinevere gasped, as Marcus grabbed her and held her. "I must go to her! Let go! Let go!"

"No, princess. There's nothing you can do. I'll go, if you'll promise to stay here."

Guinevere struggled to free herself. "Don't you see? He doesn't care any longer. He's not looking for reward from Sir Darric. All he wants now is his life."

"I'll circle around back and—"

"How can you help her? One look at you and he'll kill her so he can fight you unencumbered. But he'll see no threat in me. Maybe I can talk him into letting her go, if you will let him flee. I've got to try, Marcus. *Please*."

Marcus shook his head. "It's out of the question—" he began, and then stopped. The cloak he still held in his hand was empty. The girl had unlaced it and gone. He saw her now in the gray light, running toward the cave, bright hair flying. "Struth," he muttered, and ran for the horses.

"Gwen!" Elaine shouted. "Don't come near him—he's crazed with drink!"

Guinevere stopped at the cave mouth. "If you want to live," she said to Drako, "you'll have to let the princess go."

Drako was drunk, frightened, and sweating heavily. In his right hand, he held a bared blade, and in his left, he held Elaine. The hem of her gown was only inches from the fire. He did not look in the mood for reasoned argument. "Where's Jordan?"

"He's dead."

Drako glanced left and right. "Who killed him?"

"A man I had with me. A brave man, a soldier. Jordan cut him, and he's just now died of his wounds."

"Only one man?" Elaine's voice rose, dismay struggling with disappointment.

Drako's eyes were red and tired and his face dark with dirt and stubble. Thinking seemed to be a labor for him. "How do I know that's true?"

"If he weren't dead, do you think he'd have let me come out here alone?"

"You came before."

"That was to trick you into following me into the ambush. But there's no ambush anymore. There's no one left but me."

"For God's sake, Gwen!" Elaine's eyes were full of tears. "How could you come with just one man?"

Drako jerked her rudely. "Shut your mouth. I'm tired of all your yammering."

"Listen to me, Drako." Guinevere came closer. "There's a battle going on down at the castle, as I think you know. Queen Alyse is winning. If you value your life, you'll let the princess go. The queen's men will come looking for her as soon as dawn breaks, and if she's been harmed in any way, they'll have no reason to show you mercy. Sir Darric warned you not to harm her, didn't he? Yet you've bound her wrists, and you're threatening to burn her alive."

Drako stared at her as if she were a spirit from the Otherworld, as if her speech were incomprehensible to him. She tried again.

"Why do you threaten her? There's no one's hand to force. There's no one here but me, and I have no weapons. If you leave now, you can slip unseen into the hills. You can escape. Survive. But you must get away before the queen's men come looking for Elaine."

Drako sucked in his lips and pushed them out again. He seemed to teeter on the verge of speech. "You're the queen's ward, aren't you?"

"Of course she is," Elaine said impatiently. "She's my cousin. Our mothers were sisters."

Drako grunted. "Family, eh? Then she'd do just as well." He beckoned Guinevere forward. "I'll let your cousin go if you'll take her place."

"Leave her alone!" Elaine shrieked. "Don't do it, Gwen! Run back down the mountain and get more help!"

"You do and I'll take this one with me." Drako looked straight at Guinevere, and she could see he meant it. "If I'm slipping off, I'll want a hostage for protection, won't I? I can buy my life with her or take her with me. She can be my servant in some other kingdom."

Elaine shrieked and struggled, but could not loosen his grip on her arm. "Let me go, you foul traitor! Let me go!"

Guinevere stood on the rocky ground, shaking. In the east, above the mountains, the sky was lightening. The breeze was stronger now and cold. She was so numb she could barely feel her feet moving over the dead grass toward him.

She stopped just out of his reach. "Let her go. Please."

Drako glanced around again from side to side. He saw nothing suspicious. He could hear the horses moving uneasily in the pen, but Jordan's roan was always spooked by wind. In one quick movement, he shoved Elaine aside and lunged for Guinevere. He caught her arm and threw her spinning to the cave floor behind him. In the same moment, he heard a hissing in the air. Light broke and shattered before his eyes as something hard struck his chest and knocked him backward. He gasped without breath and fell over, a long fall forever into darkness.

Someone screamed. Hooves clattered on stone. Guinevere struggled to rise but could not move. She could hear voices, but they seemed a great distance away. She opened her eyes, but the world had gone black and breathless. Her body ached, and her cheek was flattened hard against the ground by a great, suffocating weight.

"Gwenhwyfar!" She heard another voice and then a succession of grunts. The weight lifted, and sweet air rushed into her mouth and nose. Light filled her vision. Strong arms raised her and wrapped her in the warmth of fur. She looked up groggily into Llyr's face, Marcus's face, Elaine's face. They looked with sheer relief down into hers.

"The brute fell on you when Llyr shot him," Marcus explained. "I'm amazed he didn't crush the life out of you."

"Oh, Gwen!" Elaine cried, clutching Guinevere's hand and spilling tears on it. "It's over. It's over at last. You saved my life. You were so utterly brave—how did you do it? How can I ever thank you?"

Guinevere saw the raw flesh on Elaine's wrists where the bonds had rubbed. "Are you hurt, Laine? Your gown's torn, and your wrists—"

"Don't be ridiculous." Elaine hugged her, and Guinevere wrapped her arms around her cousin. The nightmare of the past day and night dissolved in a steady waterfall of tears, to which Elaine responded with reassurances and hugs but which discomfited the men.

Llyr offered an awkward apology. "I could not shoot sooner. You were in my line of sight."

"Drako is dead, then?" Guinevere asked, recovering her breath. "And no one else is hurt?"

"You have Llyr to thank for that," said Marcus. "I had some idea of bringing the horses out and attacking the brute from behind them, but one of those animals is afraid of wind. I couldn't catch him. You owe your rescue to your guardian."

Elaine looked askance at Llyr and addressed Marcus. "Is there really a battle going on in the castle? I thought she made that part up."

"I'm afraid it might be true. The captain of the house guard and some of his men are in Sir Darric's pay. Last night they rebelled. Add to them the force that Sir Darric brought with him, and they outnumber the queen's loyal followers."

Llyr smiled shyly. "Perhaps not."

Marcus turned to him eagerly. "You were able to get word to your people?"

Llyr nodded. "We took all of them. And the man the Marsh Lord's son sent to summon them. They cannot help him now."

Marcus slapped his own knee in excitement. "That's great news! There's a chance, then, that Queen Alyse can repel the attack herself. I wouldn't put anything past that woman."

"Mother's being attacked?" Elaine quavered. "Can't we help her?"

"Certainly we can," Guinevere responded. "We have three horses now."

Marcus smiled. "All right, then. Let's go down and rescue the queen."

CHAPTER THIRTY-FOUR

Queen of Gwynedd

With a candle in her hand, Queen Alyse made her way slowly around the hall of meeting. The torches had been doused for the present, and the great chamber was in darkness except for scattered, small pools of light where the women gathered around oil lamps on the floor. All the furniture had been used to barricade the doors. The men waited in their assigned positions, some silent, some talking in quiet voices. No one slept.

A good fire was burning on the kitchen hearth, and everyone had been well supplied with willow tea, leftover meal-cakes, and heels of stale bread. There would be no more, for the bakehouse outside was inaccessible now. There was food enough in the storerooms to keep them for weeks and mead enough in the cellars to serve them once the water ran out. That was not what worried Queen Alyse. Morale was the problem. Her people were afraid.

In her progress around the hall, she spoke to them all. She thanked them for their loyalty, encouraged their wakefulness, and showed them more confidence than she felt. When she paused in her progress to listen, everyone listened with her. No one breathed. The cool night air flowed in through the high windows, but the only sounds it carried were the normal small rustles and flutters of night. The queen moved on, and the room breathed again.

Ailsa and Grannic huddled together against one dark wall. They were eager to keep out of the light and away from the queen's notice. Grannic's bony face was haggard, and her hands twisted in her lap. She feared for her future. Ailsa, who knew hers only too well, could not spare a thought for Grannic. She could think only of Guinevere.

Somewhere out there in the chill, wet night, her dear girl was struggling against evil forces too strong for her. Stannic should never have let her go—Marcus should never have let her go—what fools these men were! How could they risk her, even for the queen's daughter? Did they not know who she was? What she would one day be?

Her perfect belief in the prophecy made at the child's birth did nothing to relieve Ailsa's fears. All gods required the sweat of human labor to bring their wills into being. Even Arthur's coming, foretold a good hundred years before his birth, had required the assistance of men to bring about. What if Gorlois, Duke of Cornwall, had stayed at home and not led his troops against King Uther's on that fateful night of

Arthur's begetting? What if Uther, disguised as Gorlois, had been recognized by the porter who let him into Tintagel? What if Ygraine, Duchess of Cornwall, had not taken King Uther to her bed in her husband's place? What if Ygraine, as High Queen nine months later, had not been able to give up her firstborn son on the night of his birth, or if Merlin had been unable to receive the child after Uther refused to raise him? A million things might have gone awry. The truth of a prophecy did not, in Ailsa's eyes, ensure its coming to pass. That required the assistance of human beings, the most fallible of creatures. If Guinevere was to become a great lady someday, the highest lady in all the land, the utmost care must be taken of her. She must be protected, not allowed to ride off on dangerous rescue missions in the middle of the night! That, as she had told Stannic in no uncertain terms, must be as plain as the nose on his ugly face. His apologies, his explanations, could not excuse him. Guinevere was gone, and he had let her go. The fact that she herself had slept soundly through the girls' escape was no comfort at all.

Queen Alyse passed by without a pause. She saw the dim shine of Grannic's tears and Ailsa's head bent low, but they did not move her. Let them fear, let them tremble, let them reap the bitter harvest of their neglect. She could not spare a thought for them now. She would deal with them when she had her daughter back. When she had her daughter back . . .

Where was the traitor Darric? Why hadn't he come? Could he not find her? Could he still be fighting the fire? The longer she waited for him, the more she believed that setting fire to Pellinore's apartments had been a brilliant move. She had expected a battle long before this. Judging from the amount of oil left in the lamps, this was the ebb of night, just before dawn, when the old folk believed spirits roamed the earth to collect the souls of the dying. Certainly, more people died at this time of night than at any other.

She shivered and hoped that the breeze meant dawn was near. The coming of day would instill new hope into all her people, for she saw in their faces the expectation of imminent death. For Sir Darric's men, dawn could bring only discouragement. They had probably expected to be in possession of the castle by morning. Daylight would make them realize how long they had been struggling against the fire and how much was left to be done. With luck, they might even be downcast and fatigued. But perhaps they would just be angry. Queen Alyse stilled another shiver. The fire had kept them at bay for more than half the night, but she knew it could not hold them off forever.

She was at the door to the kitchen stairs when she heard a noise and turned back. The clamor of voices and the thunder of boots on stone grew louder and louder. She went to the barricaded door and nodded to Lucius, the guard in charge. "At last, the villain comes. Now we shall see what he has to say for himself."

Lucius bowed, and his men drew their swords.

A heavy fist pounded on the door, and a wild voice cried, "Alyse of Gwynedd! Come out, you coward queen, and yield to me!"

Queen Alyse waited until the pounding stopped. She pitched her voice so it would carry. "I do not yield to traitors."

The door shuddered as bodies thudded against it, but it did not budge. "Come out! I command you to come out! I'm master of this castle now."

"Are you? Then come in and get me."

They tried. They battered at the door with a united strength, but with the weight of the barricade behind it, it proved as impenetrable as stone.

At length, Sir Darric paused for breath. "Did you set that fire, you vengeful bitch? Come out or I'll burn you out, so help me God! I'll finish the job you started."

The men around her stiffened, but the threat did not surprise the queen. It was what she would have done herself, in his place. But she knew something that Sir Darric didn't: there had only been oil enough in the lamps to burn until dawn, and her own men had taken most of the torches. Without access to the oil in the storerooms—which she controlled—it would not be easy to generate enough of a blaze to burn a way into their sanctuary. Indeed, if she was not mistaken, his own men were pointing out that fact to Sir Darric now.

She stepped closer to the door. "Did you really expect me to sit quietly by and let you take my kingdom? You gave me warning last night, and I took it. I don't apologize if the measures I've taken have kept you busy and soured your temper. They were meant to."

An argument flared beyond the door. "What warning?" "You gave her a warning?" "You *told* her what you were going to do?"

Sir Darric subdued the dissension with difficulty. "Come

out, Alyse," he said again, sounding tired now. "You have the hall of meeting and the throne, I grant you, but I have the castle. And the land. Your sanctuary is your prison. Come out, and you will be honorably treated."

"Honor! I wonder you can speak the word."

"I've got the upper hand," he insisted. "Gwynedd is mine. You can do as you wish in there. Starve, if you like. I am only offering you my protection."

Queen Alyse laughed. "Protection against what? I doubt very much we'll starve before you do. We've got the kitchens and the storerooms. We've got everything we need until King Pellinore gets home."

As she expected, this statement produced a hubbub among his men. She knew they must be tired and thirsty from their long night's work and eager for a cool drink, a meal, and a rest. The clamor of dissension grew and was cut short only when Sir Darric assigned Regis to take half the men and find a way into the storerooms.

"Lucius," Queen Alyse said quietly, "send someone to warn the men downstairs and check all their defenses. I want no displays of heroism. The doors stay shut. We are playing a waiting game, at least for now."

Lucius obeyed, and the queen turned her attention back to the door. "So Regis is with you, is he? I suspected as much. You could not have stolen so many cattle without his assistance."

Sir Darric's voice was cold; he, too, had been looking forward to a meal. "Still worried about your precious cattle? I tell you, the hillmen took them."

"And sold them in the market at Segontium? I have records of the sales. I also have the severed heads of cattle, dug from your own slaughter pits, with King Pellinore's mark on their ears. And I have a witness who last week counted three of the king's animals still grazing in your fields."

Sir Darric began to curse. "So you're the one who's been spying on me. I thought as much. Who hires a one-armed man to write?"

Shouting came from the kitchens and the noise of battering at doors. At the queen's signal, Lucius took a handful of men and went to help.

"You shouldn't be surprised," Queen Alyse said, raising her voice to cover the sounds of mayhem below stairs. "All kings use spies. I sent a man to track my cattle even before you came to visit."

"Impossible. I looked myself. There were no tracks."

"Because you covered their feet in canvas shoes? Even canvas leaves a mark if you know what to look for. And did I say? My spy also brought me three of the canvas shoes that had ripped and been thrown away. Your men are careless, Darric."

"What does it matter?" Sir Darric cried hotly. "It was a game—a ploy to swell our larders and fatten my purse. And give me something to do while everyone was away. Are you really so upset about the loss of twenty cattle? It's nothing to a wealthy king like Pellinore."

"It's a small crime compared to treason," Queen Alyse agreed. "But it's still theft. It's the lambs and heifers I mind the most. They are the future of the herd."

"Set your mind at rest, then. We took no lambs."

Lucius appeared at the head of the stairs and signaled to Queen Alyse. She crossed the room to him.

"I don't know how long we can hold them," he said quickly. The kitchen door is secure, but they're battering at the storeroom door with a solid wooden post. Even with twenty men behind the barricade, it won't hold much longer."

He did not say the rest; he did not have to. Even if they killed those who entered, word would reach the main force at the door to the hall of meeting, and their little corps of loyal followers would be overwhelmed by trained troops with better arms.

"Hold them off as long as you can," Alyse said. "I'll send down more men. Set the cook's boys to carry food from the storerooms into the kitchens, as fast as they can. If you have to, you can fall back and barricade the inner door to the kitchens."

Lucius saluted and disappeared back downstairs. Alyse dispatched more of her men to follow him. Now there were only three standing with her at the door to the hall of meeting. One glance toward the dais behind her convinced her she could not spare Yvonet or Bredon. Prince Maelgon was jumping up and down, shouting, "I want to fight! I want to fight!" and it was all both men could do to prevent him from running downstairs himself.

Queen Alyse drew in a long, deep breath and faced the door.

"Men of Gwynedd, hear me. You are engaged in treason. If Sir Darric fails to gain the throne, you will surely die. Your families will never recover from the disgrace. Your names will all be forgotten.

"In what cause do you risk your lives and your reputations? In the cause of a confessed cattle thief who has promised you riches? In the cause of a younger son who has no future without your help? In the cause of an arrogant, careless boy who has no experience of ruling men? I advise you to think twice about it.

"In changing masters, will you be any better off? I ask you to consider the lives you have led under King Pellinore. When you were starving, did he not feed you? Does he not provide clothes and goods to the poorest among you? In the black year of King Uther's death, when the crops burned in the fields from drought, did good King Pellinore not open his storerooms to you and your kin? We all went hungry that year, highborn and low alike. Do you think it is so in every kingdom? It is not.

"When the Gaels attacked and burned the lower village, did King Pellinore not send men to repel them? Did he not send men and materials to help rebuild your homes? Do you imagine all kings treat their subjects with such generosity and care? Let me assure you, they do not.

"If you have complaints, does the king not listen to you? Has he not set aside one day in every week to hear you? Do you think all rulers listen to their people or care how they feel? They most certainly do not.

"Darric of Longmeadow has no doubt played upon your resentments, called good King Pellinore a tyrant, and promised you riches. Are you so credulous that you believe him? *He* is the one who is full of resentments. *He* is the one who longs for a tyrant's power. *He* is the one to whom riches mean everything. That is why he worked so hard to extinguish the fire in King Pellinore's apartments—to save the riches there. A smarter, less greedy man would have secured the queen and the heir before thinking about riches.

"A man who is consumed with the desire for power cares little about his fellows. From your own experience, you must know this to be true. Who cares more about you and your families: King Pellinore or Darric of Longmeadow? Who will be able to repel the next Gael attack: King Pellinore or Darric of Longmeadow? Why, Darric has not even yet wrested this castle from your queen, though he has had three days to do it! Who will keep you from starvation and misery in the years of drought? Can you even imagine this arrogant nobleman opening his storerooms to you? Rebuilding your houses? Listening to your complaints? Do you really think he cares a fig what happens to you once his own goals are accomplished?

"Men of Gwynedd, you have your futures in your hands. Renounce this upstart lord and join us. All your transgressions will be forgiven. I promise you that. King Pellinore will be back in a few days' time. He will honor any among you who come to my aid. He will destroy you if you do not."

"Silence!" Sir Darric cried, panic making his voice rise to a squeal. "Silence, you brittle whore! Pellinore himself will yield to me! I have your daughter!"

Queen Alyse heard a chorus of mutters from beyond the door. "Men of Gwynedd, hear me! This despicable coward has abducted my daughter, a child who cannot defend herself. I ask you all: Is this the action of a brave man? Has Darric of Longmeadow yet lifted his sword against a foe of merit, or does he content himself with blustering at women and servants? I ask you again, whom would you follow: King Pellinore or Darric of Longmeadow?"

Voices rose on the other side of the door, rose and swelled into a veritable chorus of shouts and cheers. But from outside rose a new tumult of noise—thuds, shouts, jeers, cries of fury and of pain, and the unmistakable clash of swords.

Queen Alyse backed away from the door. She was too late. The battle had begun.

CHAPTER THIRTY-FIVE

A Measure of Mercy

Knowing that she could be of no more use to her men, Queen Alyse retreated to the dais. She released Bredon and Yvonet to join the fighting and sat on her throne with Prince Maelgon on her lap. Julia stood beside her, little Peredur asleep on her shoulder.

"There is nothing to do now but wait," Queen Alyse said quietly. "They know where to find me."

Young Maelgon fidgeted and squirmed and begged to be allowed to join the contest, but she controlled him without a reprimand. She could not bear to speak harshly to him during what might be the last morning of his life.

The women gathered in a group in front of her. A few of them had daggers, the little, thin-bladed knives they used to cut their food, but most of them were weaponless, and all of them were frightened. Ailsa and Grannic, she saw, had gathered up the oil lamps from the floor and poured what oil remained in them into the two largest lamps. These they had lit and now held ready to fling at an attacker. Queen Alyse appreciated the gesture. By all the rules of war, any woman who attacked a man was considered one of the enemy and could be killed by any warrior without other justification.

They waited. Beyond the windows high in the wall, the sky turned pale gray and then pale gray-blue. The noise of fighting increased downstairs and could be heard now beyond the barricaded door to the hall of meeting. The queen wondered if the cook's boys would remember the pokers heating these long hours in the embers. A sudden shriek followed by a volley of cursing rose up the stairs and made her smile.

All at once, a great shout went up, and a chorus of male voices raised a victory paean. Footsteps thundered up the stairs. Queen Alyse clutched her son to her and waited with a frozen face for the first man to appear. Would he be hers or Darric's? All their futures rested on that.

Stannic burst from the doorway and fell on his knees. His great, broad face was split by a grin. "Victory, my lady queen! We have carried the day! They are defeated!"

Queen Alyse released Prince Maelgon and rose shakily to her feet. "Is Sir Darric taken?"

"Aye, lady, and Regis, too. Lucius has him. It is safe to open the doors now."

The women hurried to help pull back the furniture and to arrange the benches in some sort of order around the room. Regis and a handful of others were dragged upstairs, bound and bleeding from sword cuts, and thrown down at the foot of the dais. People flooded upstairs after them. The main door to the hall of meeting was at last thrown open, and a throng of men pushed in with Sir Darric in their midst, weaponless, bedraggled, and bleeding from a cut on his cheekbone. He, too, was shoved to his knees before the dais.

Queen Alyse looked in astonishment over a hall crowded with men. Half of them were neither guards nor warriors, but villagers with clubs in their hands. Everyone was laughing and jesting and making noise. Pale shafts of sunlight fell from the high windows and lit their buoyant faces.

The queen beckoned to Stannic. "Where did all these people come from? They cannot be Sir Darric's reinforcements?"

"No, my lady," Stannic said with a broad smile. "These men came up from the village when they heard there was trouble. Old Argus roused them. He knew something was amiss when Marcus didn't come home at dawn. Seems he knew there was treachery in the house guard, and he couldn't sleep on account of it. So he raised the village. They took Sir Darric's men from behind. It was short work after that."

Lucius came forward and knelt on one knee. "That is how the force that Regis commanded was taken, my lady," he said. "But Sir Darric was taken by the men of yours he had turned. It was your speaking to them that did it. You turned them back, and they rounded on him."

With tears in her eyes, Queen Alyse looked out at all the smiling faces. She called Old Argus forward and thanked him from her heart in front of everyone. From her pouch, she withdrew the jeweled dagger Sir Darric had given her last evening—it seemed a lifetime ago—and bade him keep it as a token of her gratitude and esteem. She thanked the villagers for their bravery in coming to her defense and asked if any had been wounded in the action. A few, she was told, had suffered sword cuts and were being treated and bandaged below stairs. Queen Alyse offered the villagers all the mead they could drink, and with a great cheer, they went back downstairs to the kitchens to take immediate advantage of her hospitality.

She looked around at the men who remained. They were all warriors of one class or another, even the traitors who lay prostrate at her feet. To the men loyal to King Pellinore she owed her life. She thanked them, each one, for their service and promised them honors from the king when he returned.

To the waverers, those whom Sir Darric had bribed and who had changed their minds when the going got rough, she acknowledged herself in their debt and promised to put in a good word for them when the king returned. Until then, they were free men. She wondered privately how many would be left in Gwynedd by the time Pellinore got around to passing judgment.

Finally, she turned to the vanquished. "Get up on your knees. Lucius, help them. Darric may stand."

He was already standing, having risen from the floor with catlike grace even before she spoke. He regarded her with the sullenness of a spoiled child. "You don't frighten me, Alyse. You have more men, but you don't have the upper hand. I still have your daughter."

An angry mutter ran through the standing men. Queen Alyse stilled it with a look.

"If you want to live, you'll tell me where she is."

He smiled his charming, wicked smile, which had so piqued her interest a mere three days before. "You've got it backward. If you want to see your daughter again, you'll do as I say. You'll do whatever I say." He lifted a sleeve to the cut on his cheek and dabbed at it delicately. "The first thing you'll do is order your men to keep their distance."

Queen Alyse stiffened, and his smile broadened. "Or don't you want her back? Is that it? You've got your sons close at hand, safe and sound, so the daughter doesn't matter?"

"Nonsense," she snapped. "But I will not submit to threats, especially not from you. I'd sooner cut your throat and spend the rest of my days looking for her. She can't be that far away. There hasn't been time."

Sir Darric made her a mock bow and gestured toward the door. "Then go and find her. She's probably still alive. I told the men not to touch her, but," he added with a shrug, "it's been a long night, and who knows what they do when I'm not there?"

"You are a cruel man," Queen Alyse said evenly. "And for what you have done, you deserve death. But I will yield this far: if you tell me where to find her, I will spare your life."

Sir Darric's expression hardened. "So you said before. That offer's already been rejected. Have you nothing more?"

"Let Father kill him!" Prince Maelgon cried. "Father will surely kill him when he comes home!"

Julia reached out a hand to shush him, but Queen Alyse looked at her son with a cold smile.

"Prince Maelgon reminds me that I have one more thing to offer," she said to Sir Darric. "I will vouch for King Pellinore's mercy. Tell me where Elaine is and I will not let him destroy you."

Sir Darric's lips curled in a sneer. "She's not worth the kingdom, then? She's only worth my life? I know how little you value *that*, Alyse. You hold your daughter's life cheap, it seems."

Queen Alyse signaled to Lucius, who drew his sword and placed its sharp edge against Sir Darric's throat. "Are you ready to die, Darric? Or are you going to tell me where she is?"

"For God's sake," grumbled Regis beside him. "You might as well tell her, my lord. It's over."

Lucius let his blade edge bite into Sir Darric's neck until it drew blood.

Sir Darric spat viciously at the foot of the dais. "In a cave. Up in the hills. Near the north pass."

Alyse exhaled carefully and, with an effort of will, unclenched her fists. "Very well. If she's found alive and well, I will let you live. Lucius, lock them all downstairs in the dungeons. Stannic, get horses ready. We've not a moment to lose."

But Lucius and Stannic were not listening. They were staring at the open door. One by one, heads turned as voices echoed down the corridor, girls' voices, clear in the morning air.

"I'll tell her. Gwen, let me tell her. You're hurt, and Marcus didn't see it all, and those other two don't speak Welsh."

"Mapon does."

"Well, I'm the one that was abducted. I'll be the one to tell it."

Color drained from the queen's face. She turned to the door and began to shake.

Marcus appeared first in the doorway. There was dried blood on his clothes and dirt on his face, but his look was cheerful, and he smiled at the queen as he made his reverence.

"My lady Queen Alyse. It is my great honor to return your daughter to you, well and whole."

He stepped aside, and Elaine ran into the room, followed by Guinevere.

"Mama!" Elaine cried, as the hall erupted into cheering. She ran up to the dais and flung herself into her mother's arms. "Oh, Mama! I am so glad to be home!"

"Elaine." The queen's voice was a whisper of disbelief. "Elaine. Thank God."

Sir Darric swore furiously under his breath. "That damned cripple again! Who is he? How did he find her?"

Regis gasped. "Marcus!"

"You know him?" Sir Darric whipped around.

Regis swallowed. "Yes, my lord. He is—he was—my second-in-command."

Sir Darric stared. "A one-armed man? How does he fight?"

"With knives."

"You never said anything about him."

Regis shrugged apologetically. "He's been home abed with fever since before you arrived."

"You incompetent fool! He was spying on me in

Longmeadow all the while you thought he was ill. *He's* the one I should have paid my money to. He has twice your brains."

Queen Alyse, at last loosing Elaine from her embrace, heard the end of this conversation. She turned to Marcus, still in the doorway, and made him a deep reverence.

"Marcus, son of Argus, I owe you more than is in my power to repay for the safe return of my daughter and my ward. You are hereby made captain of the house guard. King Pellinore will confirm the appointment as soon as he returns."

Marcus bowed and thanked her for the honor as the men began to cheer his name. "I will serve you faithfully, my lady queen. But you hardly need me. You subdued the rebellion yourself."

Queen Alyse smiled at him. "Not without the help of your loyal men."

"What shall we do with your prisoners, my lady? Take them out into the yard and dispatch them? I think we have spikes enough."

Regis whimpered. The queen looked down at the men kneeling before her. Sir Darric was the only one who met her eyes. His gaze was calm, cool, and unafraid.

"I should have liked to see your head upon a spike," she said in a tight voice. "It is what you deserve. But I will keep my word. You'll have your measure of mercy." She glanced swiftly at Marcus. "Take them below and lock them up. King Pellinore will decide what to do with them."

While Marcus formed a guard and marched the prisoners away, Queen Alyse directed her women to see if the kitchens were operable and to bring refreshments up for the rest of the men. She excused only Grannic and Ailsa from this duty, since Ailsa had her arms about Guinevere, and Grannic, suitably humbled and miserably anxious, hovered nearby, eager to take charge of Elaine. Queen Alyse found herself so full of pleasurable emotions that she could not chastise them. The long night of waiting had been punishment enough.

Released from her mother's arms, Elaine plunged into the story of her capture and release. Queen Alyse listened in growing astonishment to the tale. Elaine seemed to regard the entire night's events as one great adventure. Although she bore on her wrists the marks of bonds, and although she had spent the night in the power of ruffians, she had no sense of personal danger or of the greater tragedy that had threatened the kingdom.

Guinevere's part in the adventure was still more astonishing and more difficult at first to accept. She appeared to have engineered Elaine's rescue all by herself. Men had played their parts, but the initiative had been hers. That she had dared to try, and against such staggering odds, displayed a courage and resourcefulness Queen Alyse had not dreamed the child possessed.

She turned her head to look across at Guinevere, still held hard in her nurse's arms. For an instant, she saw Elen's face looking back at her, pale and lovely, her dark blue eyes luminous with tears, and she saw in the girl what Sir Darric must have seen. She saw also in that grave, tear-stained face a recognition of the dangers to which Elaine was still oblivious.

Queen Alyse was the first to look away. The women were coming up from the kitchens now with jugs of mead and strips of jerky from the storerooms. The bakehouse fire had been relit, they reported, and bread was baking. The cook was frying sausages on the fire, and in a little while, a proper breakfast would be ready. The men sat on the benches, grateful for the mead and jerky and the promise of hot food. The hall was full again, but quiet, as everyone wanted to hear the tale of the night's doings from Princess Elaine's own lips.

Elaine related all the details of Guinevere's escape from Sir Darric's chamber, which Guinevere had shared with her on their ride back down the mountain. Marcus returned in time to furnish a fuller account of their ascent into the hills and the action at the cave. Queen Alyse listened to it all in utter silence. The bravery of a girl not yet thirteen, escaping Sir Darric and riding out on a dark night into hills guarded by Sir Darric's men, took the queen's breath away. It was not a thing she herself would ever have attempted, but it had saved Elaine's life.

Elaine herself told proudly how Guinevere had offered to switch places with her. "Drako meant to take me off with him, over the mountains and into another kingdom, Mama! And Gwen was willing to take my place. Was that not wonderful of her? I said she shouldn't do it, she should go back and get more help, but she did it all the same, because there wasn't time. Oh, I was so happy to be free! And then Llyr shot him, and he was dead, and it was over all at once."

Queen Alyse looked at her daughter blankly. "*Who* shot him?"

Elaine pointed to the doorway. "Llyr."

Two figures stood in the passage beyond the open door.

They were not visible to most of the people in the hall, but Queen Alyse could see them. She knew at once they were hillmen. They were both small in stature, one old and grizzled, the other young and dark. After a moment's hesitation, she beckoned them forward.

Her own men jumped up from their seats as the Old Ones entered the room. Some of them drew their swords. Guinevere pulled away from Ailsa and went to stand beside Llyr and Mapon as they sidled cautiously through the door.

"My lady," she said, making the queen a reverence, "allow me to present two friends of mine. This is Mapon, leader of the Long Eyes who live in these hills, and this is his foster son Llyr, son of Bran, leader of the White Foot of Snow Mountain. Llyr is the one who killed Drako and who took Mapon the news of our distress. Mapon and his men have rounded up the men Sir Darric stationed in the hills. He tells me they await you in the orchard, bound hand and foot."

Queen Alyse signaled the guards to back away. She came down from the dais, holding Elaine and Maelgon each by the hand, and walked up to the strangers. They ducked their heads shyly and kept their eyes lowered.

"Do they speak Welsh?"

"Yes, my lady. Mapon does."

Queen Alyse made them a low reverence and made her children do the same, to the wonder of all the people in the hall. "I owe you my daughter's life," she said simply. "It is not a debt I can repay. Ask of me any favor you wish, and I shall grant it."

Guinevere translated into Mountain Welsh for Llyr, who glowed. Mapon, however, looked decidedly uneasy.

"Thank you, lady. But I do not come into your abode to receive your thanks. I come to confess a transgression."

Queen Alyse cast a swift glance at Guinevere, who seemed as startled as she was. "Whatever it is, sir, I forgive you for it."

Mapon grunted, looking away briefly and shifting his weight onto the other foot. "The Long Eyes did not steal your cattle, lady, but we did take lambs. It was necessary. The skin and blood of a newborn lamb can cure childbed fever. And my woman—" He stopped. His face grew hard as his eyes grew bright. "The winter was a hard one, and our own flock was attacked by wolves. When my woman gave birth at the equinox, we had only two lambs on the ground. Both were sacrificed for her but . . . it was not enough."

"I am sorry," Queen Alyse said gently. "Did she survive?" Mapon's stony face supplied the answer. "And the child?"

He shook his head.

"A tragedy. I am very sorry. Thank you for coming to tell me. Your people have saved King Pellinore's kingdom as well as his daughter. I do not think he will begrudge you his lambs. I only wish they might have saved your wife."

Mapon made her a stiff bow and retreated. Queen Alyse turned to Llyr.

"Guinevere, please thank this young prince for his bravery. Tell him I will grant him anything he wishes."

She watched as Guinevere spoke rapidly to Llyr. Llyr

flashed the girl a brilliant smile—too brilliant, by far, for the queen's comfort—and his reply brought a flush of color to Guinevere's cheeks.

"What did he say?"

Guinevere lowered her eyes. "He asks that you not restrict my . . . my riding out into the hills alone. He is sworn to guard me. He says it is his duty and his life's work." She looked up at the queen, wishing her to understand. "It is not just the task they have assigned him. The wise woman of his clan has appointed him my guardian. It is now his life." She flushed brightly and lowered her eyes again. "I know it's foolishness, my lady, but the Old Ones believe in the . . . in what the hill witch told my father when I was born."

The queen's eyes flickered. That wretched prophecy again! But it was a glorious morning, the kingdom was hers, and Elaine was safe and whole. This was not the time to worry about the future.

"Tell him that King Pellinore and I are also your guardians. We were given that charge by your father. I cannot . . . I really cannot . . . Oh, Guinevere, will you give me your word to stay close to the castle and not take chances?"

The girl's face lit. "Oh yes, my lady! I promise it faithfully."

"Very well, then. I grant his request. Although I cannot see that banishing you from the stables ever had much effect."

Queen Alyse turned and saw Stannic's smiling face and Ailsa's and Leonora's and Marcus's at the top of the kitchen stairs—everyone in the hall was grinning. Did they love Guinevere so much? Her sister Elen had been gifted with the power to inspire love and admiration in people in every walk of life. Could such a gift be passed on to a child? Queen Alyse pushed the thought aside. There was no time to worry about it now. She could see by Marcus's signal that breakfast was ready. It was time for the victory feast to begin.

As she sat down at the family's round table with her children and their nurses, with Guinevere, Cissa, Leonora, Marcus, Lucius, Stannic, Bredon, Yvonet, and the two reluctant hillmen, she reflected that things could hardly have turned out better. Gwynedd was safe and stronger than before, with Marcus in charge of the house guard. The children were safe, and their nurses had learned a lesson. Pellinore would be distressed to find his apartments in ruin, but she could make room for him in her own apartments until his were set right again. Not all his treasured belongings had been lost. Marcus had already found a cache of them that Sir Darric had saved from the fire.

As to the stolen cattle, not only did she have the culprit, but she had proofs of his deeds to show Sir Gavin. She was certain that when Sir Gavin returned the remaining stolen cattle still grazing in his meadows, he would make good the others his son had sold in Segontium. There would not be a cow lost.

She smiled, turning all the heads at the table. To think, after all his lies and schemes, that Sir Darric had told the truth about not stealing any lambs!

CHAPTER THIRTY-SIX

Riding Out

Guinevere stood on the battlement overlooking the courtyard gates and the approach to the main road through the forest. It was a warm afternoon, sunny and calm. Off to her left, the smiling sea stretched blue to the horizon, and on her right, the hills rose in a hundred shades of green straight up to a robin's egg sky. The orchards were strewn with apple blossoms, the gardens ablaze with daffodils, and the air alive with birdsong. She could not remember a moment of more splendid happiness. She was high in the queen's graces, and King Pellinore was coming home.

Today was Beltane and her thirteenth birthday. Down in the village, where the festival was still observed, she could see the smoke of bonfires threading upward to the cloudless sky.

For the first time since leaving Northgallis, she had no wish to join the villagers in their celebrations. Recent events had put games and dancing into perspective, and the rites as she had known them held less attraction for her now. She had outgrown them, somehow. She had crossed some kind of threshold in the last three days, for even though she still had not begun her monthlies, she felt that something essential within her had matured and changed.

She glanced down at her new gown for the twentieth time. The thick green silk whispered pleasantly when she moved and slid milky smooth across her skin. It fit perfectly, and the sleeves reached all the way to her wrists. Queen Alyse had finished the gown herself, although how she had found the time for it during the bustle of the last three days, Guinevere could not imagine. There had been more than enough to do. Taking charge of the prisoners Mapon's folk had brought down from the hills, deciding which to imprison with Sir Darric and which to send home to the Marshes, rebuilding the house guard, clearing out the king's apartments, and beginning the long process of washing away the soot and ash— Queen Alyse had supervised it all.

She had also overseen the preparations for the great feast to celebrate King Pellinore's return, had sent men into the hills to recover the bodies of Jordan and Drako so that they might be properly buried, had sent gifts of meat, tallow, and animal hides to the hillmen as practical tokens of her gratitude, and somehow, amid all this, had found time to sit down with her women and finish the gowns the girls had begun.

The queen had done all this without anxiety or fuss, with an even temper and a certitude that bore down all obstacles before her. Everyone stood in awe of her.

In this mood, she had directed her women to finish Elaine's gown and had finished Guinevere's herself. With her own hands, she had sewn on a collar of creamy lace the exact shade of Guinevere's hair. Lace was costlier than jewels, being so rare, and Guinevere still could not believe Queen Alyse had given it to her. She reached up a tentative hand to touch it. Perhaps it was the queen's way of thanking her for her efforts to save Elaine, or perhaps it was her way of ensuring ladylike behavior. One could not ride or roughhouse in a gown like this.

Voices from the gatehouse broke into her reverie, and she looked down to see a rider cantering toward the castle along the forest road. She judged from his easy pace that he was an outrider sent to give them notice of King Pellinore's approach. The courier who had come last night had brought them all the news.

The man rode to the gates, gave the password, and was admitted into the courtyard below. He laughed and gossiped with the guards as a groom led his horse away.

"Be here by sunset," Guinevere heard him say. "And bringing a couple of guests with him, too. Another Welsh king and his son. Didn't catch the names, but I'll wager the son's a suitor." He laughed. "He weathered his first battle well enough, but now he looks scared to death."

The guards laughed at the jest and escorted him inside to see the queen.

Guinevere gazed thoughtfully after him. She hoped with all her heart that the king's son was not a suitor. If he was, he had timed his visit poorly. Elaine had been abed and weeping more than half the day, and no amount of cool water or compresses would make her presentable by the time the feast began, even if she agreed to attend it. This did not seem likely. She had thrown herself into a tantrum at midmorning and now, hours later, was still causing everyone as much trouble as she could.

Guinevere knew, alone of all Elaine's attendants, that she enjoyed these storms of emotion. It made her the center of attention and the object of sympathy. It also usually gained her the end she sought, but that would not be so today. There was no cure for this distress.

That morning, Queen Alyse had gathered the ladies of her household to give them the news King Pellinore's courier had brought her the night before. They learned all about the great battle against the Saxons, how King Arthur had devised a trap, and King Pellinore had sprung it, and half the Saxon force had been destroyed. Only twenty Welshmen had been killed, and King Pellinore was bearing their bodies home. The king was also bringing a surprise home with him, which Guinevere now guessed must be Elaine's first suitor.

And finally, they learned that King Arthur would begin that summer to build himself a fortress on a hill near the River Camel, which ran through the Summer Country southeast of Avalon, and that, come autumn, he would take a wife. The girl had already been chosen. She was the daughter of a Dumnonian king who had died in the service of Cador, Duke of

Cornwall, old Gorlois's son. What was more, she had been raised in the household of Queen Ygraine, Arthur's mother, and was high in her favor. Her name was Guenwyvar of Ifray.

This news had upset Ailsa, who kept muttering under her breath about some dreadful mistake, but it had devastated Elaine. She had run to her room, inconsolable with grief. Guinevere had tried to comfort her but without success, and she had left Elaine to the more expert ministrations of Grannic and Ailsa.

That Elaine had long admired King Arthur, Guinevere knew well. Almost from her first days in Gwynedd, Elaine had spoken to her of Prince Arthur, King Uther's hidden son, whose coming had been foretold by a firedrake across the heavens. Since his birth, his whereabouts had been shrouded in mystery.

Four years ago, no one had been more excited than Elaine when news came of Prince Arthur's sudden appearance at King Uther's side on the eve of the battle of Caer Eden. To the amazement of all, the fourteen-year-old boy had taken the field with his ailing father's sword and won the battle for him. Elaine had always been certain of his virtue and his prowess. She believed every story told of him, no matter how exaggerated or unlikely. She refused to hear a word said against him. Any attempt on Guinevere's part to make her take a more reasonable view always ended in a quarrel. To Elaine, King Arthur was a hero, like Hercules of old, capable of anything and the finest warrior in the world.

Until this morning, when Queen Alyse broke the news of the coming wedding, Guinevere had not believed that Elaine truly expected even to meet King Arthur, much less to marry him. But there seemed no other interpretation of Elaine's weeping fit or of her genuine despair. Ambition was one thing, but common sense was quite another. King Pellinore was high in King Arthur's graces just now, but he was merely one of a handful of Welsh kings and only one of several hundred kings in Britain. What gifts did Elaine think she possessed that raised her above all the other princesses in the land, most of whom were probably as calf-eyed as she?

Guinevere grieved for Elaine, but she could not understand her. Did she really want to leave her parents and the country of her birth to move to a distant land where she knew no one, where the people and even the language would be strange to her? Could she not understand that the girl who married the High King of Britain would be forced to spend most of her life alone? The High King was always on the move, as the last four years had proved. He went where the Saxons called him, with whatever forces he could muster, in his eternal battle to unite the kings of Britain against their enemies. She could not believe Elaine had ever really thought about what life would be like for King Arthur's queen.

Elaine had never questioned any of the fabulous tales about King Arthur. His seemed to be a personality that attracted stories the way a still stone did moss. But Guinevere had once heard a tale about Arthur Pendragon that tarnished, if not destroyed, the luster of his reputation. She had never told it to Elaine; she could not imagine repeating it to anyone. It was a dark tale of incest, revenge, and the massacre of innocent children. The blame for the entire tragedy had been laid at Arthur's door by the royal courier whose gossip to Stannic Guinevere had accidentally overheard. Even if it was not true, the fact that one of his own men could believe it of the King sent a shiver up Guinevere's spine. Imagine having to live with such a man! She pitied the Dumnonian princess with all her heart.

She crossed the battlement to the stairs and made her way back down to the women's quarters. She would tell Grannic and Ailsa that King Pellinore was expected by sundown and urge them to ready Elaine in time. She resolved to say nothing of the suitor.

In spite of Guinevere's best intentions to behave like a lady all day, it was she and not Elaine who was late to dinner. The day was too mild and her heart too high to resist a quick gallop through the woods. There was plenty of time before sundown, and Peleth had not been outside for a run in three long days. Since Queen Alyse had granted Llyr's request, Guinevere could ride to her jumping field with a carefree heart.

Peleth seemed as ready for a romp as she was. He cleared all his fences with room to spare and still had energy to burn. She whistled for Llyr and saw him step smiling from the woods.

"Shall we go for a gallop along the shore road, Llyr? You've never ridden a horse that fast, have you?"

He shook his head. "I am willing to try."

She laughed as he leaped up behind her. "You've got the

knack of balancing on a horse. We shall have to find you a mount of your own before long."

Llyr's eyes widened. "To ride?"

"Of course to ride. What else? It won't take you long to learn. I can catch you a mountain pony, and we can train him together over the summer. It will be lots of fun. Horses are amazing creatures when you understand them."

"And amazingly good to eat," Llyr said with a smile. "I will have to warn Mapon that Earth's Beloved must not eat my pony."

Guinevere turned to him in shock. "You *eat* ponies?" She turned away again so that Llyr might not see the revulsion in her face.

"We have no other use for them," he said gently. "We do not hunt with them, for they are too noisy. We do not need them for travel, for our territory is not large. In the heights, they cannot go where we go, for their feet are too big. They are not like sheep; they are wanderers and must always be corralled. But their flesh is wholesome, the hair of their manes and tails is wonderfully strong and has a thousand uses, and the marrow from their bones can save a life. Forgive me. I see this pains you. But we sacrifice to Rhiannon before we hunt horses, and the ones we take are taken with her blessing."

Guinevere could not still a shiver. All deities had a dark side. The Good Goddess, mother of men, whose gifts were bounty, fertility, and life, was also the Great Goddess, whose gifts were victory, justice, and death. Likewise, the God of Christ was both a merciful God who forgave sins and a wrathful God who destroyed whole cities in a single breath. There was no reason her beloved Rhiannon should not be the same, but it grieved her to know it. The ivory carving of the horse goddess still rode in her pouch, but she did not touch it.

Llyr enjoyed his gallop along the shore road. At full stretch, sitting the horse was easy, and he did not need his arm around the girl's waist to balance. But he did not withdraw it. He liked the sensation of her nearness; he liked the loose strands of her hair whipping against his cheeks. For her, he would learn to ride a mountain pony, even though it took him one more step away from the life he had known as one of Earth's Beloved and one more step closer to the life of the Others. His father would grieve over it, but Llyr would never be leader of the White Foot now. His fate had changed the day he first spoke to She With Hair of Light. His future, like hers, lay shrouded in mystery, or "in the smoke," as his people put it. He was content that it should be so.

They were halfway back to the castle when Peleth threw a shoe. They slid off the horse at once and searched for the shoe but could not find it.

"Is it a cause for distress?" Llyr asked, as Guinevere emerged from a clump of roadside brambles with scratches on her hands and tears in her much-worn tunic. "We can walk back, surely?"

"Yes, of course we can. We shall have to. But if I had the shoe, Stannic could nail it back on. Without it, I can't ride again until the smith makes a new one. That will take days. No one works on Beltane or on the day after. They are all sleeping it off."

Llyr smiled sympathetically. "Perhaps you, too, will be 'sleeping it off.' The queen is preparing a feast tonight, I think, to welcome the king back home?"

"The feast!" Guinevere gasped. "I forgot all about it! Oh, how could I?" She stared in disbelief at the sun hanging low in the western sky and at the long shadows the trees cast across the road. She would never make it back to the castle in time. She would miss King Pellinore's arrival, and Queen Alyse would be furious. All the ground gained by her rescue of Elaine would be lost by one impulsive decision to ride out! For the first time, she recognized the justice of the queen's complaints. Had she given Queen Alyse the obedience owed her, she would have been ready for the long-awaited moment of the king's return. Her lateness was bound to be seen as an insult to King Pellinore. In her grief, she saw it so herself.

"Come," said Llyr. "I can see you wish to hurry. I will teach you how to walk before the wind. It is the step we use to cover open ground on a long journey. Six steps walking, six steps running. Like this." He demonstrated. "You will get there in half the time and will not lose your breath."

They moved off at once, leading Peleth back home at Caesar speed while the shadows lengthened and the brightness of the day slid into dusk.

CHAPTER THIRTY-SEVEN

King Pellinore's Surprise

Ailsa was not pleased. After a long day nursing a spoiled girl in a weeping fit she was in no mood to countenance Guinevere's tardiness. She stripped the girl of her clothing, bathed her hastily with a wet cloth grown cold with waiting, ruthlessly combed out the tangles in her hair, yanked the green gown over her head, pulled the laces tight, and rebraided her hair with swift, ungentle fingers.

Guinevere submitted meekly to such fierce handling. She welcomed the cold sting of the water and the sharp tugs at her scalp as the beginning of her penance. They were alone in the room, which meant that for once, Elaine had had the wisdom to obey her mother and go down to dinner. When Ailsa released her, Guinevere hurried downstairs, hoping to slip unnoticed into the gathered crowd.

She was foiled by King Pellinore himself. He saw her the moment she entered the hall of meeting and called out her name. Heads turned. Guinevere dropped into a curtsy and fumbled for the right words to beg the king's pardon. He cut her short with a hearty laugh.

"Come, come, none of this, lass. All the world knows where you've been." He wrapped his arms around her and squeezed her breathless. He looked just the same despite six weeks on campaign. His bearded face creased with laughter, and his eyes shone bright with merriment. "You and your horses. Can't keep away from them, eh? Just as well, just as well." He winked at her, and the men around him chuckled in agreement.

"See who I've brought home with me?" he said, grinning. "Do you know them after all these years?"

Guinevere turned to his companions, and her eyes widened. The elder of the two men, dark-bearded and swarthy, opened his arms to her.

"Gwarthgydd!" she cried, running into his embrace. "Gwarth, my dear brother, how wonderful!"

"Birthday greetings, little sister," he rumbled in a deep bass voice. "I hardly knew you, Gwen, you have grown up so. I hope you remember Gwillim?" He indicated the young man at his side, and Guinevere stared in disbelief at her first and oldest friend.

She did not recognize him. Her childhood playmate was a stranger. He had grown into the twin of his father, only slightly shorter and a little less muscular, with a beard nearly as full and as dark. But the change in him went deeper. His eyes avoided her, lifting for a moment to her face and then dropping instantly to the ground. He shuffled his feet uncertainly and mumbled a halfhearted greeting.

"Gwill?" She made to give him a kiss of welcome but hesitated as he shied away and instead made him a reverence. "It is wonderful to see you. I am so glad you've come to visit."

He bowed, but civil speech was beyond him.

Gwarth laughed and slung an arm about Gwillim's shoulders. "He's shy around girls yet. Doesn't know enough of them. We're hoping a brief stay here might cure him."

"Let him sit near me and Elaine at dinner. We'll get him talking."

She looked around for Elaine and saw her sitting with Grannic and the other women on a bench before the fire. She was dressed in her new blue gown and her hair was braided with ribbons, but she seemed insensible of the occasion. She sat sullenly with downcast eyes and a face still swollen with weeping. Guinevere had to bite her lip to keep from smiling. A suitor who was shy of girls and a princess who had clearly been made to appear in public against her will—it was not an auspicious beginning.

Queen Alyse came to her husband's side and laid her hand upon his arm. "Now that we are all gathered," she said, with a pointed look at Guinevere, "we shall take our seats."

As the crowd of people moved to find places at the long tables, Queen Alyse leaned close to Guinevere. "Say nothing about what has happened here. Say nothing to anyone. I don't want his men to know until I have had a chance to tell Pellinore in private. Do I have your word?"

Guinevere nodded. "Of course." She glanced quickly at Elaine, who moved sluggishly forward at Grannic's fierce insistence. No, Elaine would not speak, either. Her very presence was proof of her submission to her mother's will.

The feast was a noisy affair. Guinevere reflected that Queen Alyse need not have worried about gossip spreading far, when each diner had to strain to hear his neighbor's voice. Since neither Elaine nor Gwillim spoke at all, she had leisure to notice other precautions the queen had taken. It was usual to include the entire household on occasions such as this, but the tables were filled only by the men King Pellinore had taken into battle. The few members of the household present were the children's nurses, and they all sat at the round table with the family, directly under Queen Alyse's eye. No one else who had stayed at home was there.

Regis usually stood behind the king's chair on feast nights, with six of his men stationed around the hall to check any overexuberance once the wine went round. Tonight, however, the house guard was posted outside the hall, and the space behind the king's chair was empty. If King Pellinore noticed any of these changes, he gave no sign of it. He ate and drank with all his usual gusto, as merry as ever, glad to be home, and frowning only when his glance alighted on Elaine.

Toward the end of the meal, when bellies were full and voices hoarse, and the air was thick with smoke from the torches and the fire, Queen Alyse rose to lead the women out. At the same moment, Guinevere saw Marcus come through the door, pause to assess the condition of the half-drunk men, and proceed swiftly to the round table on the dais. She knew from his guarded expression that something was amiss.

Marcus stopped at a point halfway between the king and queen and saluted. Guinevere could not hear what he said, but King Pellinore could, and she watched confusion, bewilderment, and consternation cross his face as Marcus spoke and Queen Alyse replied. Gradually, conversation died at the table, and she heard King Pellinore say in a voice thick with shock, "Escape? Escape from what?"

One by one, the tables in the hall fell silent. All heads turned toward the dais. King Pellinore pushed his platter away and rose. His voice, never dulcet, was rough with anger. "Explain yourself, man. Why was he imprisoned? And where is Regis?"

Guinevere glanced at Elaine, who shot her a look of triumph. Instantly, Guinevere understood. Elaine wished the whole tale to be told in public, that she might regain the attention and sympathy of all the court. For the last three days, no one had paid her the deference she felt she was due as a victim of abduction. Now, when her mother told King Pellinore the truth, all that would change.

"What do you mean, Regis is locked up, too?" King Pellinore roared, his face red with temper. "What's been going on here?"

"*Was* locked up, my lord," Marcus said ruefully. "I'm afraid they have escaped together. Along with Darnal, who stole the keys and let them out. We have traced them as far as the coast. They may have taken ship to Ireland. There was a trader in port that sailed on the afternoon tide."

King Pellinore's nostrils flared, and he banged a fist on

the table. "You go too fast, man! Will someone please tell me what has being going on in my kingdom while I've been away!"

Queen Alyse rose. "I will," she said with cold precision, "if you will be so good as to sit down and give me the courtesy of your attention."

King Pellinore opened his mouth to object, saw the queen's resolve, and decided against it. "Very well," he grunted, thudding into his chair and reaching for his winecup. "Begin."

Queen Alyse gazed coolly out at the expectant crowd, and as one, each man turned back to his meal and his wine. The low hum of their conversation made the queen's words audible only to those around the king's table. She told him the truth, without hesitation or excuse, in short, clipped tones that brooked no interruption. She did not dwell on anyone's villainy or heroism but gave him the facts as she knew them, the measures she had taken, and with what results.

Elaine's expectations were rewarded. King Pellinore beckoned to her with tears in his eyes, held her on his lap, and hugged her to him while he listened to the end of the tale.

"I held them in the dungeons until you could come yourself to pass judgment on them," she finished wearily. "But it seems they have defeated me there. I have promoted Marcus to captain of the guard, since without him, I could not have proved Sir Darric's guilt, and I hope you will confirm him in the post. You have him and Guinevere to thank for Elaine's safe return. Oh yes, and Llyr, son of Bran, a prince among the Old Ones. Guinevere knows how to summon him from his fastness. I do not."

King Pellinore looked solemnly at Guinevere. The emotion in his face was clear enough for all to see.

"Alyse, my dear," he said at last, turning to her, "you are a woman in a thousand. Without you, I'd not have had a kingdom to return to. I bless the day God gave me a woman with wits."

Queen Alyse colored faintly. "Thank you, my dear. You will have to send a courier to Sir Gavin tonight, for by now, he has arrived home and discovered the absence of his son. And if you will confirm Marcus in his post, I believe he is eager to continue his investigation of the ruffians' escape."

"Of course," the king replied. "Marcus, you are captain of my house guard. Send a man to the Longmeadow Marshes and tell Sir Gavin I would see him here tomorrow. You may let him know it concerns Sir Darric, but nothing more."

"Yes, my lord."

"And you will find that scoundrel for me, however long it takes. Any man who endangers my daughter," he growled, with eyes growing moist as he pulled Elaine closer to him, "has forfeited his life and will die by my hand." He paused and steadied himself. "You're a good man, Marcus. You have my sincerest thanks for your bravery and your skill. I confess I did not know you were so accomplished."

Marcus bowed. "My lord is kind. But there is one who is braver than I, for she is young, female, and without the use of any weapon but her wits." He flashed a smile at Guinevere. "And her horse."

King Pellinore's grim face relaxed. "Yes, indeed. Such

courage is astonishing in a maid." He turned to Guinevere, his kind face shining. "Guinevere of Northgallis, I thank you with all my heart."

Guinevere flushed and hurried to explain. "My lord, it took no courage. I couldn't just let them . . . I had to find . . . it was *Elaine*," she finished simply, as if that explained it all. And to King Pellinore, it did.

"My dear girl," he said gently, "it was a lucky day for us when you came to Gwynedd."

"Yes, it was," Elaine agreed. "Gwen is the best friend anybody ever had."

"Hear, hear," Gwillim breathed.

Queen Alyse rose once more to lead the women out, but the king laid a hand on her arm. "One moment," he said. "I have brought home a birthday gift for Guinevere, and there is no better time than this to present it."

The queen looked at him sharply. "Not jewels," she warned. "She is far too young."

King Pellinore smiled. "Not your kind of jewel, Alyse. Guinevere's kind of jewel. The High King himself gave it to me."

The chatter in the hall died away. The king had everyone's attention now.

"The High King?" Elaine whispered, wide-eyed. "He honored you with a gift?"

King Pellinore's eyes were dancing. "Arthur's a generous man, and one who appreciates honest service. I sprang the trap he set, and he asked me what I would take in return. He said people would think poorly of a king who did not reward such loyalty. So I asked him for something I thought my niece might like for her birthday treat."

Guinevere's mouth went dry. She felt Gwarth's eyes on her and Gwillim's, shining like shield bosses. Elaine could hardly contain her excitement.

"Pellinore, for heaven's sake," Queen Alyse said irritably. "Stop teasing the girl and tell her."

King Pellinore winked at Guinevere. "I brought you a mare from the High King's stables. You can finally turn poor old Peleth out to grass."

Guinevere stared at him. A thousand thoughts raced through her head, but the foremost was, it wasn't possible. She must have misunderstood. Stannic had told her all about the High King's breeding program, how King Arthur had sent one of his best knights to southern Gaul early in his reign to bring back horses of exquisite beauty and stamina to cross with their own sturdy native breeds. Now and again, when a stallion didn't measure up, they gelded him and gave him away. Stannic had seen one once. The horse had made an impression on him. But they never let go of mares. Mares were the very heart of the breeding program and much too valuable to part with. "A—a mare, my lord?"

King Pellinore laughed. "Well, a filly, then. She's only two years old. You can have the training of her. Sir Lancelot du Lac didn't want to part with her; she's the best of her year, but the High King said a valuable gift bestows more honor than one they'll not miss much. Now, how's that for a courteous gesture?"

Both Elaine and Guinevere looked at him with shining eyes, and Guinevere spluttered out her thanks. For the third time, Queen Alyse rose to lead the women out. As they moved from the table, Guinevere ran to King Pellinore and hugged him. He laughed, patted her in his fatherly fashion, and wished her joy of her gift.

"Well," said the queen with a little smile as they moved to the door, "it's just as well you earned back your riding privileges. I'll never get you away from the horses now."

"Oh, Aunt Alyse, may I not just run down and have a peek at her tonight?"

Behind her, Ailsa tugged sharply at her sleeve.

"No," said the queen, "you may not. It's only a horse. It will keep until morning."

"I won't get a wink of sleep," Guinevere pleaded.

"But, Mama, it's the *High King's* gift," Elaine said in an awed voice.

Queen Alyse stopped in the doorway and looked sternly at them both. "It is King Pellinore's gift. And tomorrow is soon enough." In a swift and unexpected gesture, she bent and kissed Guinevere's brow. "You may go as soon as it's light. Happy birthday, Guinevere."

CHAPTER THIRTY-EIGHT

Promise

In the still predawn, Guinevere slipped silently out of the castle and darted downhill past the outbuildings to the stable. Entering by the side door, she went right to the box stall, keeping her breathing as normal as she could. Surely, Stannic would have put her in the box, a filly among so many stallions and geldings, a new filly in a strange land. With her heart hammering in her ears, she lifted the latch, opened the plank door, and slid inside.

It was dark as night in the stall. The single, high window looked west, toward the sea and the fading stars. She stood perfectly still and waited. Around her, she sensed only utter stillness. The straw lay ankle-deep and would rustle at the slightest movement, but she heard nothing. For a frantic moment, she thought the stall must be empty—Stannic had housed the filly elsewhere—the animal had died overnight, and her body had already been removed—King Pellinore had been pulling her leg; the High King would never part with a mare from his own stable—the master of horse, the knight with the strange name, had put his foot down. And then she heard a soft exhalation that was not her own, could not be her own, for she was holding her breath. Again it came, a drawing of breath, a testing of the air, and another gentle exhalation whose warmth reached her across the bed of straw.

There, under the dim light of the window, a dappled, dark gray filly stood in perfect stillness, her lovely head turned toward Guinevere, her dark nostrils wide, drinking in the new scent.

"Oh, you beauty," the girl whispered, hardly knowing she spoke. "You angel, you wonder, you lovely, lovely thing."

She hummed a little tune as she took a step forward. It was an old Welsh melody, handed down through countless generations, a favorite among wet nurses and stablemasters for its power to comfort. The filly's ears flicked forward to the girl, then backward to the window where the first birdsong erupted from the hills, and forward again to the girl. Her dark eyes fastened on Guinevere. She blew once, then lowered her head and nickered. The girl came closer, hand outstretched. There was something in the hand, something recognizably edible. The filly stretched out her neck and took it.

The touch of those velvety lips against her palm made Guinevere shiver with delight. It was only an apple from the storerooms, slightly shriveled and more tart than sweet, but the filly chewed it gravely, swallowed, and looked for more.

Guinevere ran her hands over the bony face; down the long, muscled neck; lifting the black mane and scratching where she knew horses could not scratch themselves. The filly responded, leaning into her touch, swinging her head around to examine the girl more closely, gently lipping her tunic and snuffling her hair.

"Well," said a low voice from the doorway, "I see you've met."

Girl and filly turned as one to face the broad figure of the stablemaster at the entrance to the stall.

"Oh, Stannic, isn't she beautiful? Isn't she magnificent?"

Stannic grinned. "I knew you'd be up early. Just not this early."

"I had to come, I couldn't sleep. I couldn't sleep a wink until I'd seen her."

"Here." He handed her a halter and lead rope. "I know you won't be satisfied with patting her in the stall. Take her outside into the paddock and watch her move."

Guinevere led the mare out into the cool dawn of a May morning. In the east, the sky had turned an eggshell blue, and the dew was already drying on the grass. She turned the filly loose in the paddock and watched her trot along the fence line, floating, tail held high and mane flowing, drinking in the new scents of woodland, mountain heights, and sea.

Guinevere watched her in silent awe. She sought for a name for this wonderful gift, something to capture her quickness, her youthful spirit, her infinite grace. She could think of nothing. The quality of this animal was beyond her experience. She glanced back quickly at the stables. The grooms were up now and grumbling sleepily as they began their morning chores. There was no sign of Stannic.

Guinevere slipped into the paddock and called to the filly, holding out her hand, although this time there was nothing in it but the lead rope. The filly shook her head, burst into a gallop, bucked twice, spun, raced three times around the paddock, and finally trotted over to Guinevere, blowing with pleasure.

Guinevere laughed and patted her neck as she fastened the lead rope to the halter. "Feeling good, are you? Me, too. Let's go for a ride."

With the help of the fence, she slid quietly onto the filly's back. The horse stood calmly enough, flicking her ears back in anticipation of the next command. Guinevere leaned forward and stroked her glossy neck. "What excellent manners you have," she murmured. "The knight who trained you knew what he was doing."

She turned the filly away from the fence and asked her for a trot and then a canter and then a walk. The filly responded willingly. Guinevere rode her in a circle, reversed direction, and completed another circle, first at a trot, then at a canter. The filly happily complied, pulling a little against the single rope rein, wanting more speed but not insisting on it. Firmly, with hands, seat, and legs, Guinevere asked her to slow and then stop. The filly yielded without argument, coming to a halt by the gate. Guinevere leaned down to open it, and, after a quick glance around for Stannic, they slipped through.

By the time they reached the shore road, the sun had risen clear of the eastern hills and touched every leaf, every blade of grass, with light. The filly walked in a limber, ground-covering stride, her head lifted to the sea breeze, her wide nostrils drinking it in. Guinevere tried hard to quell her own excitement. Never in her life had she ridden such an animal as this. This was no mountain pony from the hills of Wales, no aged cavalry mount grown stiff in the knees. This was a young mare with all the eager quickness of youth, with power and agility and speed, to judge from the muscling of her hindquarters. It was said that the High King's master of horse had brought to Britain stallions of Eastern blood, finely made animals who could run all day on a handful of grain and a bucket of water. If the filly descended from such horses—as she must, she was so unlike the native Briton breeds—then it was even possible she carried in her the blood of the royal line of Bucephalos, Alexander's great stallion, who was himself descended from the god-horse Pegasus, who could fly.

Guinevere held the mare lightly, letting her take in her surroundings, feeling the suppressed eagerness in the warm body beneath her. The filly wanted to run, she could feel it in her, but the beach was the place for that. The tide would be halfway out and the shingle hard and smooth, perfect for a gallop. On the beach, she would discover if her filly, too, had wings.

When the shore road turned north, Guinevere urged the filly down the path to the beach. Gradually, the trees around them thinned to shrubs and then to windblown scrub as they came in sight of the sea. Without warning, the filly shuddered to a dead halt, flung her head up, and screamed. The next instant, she reared on her hind legs, pawing the air frantically with her forefeet, landed with a jolt, whirled, and tried to bolt back up the path. Breathless, Guinevere just managed to hold her, turning her in tight circles until she stood, shaking and sweating, staring at the vast, restless, terrifying expanse before her.

"It's the sea, my lovely girl. That's all it is. Have you never seen it? You don't have to go any nearer if you don't want to."

What had that master of horse been thinking, not exposing the horse to the sea? Caerleon, where King Arthur had his headquarters, was on a river, but according to the map of Wales that Iakos had drawn for her and Elaine, it wasn't all that far from the coast. Perhaps he took only colts to the sea and left the fillies at home to grow up into broodmares.

Impatiently, Guinevere pushed all thoughts of King Arthur's master of horse from her mind. She tried walking the filly along the shingle, but the animal shied violently every time a wave broke. She could think of only one way to distract the filly from the horror of the sea: she gave her her head.

The filly bolted down the beach. In four strides, she was at full gallop. Guinevere crouched over her withers and buried her fists in the flying black mane. The wind made her eyes tear and blurred her vision. She clung to the filly's back as the animal settled into her stride, lengthening her long body and increasing her speed. Speed! Guinevere shared the filly's exultation as the shoreline whipped past them. All fear had fled. In its place were only joy, eagerness, and the release of something long held in.

Guinevere kept a firm pressure on the rope, and the filly leaned into it, using the pressure to balance her racing strides. She ate up the ground, flying past the place where Peleth always pulled up, blowing with fatigue. She ran in a seamless, four-beat gait, ears and neck stretched forward, wanting more. They flew past the point where the rocks ran out almost to the tide line. The filly ignored the closer approach of the sea and kept to the narrow shingle, exploding forward in a new burst of speed as another long stretch of beach came into view.

In the far distance, a series of huge, rocky outcrops protruded from the shingle, running from the woodland all the way down to the sea. They resembled a series of giant wolf's teeth, upturned. The Fangs, as the locals called them, were a landmark for fishermen up and down the coast. There was no way around them, and the passage through them was tricky, even at a walk. Guinevere began to speak to the mare, calling her pet names and praising her strength, her speed, her will. She was rewarded with a brief backward flicking of one ear. Gradually, she straightened a little from her crouch over the withers, made her pressure on the rope intermittent, and called to the mare in a low, beseeching voice. She sensed a moment of indecision, little more than a moment's flicking of the ears and a fractional lifting of the head, before the filly gave her consent and began to slacken her speed.

By the time the Fangs approached, Guinevere had persuaded her to an easy canter. Her stride was still buoyant and full of joy, but she was willing now to slow to a trot and even to a walk. Her sides were warm and her breathing fast, but she was not really winded. When Guinevere turned her to head back home, the filly was eager to gallop again. Laughing, Guinevere restrained her.

"By all the gods, you are a marvel!" she cried, stroking the dappled neck. "Your gaits are as smooth as honey, and you can run forever. I have found a name for you at last: I shall call you Zephyr, after the west wind, for your beauty, your endurance, and your joy of heart. And look, you have lost your fear of the sea."

The filly stretched her neck forward and splashed through the surf in her long, limber stride. Guinevere let the rope lie slack across the withers and smiled to feel the relaxation in the supple body beneath her. She was filled with a joy she could not name. It was more than joy of the ride or of the gift of the horse or of Elaine's escape from tragedy, and yet it encompassed all these. It was joy of a renewed sense of freedom, of independence, of escape from rules and watchers and protection. This was the joy of living in a perfect present with no fear of the future and no regret of the past.

She lifted her face to the morning sun and made herself a promise. *I shall remember this moment forever. And someday, I shall find the knight with the foreign name who made this possible, who trained my filly with such consummate gentleness and understanding, and I shall thank him from the bottom of my heart.*

A Note to Readers

This is the story of the girl who grew up to be King Arthur's queen. It is important to remember that this book is a work of fiction. If King Arthur existed—and this is still a matter of debate among scholars—he lived in late-fifth-century to early-sixth-century Britain (somewhere between 485 and 526 CE), not in the Middle Ages. This was the beginning of the Dark Ages, so called because we know very little about that period. There is only one contemporaneous account of Arthur's time, as far as we know, and it does not mention him.

Arthur would have lived around a hundred years after the last Roman legions pulled out of Britain, leaving the Britons to defend themselves against the invading Saxons (from Germany), Picts (from Scotland), and Scots (from Ireland). Legend holds that for a short time, the invaders were kept at bay by a strong war leader who united the Britons and gave them perhaps two or three decades of peace. He was called Pendragon, or "High King." Arthur may have been that leader, though his parentage, marriages, offspring, friends, and fortresses are not matters of fact but of legend.

Archaeologists have discovered that there was a brisk trade between Roman Britain and the Mediterranean, which continued even after the Romans left. I have therefore assumed that any objects used in a Roman household might have been used in a British one as well.

Names of characters are drawn from historical tradition (Arthur, Guinevere, Merlin, etc.), other authors of the Arthurian legend (from Sir Thomas Malory to Mary Stewart), Ronan Coghlan's excellent *Encyclopaedia of Arthurian Legends*, and my own imagination. The genealogy of the "House of Gwynedd" is entirely invented.

I am not a speaker of Welsh or Gaelic and can give you only one clue to the pronunciation of the names and place-names in the book. I am indebted to Mary Stewart (author of *The Crystal Cave, The Hollow Hills, The*

Last Enchantment, and *The Wicked Day*) for the advice that the *dd* in *Gwynedd* and *Gwarthgydd* is pronounced like the *th* in *them* (not like the *th* in *breath*).

Whether you are new to the Arthurian legend or an established fan, I hope you enjoy this journey into the days of King Arthur.

Acknowledgments

Little did I guess when I went out to lunch with Marian Borden, a friend and fellow writer, that the direction of my writing was about to change. Knowing that I was in the midst of getting my three novels about the Arthurian legend published (*Queen of Camelot*, *Grail Prince*, and *Prince of Dreams*), she asked if I'd ever considered writing a series of young adult novels about Guinevere's early life. I hadn't. Marian and her daughter were reading young adult literature in a book group, and Marian was impressed by the level of understanding the authors expected of their readers. These were not children's stories; these were novels for adults of any age. Intrigued, I began to read some YA books myself and then, at last, to try to write one. Thank you, Marian, for planting the seed.

I also thank my daughter Caroline for the hours she spent as my sounding board. She listened with admirable patience and made intelligent suggestions. Every time we talked, I came away with a new idea. Thank you, Caroline, for your fertile conversation.

I am happy to thank my wonderful agent, Jean Naggar, and her hardworking staff for finding me a home at Alfred A. Knopf Books for Young Readers. Once again, I've been blessed with gifted editors. Thanks to Michelle Frey for the broad scope of her vision and the clarity of her focus. She framed the story so that it made more sense, even to me. Thanks also to Michele Burke for her excellent, insightful editing and for keeping me abreast of events. For the lovely design of this book, I thank Isabel Warren-Lynch and Stephanie Moss, and for the arresting cover art, I thank Tristan Elwell. Their work is a seamless combination that exactly reflects what I had in mind. Thank you all for the care you have taken in turning my story into a beautiful book.

Finally, I want to thank Deborah Hogan and Shelly Shapiro for their help in bringing this work to fruition. Without them, *Guinevere's Gift* would have withered on the vine.

Nancy McKenzie
February 2008